THE FALL OF '68

Paul Densmore

Order this book online at www.trafford.com
or email orders@trafford.com

Most Trafford titles are also available at major online book retailers.

Printed in the United States of America.

ISBN: 978-1-4907-4760-6 (sc)
ISBN: 978-1-4907-4761-3 (e)

Library of Congress Control Number: 2014917351

Trafford rev. 09/26/2014

 www.trafford.com

North America & international
toll-free: 1 888 232 4444 (USA & Canada)
fax: 812 355 4082

For Alice, Alex, and Chris

ACKNOWLEDGMENT

I would like to acknowledge the invaluable help of Barbara Ardinger, my editor. She waded through my out-of-this-world spelling and punctuation with great professionalism. Thanks, Barbara!

When Johnny Comes Marching Home Again
Patrick S. Gilmore

When Johnny comes marching home again,
Hurrah! Hurrah!
We'll give him a hearty welcome then
Hurrah! Hurrah!
The men will cheer and the boys will shout
The ladies they will all turn out
And we'll all feel gay,
When Johnny comes marching home.

The old church bell will peal with joy
Hurrah! Hurrah!
To welcome home our darling boy
Hurrah! Hurrah!
The village lads and lassies say
With roses they will strew the way,
And we'll all feel gay
When Johnny comes marching home.

Get ready for the Jubilee,
Hurrah! Hurrah!
We'll give the hero three times three,
Hurrah! Hurrah!
The laurel wreath is ready now
To place upon his loyal brow
And we'll all feel gay
When Johnny comes marching home.

WEEK 1

SEPTEMBER 22, 1968–SEPTEMBER 28, 1968

FRIDAY, SEPTEMBER 27

Pete Henning was a hippie. He wore old baggy clothes and seldom washed his long hair. He wore an Indian-style bracelet and a bead necklace. He talked like a hippie too, always sounding spaced out and high, which he often was.

Pete hadn't been a hippie long. I was certain of that because both of us had been discharged from the army only months before, and you can't be much of a hippie in the army. I was also certain he hadn't been a hippie before being in the army because I had known him then too, though not personally. We had been freshman in the same dorm at Middlesex College, a moderate-sized school in Southern Ohio. We were both drafted during the summer following our freshmen year, and now two years later, here we were again, back at Middlesex as sophomores readjusting to college life.

We met while waiting in a line at registration. We were both wearing bits of our old uniforms, so we struck up a conversation. It was a relief to know someone else had shared the experience of a year in Vietnam. Pete had been an infantryman with the Big Red One, and I had been a combat engineer in the Americal Division.

Now we were both living in off-campus apartments. Pete lived in a cellar apartment in a big old Victorian house two blocks from campus, whereas I lived in an apartment with three other guys on the other side of campus. Pete lived alone but was seldom alone. He was happy and extroverted and attracted many friends. I had been over to see him a few times since school began.

On Friday afternoon, the September 27, I knocked off studying in the library around four o'clock. I walked out of the building into the late afternoon sun and, instead of heading back to my own place, decided to go see Pete, so I went down the steps and turned right and walked up the sidewalk while thinking of how Pete kept plenty of beer in his fridge. The weather had held from summer, which was good, since I was still more comfortable in hot weather like Vietnam's. The maple and sycamore trees lining the streets still had their full summer foliage. Ohio was beautiful in the fall.

As I walked up to Pete's house, I got the feeling the house itself—not someone in the house—was watching me. It wasn't a spooky feeling, though, but a warm and welcoming feeling. I suspected the house was built before the turn of the century and wondered if anyone that had lived there had gone off to World War I or World War II.

A brick driveway ran along the side of the house and led to a small detached garage out back. A side door leading down to Pete's apartment opened out on the driveway. As I walked up to the door, I could hear a Rolling Stones song through a narrow ground-level window. I knocked on the door and heard Pete yell, "Come on down!"

The door opened on a short flight of steps. It was dark because the windows were small, but Pete said he liked the dim light. The ceiling was low, and because Pete was tall and lanky, he had to duck his head in some places to avoid hitting the pipes and heating ducts. His apartment was nicely finished with a separate bedroom, a large living room, and an adjoining kitchen with an eating area. The carpet was in good condition, and he had a couch, a couple of chairs, a TV, and a stereo. The stereo was an expensive Pioneer brand he had bought through the PX catalog in the army.

"Hey! Hey!" he called out as soon as he saw me. "It's Mike. Come on down, man, and crash awhile. What's new?"

"Nothing," I replied as I carefully stepped down the stairs, letting my eyes adjust to the dark. "Nothing's new. I was just bored. What's up with you?"

"Oh, just a same old shit. I'm just cleaning up a bit. Patty and the gang should be around soon. Help yourself to a beer."

I grabbed a beer from the fridge. Pete was emptying ashtrays and piling dishes in the sink. The kitchen area seemed a little odd to me. I think it was a cellar utility sink with cabinets and countertops built around it. I helped him some with the dishes. We filled the sink and pitched into the mess.

"Just like KP," I said.

"Yup," he replied. "Thank God I can do it when I feel like it now. Were you caught often?"

"No. Only once. In advanced infantry training."

"All day?" he asked.

"Yeah, but I only had pots and pans for lunch, so it could have been worse."

"I had one day in basic and one day in Nam when the gooks were on holiday," he said.

"Ever have to burn shit?" I asked.

"Nope. You?"

"Nope. Lucky, weren't we?"

"Kind of, I guess," he said. "I knew a guy who would mess with the first sergeant and was always stirring shit."

In Vietnam, the latrines were built such that we sat over a bucket made from a fifty-gallon drum cut in half. A few inches of diesel fuel was poured in the drum, so occasionally, we would get splashed on our bottom. Every day all the drum halves were pulled out and set on fire. This job was nearly always done by hired Vietnamese civilians.

"Have you gotten a VA check yet?" I asked him.

"No. You need money?"

"No. I'll be all right for another couple of weeks."

"Just ask, man, no problem."

"Yeah, thanks, if I need it," I replied. I was getting the impression that Pete's parents had some bucks. He drove a hell of a car, a '66 Pontiac GTO.

We finished the dishes, and I took a second beer, turned on the TV, and sat down on the couch. Pete was still in the kitchen. Pretty soon, there was a knock on the door and a girl's voice called out, "Hi, Pete." Before he could answer, Patty opened the door and stood for a moment, silhouetted against the bright light behind her. The silhouette highlighted her slightly heavy hips and short stature. In a moment, her eyes adjusted, and she bounced down the steps, calling to Pete and running up to him in the kitchen. She gave him a quick kiss, which immediately made me horny. Pete was getting all he wanted, while I hadn't laid a serious hand on a girl since R & R in Bangkok. Like most GIs there, I had shacked up for the week. I never knew (or couldn't remember) the girl's name and now just thought of her as the Old Bangkok Whore. The whole week was a blur in my mind.

I had met Patty the week before when I bumped into her and Pete at the student union. It was in the evening, and she was on break from an evening class. She was a "townie" and, as far as I knew, was taking only that one class. She was reasonably good-looking, with brunet hair, slightly-larger-than-average breasts, and a round face with thin lips. She was always vigorously chewing gum. Pete had met Patty and some other townies in August when he came to Middlesex early to set up for school. I don't know how he met the group, but he and Patty sure hit it off.

After Patty and I exchanged greetings, I knew I'd better split. I got up and went out to the kitchen and told Pete I was on my way. He protested and began telling Patty how he and I were Vietnam soul mates. I laughed and said I did have to go. He made some joke, and we laughed, and she hung on his arm, and I went up the stairs and left.

The sun was about to set when I stepped out into the alley and started down to the street. The alley was empty, but after a few steps, I looked over my shoulder and saw that another guy and girl had stepped into the alley from back, up by the garages, and were going to Pete's. Pete was a popular guy.

As I walked past the front of the house, I caught a glimpse of Pete's landlady watching me from a window. She kept an eye on who came and went, but she must have been hard of hearing, since she didn't complain about the noise downstairs. I wondered if the pot smoke seeped upstairs and got her high. Or maybe she wasn't hard of hearing but put up with the noise to get a buzz now and then.

It was nearly dark when I came to the street that bordered the campus. I stood on the curb for a few seconds as a car came from my right and passed me. It turned right on to the main street through campus. It was just light enough for me to see the driver. It was Olivia, the girl I had dated the winter of my freshman year. She still wore her black hair long and straight, and her hair reflected the streetlight like a mirror as she turned the corner. I'd seen her once since I'd come back to school, but seeing her now was just as hard as the first time. After we'd dated for three months our freshman winter and spring, she had found that I didn't meet her standards.

Shrugging, I continued across the street and walked down the same street she'd taken. Cars lined the street, and a few people were on the sidewalks, coming from and going to the library or evening classes. As I approached the library, I noticed a figure standing in a shadow of a tree beside the sidewalk. It was too late to change direction when I realized it was Olivia.

"Hi, Mike," she said as she stepped into the light.

"Hi, Liv," I said in a flat voice. I had called her Liv when we were dating. She came up to me and kissed me on the cheek. Her perfume was faint, but I recognized it as her favorite, jasmine. It had been nearly two and a half years since I'd smelled that scent.

She stayed close to me and looked directly in my eyes. "I'm so glad you're back," she said. "It was hard for me when I heard you were drafted and worse when Robert told me you were in Vietnam. Did you get my letters?"

I flinched and hoped it was too dark for her to see my reaction. "Yes, yes, I got them," I began to stutter. "I, I, I guess I just couldn't think of anything to write back. I'm sorry. It was great of you to write. It meant a lot." I was lying. I had opened the first letter, read half of it, then wadded it up and stuck it in an empty C rations can and left it beside some road while on a mine sweep. I hadn't opened the other two letters. I'd stuck one letter inside my helmet where it got so sweat-soaked I couldn't have read it if I'd wanted to.

"I talked to Robert," she said. "He told me how you were and gave me your address."

"Good, good. Robert's the greatest. I'm lucky to have a friend like him. We're sharing an apartment now with some other guys."

She finally took a step back, and I asked her if she was living at her sorority house. She was. She asked me if I thought campus had changed much. I commented on the new buildings and added that, otherwise, it seemed the same. Then she said she had an editorial review meeting for the student literary magazine and had to go. She put her hand on my arm and gave me a soft squeeze and said, "Believe me, Mike. I'm happy you're back." We exchanged final good-byes, and she rushed off across the street. Sure she was glad I was back. Imagine the emotional conflicts she might have had if I'd ended up KIA.

I started walking again, feeling all knotted up inside, my heart pounding. None of the imaginary conversations I'd had with her had prepared me for a real conversation. I picked up speed as I walked past the student union, turned left at the fine arts building, which was all lit up for an evening event, then out past the girls' dorms. Finally, I cut across an athletic field and left campus.

Four of us—Adam, Brice, Robert, and I—shared a first-floor apartment a block off campus. It was in a plain house that was probably built in the 1920s and had a large porch across the front. The landlord lived upstairs but wasn't around much. I shared a bedroom with Robert McAllister, who had also been my roommate freshman year. Robert was smart, very smart, a physics major with 4.0 GPA. He was also friendly and sociable. What you noticed first, however, about Robert (and he insisted on being called *Robert*) was not his brilliance or great social skills but his limp. He had been born with a right leg that was short and slightly twisted. When he tried to run, he kind of hopped along.

Brice Winslow and Adam Hawthorne shared the other bedroom in the apartment. They were members of Delta Alpha Delta, or DAD, as everyone *not* in the fraternity liked to point out. It was one of those party fraternities full of jocks, but neither of these guys was at all athletic. I hadn't known either of them before coming back that fall, but they both seemed likable enough. They ate their meals and hung out at the fraternity house, so Robert and I only saw them in the morning and late in the evening. Living with Robert and me was only temporary for them. They were planning to live in the new wing being added to their fraternity house, but the building was months behind schedule. They would move out as soon as they could.

As I walked into the apartment that night, I immediately smelled fresh popcorn. Brice was in the living room eating the popcorn and listening to a Beatles album. We greeted each other, and I walked on down the hall and dropped my books in my room. Then I went on into the kitchen at the back of the house. Robert was there, making another batch of popcorn.

"Hi," he said. "Want some popcorn?"

I grabbed a beer from the fridge and sat at the kitchen table. "You bet! Thanks. I'll make the next batch." Our popper was old and had a crank in the lid that required constant turning to keep the popcorn from burning. "I bumped into Olivia tonight," I said after a moment.

"How is she?" There was a strong hint in his voice that said he knew what was coming. "You don't mind that I gave her your address?"

"Oh no. No sweat. It was great to get some mail."

"A couple of months after I gave her your address, she asked me again to be sure the address was okay. You didn't answer her, did you?"

"It wasn't easy to write. Hell, I doubt if I sent you more than two letters, and what would I have said to her anyway?" I took a mouthful of popcorn.

"Four," he said. "You sent me four. But I don't blame you. It's none of my business. Here, get busy and make some more popcorn."

It was a dull evening. I watched some TV, wandered back and forth to the kitchen, and sat in my room for a few minutes, working on a reading assignment. No one else seemed to be having any fun either. Sometime during the evening, Brice asked me some questions about the army. It was obvious that the possibility of being drafted after graduation worried him.

Around ten o'clock, three of their DAD brothers stopped in. One of them smoked, and the living room became stuffy, so I went out on the porch and looked down the hill. I could just see over the trees to the campus, where the white bell tower was visible. If the wind was right, it was possible to hear the clock chime.

It was chilly outside but not cold. At times like this, I wished I smoked. It would give me something to do. Instead, I just stood there with my hands jammed deep in my pockets, my arms locked stiff.

Someone came out on the porch behind me but didn't continue down the steps to the street. Then I heard Robert limp up to me. "Hey, why so pale and wan?" Robert often mixed poetry and Shakespearean quotes into a conversation.

"I don't recognize that," I responded.

"Oh," he said, "it's bullshit anyway. You going to the game tomorrow?" It was the second home football game of the season.

"No, I doubt it. You going?"

"Yeah, I might. Who knows?" He paused then continued. "I know it's none of my business, and I wouldn't blame you for telling me to buzz off but . . ." He paused again. "When did you and Olivia call it quits that spring?"

The question startled me. "Call it quits?" I repeated. "I don't know. Sometime in there."

"Yeah, right," he said. "It was dumb to ask. Forget I mentioned it."

Robert wasn't a busybody, so I wondered just what was on his mind. "Hey," I said. "I don't care, but what does it matter? What are you getting at?"

He sounded relieved I was willing to continue talking. "Well," he said, "I wondered if it had something to do with your going in the army that summer. You said you were drafted."

"Oh, you think I might have done the old French Foreign Legion stunt and run away from a lost love? No. Sorry. I was drafted, plain and simple. And Olivia and I called it quits the last weekend of April." I sounded more emphatic than I really felt.

"Okay, okay," he said. "You're not sore, are you?"

"No. I guess it might not have been obvious what was going on. We were roommates then, but I didn't exactly spill my guts to you, did I?"

He shook his head. "Well . . . then too . . . you know, getting drafted worries Adam and Brice, and I just wanted to know what your circumstances were."

"My circumstances sucked, that's what. The old World War II vets that made up my draft board thought every college student was a draft dodger. Which we were. But hell . . ." I paused to catch my breath. "I don't know . . . What difference does it make?"

"You're right," he said. "It's over. Forget I asked."

"I'm glad you were willing to ask. Shit, if I can't talk to you, I can't talk to anyone. It's good to be back, and I'm glad you were willing to take me into the apartment. I couldn't have tolerated a dorm."

"That's nothing," he said. "We needed someone, and I'm glad it worked out. I didn't want a third DAD brother in the place."

I hit the sack around midnight that night. Some nights, I fell asleep immediately. Other nights, I lay awake, often for hours. Usually, the more beer I had drunk, the quicker I fell asleep, but I hadn't drunk enough that night. I lay awake. Robert had gone to bed before me and was sound asleep. I hadn't told him the full story about how I'd come to be drafted. When Olivia told me to get lost, I stopped studying. My grades went to hell, and since the school sent my grades to my draft board, the old farts had reason to think I was dodging the draft. They had given me an interview before reclassifying me, but I guess I hadn't sounded enthusiastic enough about school. I knew of guys older than me from my high school who were drafted immediately after college graduation, one was even married and working as a teacher. Being drafted had been inevitable.

But it wasn't thinking about the draft that was keeping me awake. It was thinking of Olivia. What a name, *Olivia*. It wasn't a popular name, but it did have a classy ring to it. She had class too. Olivia had fine manners and dressed exquisitely. Maybe that was the problem. She was classy, and I was a jerk. But she enjoyed what I did. She enjoyed this jerk whenever I got my hands on her. She'd never had it so good.

It was obvious when we were dating that her high school dates had probably just held her hand. I held her boobs, her bare boobs. Classy or not, she loved it.

Now two years later, it seemed as if our relationship had gone on for a long time. Isn't December through April a long time? How many months? Five months is almost half a year. People fall in love, marry, and start a family in less than half a year.

Well, so much for her. What was she anyway? She was a prima donna who had never had any real hard knocks, not like the Old Bangkok Whore. I remembered now—the girl had called herself Susie, but the only way I ever thought of her was as the Old Bangkok Whore. At times like this, when I was trying to get to sleep, I thought about the Old Bangkok Whore and the wild things we did. It had been a wonderful education for me. Olivia had never let me get past dipping my hands into her bra, except for the one time I gave her snatch a good stroking, and then just about the time she realized she liked it, she cut me off.

I finally fell asleep. Deep in the night, I dreamed about Vietnam. It was a screwed-up dream with a couple of GIs out by a perimeter bunker yelling at the first sergeant about why they shouldn't be on guard duty. I was in the group but dressed in civilian clothes. I kept yelling that something was dreadfully wrong and that I was a civilian and had been discharged, that I didn't belong in Vietnam. In the dream, it was getting dark, and Top refused to listen to any of us and stuck us all in the bunker. There were too many of us to fit in the bunker, so I stood outside. I had a rifle but only one magazine and no clips of extra ammunition. I kept getting more and more apprehensive, and finally, I woke up. It was three thirty in the morning.

WEEK 2

SEPTEMBER 29, 1968–OCTOBER 5, 1968

MONDAY, SEPTEMBER 30

It may have been the last day of September, but the trees on campus and around town were still deep green. There hadn't been a frost yet. Monday afternoon, after my last class, I walked downtown to a news and tobacco store that didn't mind if you stood and leafed through the magazines. It was a quick, easy walk downtown. The campus was on a hill and Main Street, the main commercial street, ran by the edge of the campus. On the way down, I passed the old Congregational church, which was bright white in the afternoon sun, wooden clapboard with square windows, large columns in front, and a tall steeple. It looked exactly like a New England church should look; only it was in Ohio. The whole city looked like New England, in fact, since that's where the city founders had come from some years after the Revolution. The place was stodgy like New England too. The townspeople revered everything old, and I got the feeling they were all looking forward to being old themselves so they would be respected for no other reason than that they were old.

At the newsstand, I looked at the front pages of some of the out-of-town newspapers. Students and faculty came down to the store specifically for the big city newspapers. It even carried the *New York Times*, although it wasn't delivered until evening. I checked the headlines of the previous day's paper. It was the same old stuff, talk of the war and the Russians stomping on Czechoslovakia. Then I sneaked a peek at a *Playboy*, though I didn't open the centerfold. It pissed off the clerk if you did that. Eventually, I bought a car magazine and left.

Instead of going back to campus or the apartment, I walked through the three blocks that made up Downtown Middlesex. Middlesex was wedged in at the confluence of the Ohio and Chadicoin Rivers, and Main Street crossed a concrete bridge over the Chadicoin River. The town had a colorful history as a pioneer river port when the Northwest Territory opened.

I didn't cross the bridge though. Instead, I walked into a park that faced the river. The park was a popular place with students to take romantic evening walks and do a little smooching. We called it watching the submarine races. The river, which was about seventy-five yards wide, was running quiet and green that afternoon. After a rain, it would be brown with silt. The college had a rowing team that held their races on that section of the river, and on race Saturdays in the spring, students would line the banks with blankets and have picnics while they watched the daytime races.

I was a fool to go to the park. I shook my head at my stupidity and, like a robot, walked to a bench Olivia and I had always sat on the winter and spring we dated. I sat there and leafed through the magazine for a while then put the magazine down and gazed at the green undulations of the river. I allowed myself to imagine time had run backward and that I was waiting for Olivia and that she would come up behind me, greet me, and sit down next to me.

But Olivia never came, and after half an hour, I got hungry and started the hike back up through town to campus. Walking up the hill reminded me of a mine sweep along a busy road through the villages in Nam. During those mine sweeps, you didn't have to worry about stepping on a mine or trip wires because of all the local traffic. Now as I walked along the sidewalk, I was wishing I had my rifle instead of just a rolled-up magazine.

It took only fifteen minutes to walk across town. Back in 1820, when the school was founded, the campus must have been well past the town's limits, though by the end of the nineteenth century, fine large homes had been built up along one side of campus. Today the campus took up two square blocks on the edge of the commercial section of town.

The campus looked idyllic. Large sycamore, maple, and beach trees dotted the wide front lawn. Three brick buildings with white trim, each more than a century old, sat in a row on the crest of the gentle slope. These were the oldest buildings on campus and symbolized the school's appeal to traditional values. Adams Hall, the middle building, had a white wood-framed clock tower, the image of which appeared on the seal of the college. Westminster chimes marked each quarter hour. Every Sunday at noon, the chairman of the music department played the chimes and gave a recital of sorts.

Parts of campus had changed, of course, while I'd been gone. There was a new men's dorm and a new women's dorm, as well as a new building for the biology department. Another classroom building was under construction, but I didn't remember what department would occupy it.

More significant was the change in the atmosphere on campus. Anger and anxiety were poisoning the tranquility I'd experienced my freshmen year. Student gripes with the administration centered on privacy rights. Students wanted protection from campus cops searching their dorm rooms without a warrant. Students considered it double jeopardy when they got in trouble with the town police and then the school punished them too. There were also academic issues, such as initiating pass-fail classes and students publishing their evaluations of professors and classes. The student senate had formed committees to deal with all these issues, plus some extra committees just in case.

The paramount issue for most men on campus was the draft. Deferments for graduate school were becoming rare, which left few realistic alternatives. Only the truly desperate went to Canada, and claiming to be a conscientious objector was a chicken way out. Each day closer to graduation was a day closer to doom.

The campus had always been politically conservative; certainly, the town was. Now there was a determined group that wanted to get students more involved in national and world affairs, particularly the war, but it was difficult to tell how the majority of students felt, and so a case of schizophrenia had set in. My reaction to the campus mood was disappointment. I had just *left* a war, the ultimate chaos. What I wanted was a laid-back, peaceful place where the girls were easy. Middlesex wasn't Columbia or the Sorbonne. And I thought it shouldn't try to be.

I walked past the old buildings to a newer part of campus and headed for the student union for a hamburger. The union was a single-story building on a plaza at the center of campus. The library was across the plaza from the union, making the complex the central gathering place on campus. A large cafeteria occupied half of the union, and a TV lounge and large game room with pool tables and Ping-Pong tables took up the rest of the building. The cafeteria was called the Hideout, and the name had become and was synonymous with the student union. I ordered a hamburger and french fries. With a Coke, it cost me $1.50, a lot more than eating back at the apartment. Money was always a concern because I was trying to make it in school on army savings, loans, and Veterans Administration GI Bill checks.

When I got my food and walked out into the seating area, I saw Pete sitting at a table by a window. He was looking outside. "Hey, Pete," I said as I sat down across him, "what're you looking at?"

He turned from the window. "Oh hey, man," he said. "Yeah, sit down. How ya doin'? Nice to see ya." We'd seen each other in class that morning, but Pete always greeted people like long-lost friends.

"The Deltas won't to be happy to find you sitting at one of their prime window tables," I said, putting salt on my burger.

"Fuck the Deltas." He turned back to the window.

"Only kidding," I said. "Right. Fuck the Deltas." I started eating, and we didn't say anything more until I had nearly finished my burger. It was pleasant to sit with someone and not have to talk. When I did speak up, I asked about the friends I'd met at his apartment. "How did you bump into Patty and her friends?"

He turned back to face me, toying with the plate and silverware in front of him. "When I moved in, there was nobody on campus, and I needed a source, so I just poked around local hangouts and made friends." Pete sounded proud that he smoked dope.

"Cool," I said. "They're nice people."

"Damn sight nicer than the stuck-up bunch of assholes on campus! Look at them." He nodded at a table across the way. I knew he meant where the Sigmas sat, so I didn't turn around. Later in the conversation, I looked at the table though. Three guys and a girl were sitting there, playing with their leftover food and leaving a big mess on the table. It was a competition among the fraternities to leave their tables as big a mess as possible. Some kind of intramural sport, I guess.

Next, I asked Pete about Patty's classes. It turned out she was our age but hadn't taken any classes until that fall. He went on talking about some of the town guys he knew and told me where they worked. The chemical industry was big down the Ohio River, and many of the guys were working there and making good money. He said the two guys I'd met at his place had both been drafted out of high school and had been to Nam too.

"Where were they?" I asked him. "What did they do?"

"They were both cannon cockers," he said. "In the artillery. One was down in the Delta and the other up near Pleku. What was it you said you did over there?"

"Engineer. Combat engineer."

"Yeah. Right. A ditch-digger with a gun from what I could tell."

I sort of smiled. "That's about right. Only we considered it more like construction. Roads, bridges, work like that. And a hell of a lot of fighting too."

"Oh sure." He moved one hand in apology. "I only meant that I saw our engineers putting in culverts and stuff on the roads and slogging through the mud when the monsoon washed everything out." He didn't want to insult me. "You guys did a hell of a lot of miserable, dangerous work."

But I hadn't taken offense to the ditch-digger comment. "Yep. Our battalion motto was *Build, Fight, and Destroy*. We liked the *destroy* part best."

Pete tapped his plate with a fork. "A real party, all right." Since Pete had been in the infantry—a grunt—and had talked about "operations," I knew he'd done the worst. I wonder what weapon he'd carried, but it wasn't that important now and was probably a dumb question to ask. After a pause, he spoke up again. "Your VA check come yet?"

"No. How about you?"

"No. Just like always." He laughed. "They screw us in the end. You got enough dough?"

"Yeah, I'm getting along." I was but just barely. "I can get some cash from my parents if I really need it," I added. My parents had divorced, and each expected the other to take care of such things as helping their son. I wouldn't go to either one for help unless I was absolutely desperate.

Three girls were at the jukebox choosing songs. They were enjoying themselves, laughing, pointing, and arguing about what to play. They looked too young to be in college.

"Are they high school girls?" I asked Pete, who had noticed them too.

"I doubt it," he said, "but they sure act like it. They're young impressionable freshman," he said with a leering ring to his voice and a Groucho Marx bob of his eyebrows.

"Nah," I said. "Too young." One of them reminded me of the Old Bangkok Whore; she was that thin.

Pete moved his fork and knife again, but he wasn't really eating anything. "Don't forget, you're starting over, big guy. All the prime chicks in the freshman class have already been staked out by the fast-talking fraternity men."

"You didn't rob the cradle," I said to counter his argument. "Patty's our age."

He nodded. "I was real lucky running into her." He looked over at the girls again. "You ought to think about those girls. They're eighteen and fair game."

The girls had chosen "Love Is Blue," a nice song, and gone back to their table. I could tell they knew Pete and I had checked them out. One of them was wearing a nice short skirt, and from where I was sitting, I got a great view up the side of her leg. It was easy to imagine giving her a kiss on that thigh and then another a little higher and more and more until she went over the top. Then I heard them giggle and shook myself out of the fantasy. They were just children. I had learned too much in Bangkok.

"Anyway," Pete continued, "it would be discriminatory not to consider them just because they're just out of high school." He grinned again.

"Yeah. I have no intention of becoming a monk."

The song ended, and then the same song started over again. The girls laughed, and Pete and I gathered up our books and split.

As we walked down the steps and out of the Hideout, Pete insisted I had to come over to his place that Saturday. He was having a party, and all his town friends would be there. Obviously, my asking about the group had made Pete think I wanted to be included. He must have also thought I would fit in, even though I wasn't a toker.

TUESDAY, OCTOBER 1

Pete didn't need to encourage me to check out women. I had eyeballed every girl I'd seen on campus. Just because three weeks had gone by and I hadn't gotten around to a date didn't mean I wasn't interested. A lot of that had to do with fitting back in, seeing who was available, and then figuring out how to approach them.

There was one girl I didn't need to figure out how to approach. Twice a week, I could reach out and touch her. She sat in front of me in my ten-o-clock American literature class. I couldn't help but notice her, but I hadn't been able to figure out much about her other than the color of her hair, strawberry blond. And she wore it in a pageboy style. I hadn't seen much else because she was always seated when I came into the class, and I was always a little late, so I always rushed get to my seat. At the end of class, she'd pick up her books and bolt from the classroom. I had no reason to think she was worth following outside class.

A classroom discussion of *The Scarlet Letter* changed my opinion. The book was a bore, but at least it had a sex angle. The professor was trying to make a point about Hawthorne's writing technique of using allegory, but some girls in the class kept swinging the discussion to how men in the book victimized Hester. After a few of these remarks, I spoke up and suggested that Hester might have had an economic motivation for her plunge into adultery. It wasn't a brilliant observation, but I hadn't contributed much to the class and thought it was time to say something. Some of the girls groaned, and then the strawberry blonde in front of me turned in her seat and, with an expressionless face, said, "What an interesting thought." I couldn't think of anything to say back to her.

The image of her blue eyes and cute nose remained in my mind for the rest of the hour. My mind started to buzz. How could I approach her after class? Finally, I decided that I would apologize for any offense my wisecrack might have made. An apology is always a good opening. Girls instinctively feel men owe them an apology.

When the class ended, she bolted out the door as usual. The hall filled up quickly as the other classes let out, and the narrow stairs down to the first floor were slow-going, but I could see her ahead of me. The longer it took me to catch up to her, the more I lost faith in my half-assed idea of apologizing to her, but I pressed on, and as the stream of students spilled out on to the sidewalk, I followed her and was finally able to catch up. She was tall and unfortunately was wearing a bulky sweater pulled down over her hips, so I couldn't see much of her shape.

I finally caught up with her but walked past her for a pace or two. Then acting like someone ahead of me was in the way, I slowed and glanced over at her. She looked straight ahead. I looked at her again and said, "Excuse me. I hope my comment in class wasn't offensive."

Hearing myself say the words out loud, I wanted to crawl under a rock and never come out. It didn't help when it took her an eternity to acknowledge my existence. Finally, she cast me a look. "Was it intended to be?"

"No," I said. "I just wanted to give a different perspective, a different idea, than I heard other people giving." Before she could say anything, I added, "So I've offended you, I take it?"

"Since I don't know you, Mr. Collins, why would I think your remark was offensive?" The professor called us all by our last names, so her using my last name was no big deal. But her name wasn't easy to pronounce. It sounded French. I took a stab at it.

"Ms. Fontaine," I said, "not knowing me might make you more inclined to consider me offensive." Then as we looked at each other, we both broke into big smiles. The sidewalk was too crowded to talk, so she led me up the steps of the administration building.

"I have to go to the bursar's office," she said, "but we'll have plenty of opportunities to exchange literary opinions in class."

"Yeah," I said, "and you owe me your opinion of Hester's predicament. I gave you mine in class." She just smiled and went on up the steps.

Once again, I had proved that I wasn't a smooth operator. But she had spoken to me and smiled, so all was not lost.

THURSDAY, OCTOBER 3

It was the third week of classes, and everyone's movements around campus were regular, Olivia's in particular. Our schedules coincided on Monday, Wednesday, and Friday afternoons. I had seen her twice. She was entering the chemistry wing of the sciences building as I was leaving my geology lecture. When we were dating, she used to talk about chemistry research and her plans to go to graduate school. It looked like she was still on course. And why not? She was capable, she didn't have the draft to worry about, and her folks had plenty of money. She was an intelligent girl—so intelligent she dumped me.

I wasn't so smart. In fact, I was so dumb I decided to stage an inadvertent meeting one afternoon. I waited in front of the chemistry building for her to leave after a lab. Labs were usually from one o'clock to three o'clock. When by three fifteen I hadn't seen her, I decided to walk through the building and see if she'd left by some other door. The halls were empty, which made it easier to look in the small windows of the doors to the labs. I had no idea which lab she might be in, so I was checking both sides of the hall. I was startled when I looked in one window and saw her. I ducked past the window and then stepped further out into the hall and took another look through the door window. She was alone sitting on a lab stool, intently writing in her notebook.

It seemed like an ideal opportunity to talk to her. I had carried on many imaginary conversations with her, and now I had the opportunity speak to her for real. If I stood there and thought about the situation, I wouldn't go in and talk to her. It was like taking a rifle shot at a moving target; success is in reaction, not calculation.

She didn't turn at the sound of the door opening, but then she glanced up as I approached. "Mike!" She sounded surprised. "Do you have a lab?"

"No," I said. "I was just looking for Robert when I saw you. Do you mind?" I asked as I pulled a lab stool up next to her. A lab assistant and two students were at the front of a lab discussing a diagram on the green board.

"Oh sure, sit down. I was just finishing." It was obvious that she was flustered and didn't know how to handle the situation. "So . . . how are you?" she asked. "Getting back into the groove?" She kept her head down and worked on transposing some numbers from multiple pieces of paper on to her lab report.

"Fine, actually," I managed to say. "Everything is fitting together. It's certainly a lot better than the army. That was a nightmare."

She kept working, but then after a moment, she looked up and smiled. "Great," she said. "But I bet it's hard to adjust. I've heard of guys that have real problems." She shuffled her papers together. "There, that about does it." She looked up at the clock. "Gee—I'm late."

"So what lab is this?" I asked. She said it was an advanced organic chemistry class. Then I asked if she was planning on graduate school.

She continued to gather up her papers and notebooks. "Yes, yes," she said. "I'm hoping for Ohio State. Or maybe Case."

I had to speed up the conversation and cut the small talk. She reached for a book beside me, and I put my hand on it and held it. She looked up at me.

"Look, Olivia, it's been two years. Maybe we can see each other and get to know each other again."

Her shoulders dropped, and she took a deep breath. "Oh, Mike. I'm sorry, but no. You see, I'm really serious about someone."

I took my hand off the book. "I didn't know. It's only been a couple of weeks, and I hadn't noticed."

"Of course not," she said in a sympathetic voice. "These things just happen. It hasn't been easy for either of us."

"Yeah. Right." I desperately tried to recover. "Well . . . uh . . . we have to keep in touch. I mean, I wish you luck. But I'd still like to be able to talk to you . . . and such."

"Sure, Mike. Absolutely." She picked up her books and her purse. "We had a great time together. And now things are finally much better for you. We can always talk to each other."

There was nothing else to say. I stood up and stepped aside as she walked to the front of the lab to drop off her report. She came back to the rear door, and I opened it for her. She turned left in the hall, the same direction I had intended to go. I began turn right. Before I could say anything, she turned, smiled, and said, "I'm glad you stopped to talk. Really I am. We must keep in touch."

We each said a polite good-bye and walked toward opposite ends of the empty hall.

SATURDAY, OCTOBER 5

Pete had reminded me twice during the week about his party. When I got to his place Saturday evening, it was already full of pot smoke. It was so sweet and pungent I started coughing as soon as I stopped through the door. It smelled just like Nam when I used to walk past the hooches at night on my way to the latrine. Pete greeted me with great excitement. He was always happy to have another person join the party. There were two other couples besides Pete and Patty. They weren't as enthusiastic as Pete to see me. When I walked down the stairs, the conversation lagged, and one of them stuffed a bag under a couch cushion. I went into the kitchen to get a beer and talk to Pete.

"Jeez, Pete, where do you get this stuff? The place is so high it's going to float off its foundation."

"Oh, it's easy, man. But damn expensive. You wouldn't believe what we pay. There's no such thing as a nickel bag. Remember Nam? We could get a whole squad high on $5 bag. Not here. It's terrible. But we've got some good stuff tonight."

"Enjoy it," I said, "but you guys have to be careful. The old lady upstairs must smell the stuff."

"Yeah." He laughed. "She asked once. I told her we were cooking. Making popcorn. She doesn't know what's up."

"But she could have visitors," I said. "What about her family?"

"That's true, I guess. Well, we listen for cars and strange people talking and walking around upstairs."

I looked out into the living room area. I could see just how alert they were.

"Come on in," he said, and I followed him, holding my beer. A lamp in the corner had a black lightbulb, but there was so much other light it didn't have a good effect.

There were two other couples besides Pete and Patty. I was apprehensive about meeting them. In the army, any new person joining a group of pot smokers was automatically considered a spy that would rat them out. In the army, every new replacement was a member of the Criminal Investigation Division until proven otherwise.

The couples in the living room were arguing about something when Pete and I sat down. Pete made an announcement to the group to introduce me. "Hey, this is Mike, my buddy from freshman year." One guy looked at me with no expression and then continued arguing with the others. I sat on the floor and leaned against the cellar wall. The floor was carpeted, and Pete threw me some pillows, so I was comfortable. After a while, Patty introduced me around personally. One couple was Carl and Anna, the other was Steve and Teresa. I had seen Carl and Anna once before.

I listened to the group talk and bicker, but I couldn't figure out what they were arguing about. It had something to do with money and somebody screwing somebody over, and generally, everything was fucked up. I assumed it must be about buying pot. Pete and I hadn't been in there long when Steve gave Pete a push, and they went into the kitchen. Reading their body language, I was certain Pete was convincing him that I wasn't a cop. They came back in, and Steve pulled out his stash and started to roll a joint. The conversation stopped, and I got a couple of glances, but it seemed that if I was cool with Pete, then I was okay with the others.

They passed the joint, and I took a deliberately short toke and passed it along. Since I was a juicer, I didn't know if it was good pot or not, but when it came time, I complimented it and made a joke to Pete about it being Nook Mow 100s. Carl added something about it being as good as Mekong gold. Then he and Pete traded stories about how cheap and how good the pot was in Nam. I just hoped that pot was all they were going to do because I sure as hell wasn't going to do anything else just to be part of the party. I passed up the joint next time around and for the rest of the evening.

The group was happy with good talk and no more bickering. I talked to Carl and asked him about being a cannon cocker in the central highlands.

"So what kind of gun were you on?" I asked.

"A 105 mm and then an eight-inch battery," he said. "What did you do?"

I told him I was a "pioneer." He knew something about combat engineers and said a company of engineers had worked on one of the landing zones he'd been on. They had lifted in equipment and built landing pads covered with steel mat, ammo storage, and bunkers to live in. I told him I had done mostly mine sweeps.

"So you used those detectors?" he asked.

"No," I said. "We had them, but usually, the batteries were either dead or snitched for personal radios. Anyway, the gooks used crap the detectors wouldn't pick up."

"So you just walked along? How'd you find anything?"

"We backed a truck down the road ahead of us." I described how a driver would hang out of the side of the truck, looking backward. He'd back the truck for miles down a dirt road or trail. "That way," I explained, "when the truck hit a mine, it blew up the back wheels, and the driver usually only got a bad headache." Carl got a kick out of this.

"So what did you do on the gun crew?" I asked him.

"Oh, I prepped the fuses and humped the joes to the gun."

"Was the 105 battery mobile?"

"Yeah, and what a pain that was! Always on the move and everything a crisis, hurry, hurry, some sorry grunt unit getting its ass kicked. Damn, I was glad to get out of that."

I had seen 105 batteries at work a number of times and had always marveled at how quick they could be dropped in by cargo helicopter and set up. They could pound out an enormous amount of fire.

Pete had put on his favorite album, *Yellow Submarine*. It was a couple of years old and had some scratches, but Pete loved it and sang along.

"We do live in a kind of submarine," he announced at the top of his voice. "See, we're down here in the apartment below ground, not underwater, but it's nice and cozy anyway," and then he continued singing along. For a moment, it did seem like we had all we needed. I shut my eyes and hummed a little to the music.

Without realizing it, I fell asleep, slumping over on the pillows. When I opened my eyes again, all the girls had gone over to the kitchen area, and a different album was playing. The guys were talking about a movie, *2001, A Space Odyssey*. I hadn't seen it yet, but I'd heard talk about it around the apartment. It was a spooky science-fiction movie. Everyone always offered their opinion of what the story was about. They described scenes, and I began to worry they would ruin the movie for me, so I said, "Hey, I haven't seen it yet. Don't talk about the important stuff, or you'll ruin it for me."

Carl just laughed. "Don't worry," he said. "It's so weird we *couldn't* ruin it for you." They kept talking, so I got up and went to the kitchen to get a beer and wait until the guys were talking about something else.

The kitchen was in a commotion, with the girls making a spaghetti dinner. Teresa had brought a big pot of sauce, which she was heating and stirring. Patty was working on a salad, and Anna was cooking some meatballs. I got a beer and stood by the refrigerator and chatted with them. "So whose idea was this?" I asked no one in particular.

"This is the second time we've done this," Patty answered. "It was Teresa's idea. Her mom's from Italy, and she made the sauce."

"My mom was a war bride." Teresa smiled at me. She wasn't wearing a bra, which made it difficult to talk to her.

"Can I help with anything?" I asked.

"Yeah," said Patty. "You can get some bowls out of the cabinet to the right of the sink."

I got the bowls and put them on the table. "Are all of us going to sit at the table?" I asked. It was a small table that sat half on the linoleum in the kitchen and half on the carpet in the living room.

Patty answered, "We can make do."

Dinner was pleasant with happy conversation and lots of laughs and smiles. The spaghetti was delicious. The girls had cooked it with olive oil and herbs. All us guys had two bowls. I thanked the group and explained I hadn't expected dinner, let alone such a good dinner.

We had just finished cleaning up the kitchen when the mood took a big swing for the worse. Carl and Anna had gone back into living room, and Steve and Teresa had disappeared into Pete's bedroom. It was time I left. I was about to thank Pete and Patty, who were still in the kitchen with me, when a shouting match broke out in the living room. I ignored it and was trying to talk to Pete when Carl stomped up the stairs and left, slamming the door. We could hear Anna crying in the living room. Patty went to talk to her.

"Problems?" I asked Pete.

"Yeah," he said. "They were planning to get married when he got back from Nam, or at least that's what she thought."

"Well, that's a big plunge," I said. "Maybe it's just a matter of his settling down again."

Pete nodded. "Probably. But he thinks she was doing some dating while he was gone."

"What a mess." I was still thinking about leaving.

Patty came back to the kitchen. "I'm gonna walk her home," she said in a whisper. Anna was putting on her coat.

"It's a long way," Pete said. "I'll drive you."

"No," Patty whispered, looking back at Anna. "I offered that already. She doesn't want to be around you either. She thinks you're partly to blame for Carl being such a mess."

"Shit! My ass," Pete exclaimed. "She was dating, and you know it."

"Shit yourself. It was just for fun, and she kept writing to him damn near every day. Carl even said that." Patty got her coat on, and the two girls went up the stairs and left. Pete watched them leave and turned to me.

"Hey, do me a favor," he said, "and go with them. There may be some assholes cruising around. Somebody should be with them."

"Yeah, sure," I said. I got my coat and started up the stairs. "How far is it?" I called back to him.

"Only about a mile. Maybe a mile and a half."

When I got outside, though, I realized I didn't know which way they'd gone. I ran down the alley to the street and saw them walking away from campus. I lost all enthusiasm for the venture when I realized it would be a multi-mile hike out of my way. Nevertheless, I'd given my word. I caught up with the girls and told them I thought it would be a good idea if I walked with them. They didn't object, but they weren't any more enthusiastic than I was about my going with them. I walked as far behind them as I could and still appear to be with them. They hardly talked. It had been obvious through the evening that Patty and Anna had known each other for long time.

Half a block from Pete's place, we walked past a police cruiser sitting at the curb. The engine was running, and a large cloud of white exhaust hung in the still, cold air behind the car. The cop appeared to be writing up some paperwork and not looking at us. As I looked at his uniform with its patches, badges, and other paraphernalia, I wondered if his wife kept up his uniforms, doing all the sewing and starching. Some people liked uniforms, but I didn't miss them at all. The cop didn't look up, but I knew if he were any good, he had noticed us, as well as many details about us.

Pete was right about the distance to Anna's house. We had actually walked to the edge of town. There was still a sidewalk, but I got the feeling we were near the end of it. Patty and Anna turned up the gravel drive to a modest single-story house. A dog barked, and the back porch light was on. I stayed back on the sidewalk. When Patty came back down the drive, I said to her, "It's too bad they got into a ruckus. It was a swell evening till then."

She nodded. "It wasn't the first time they've been through this since he got back. I don't think they're going to make it."

"Have they been going together long?"

"Since senior year in high school."

"Too bad," I said. We walked on without speaking. I thought over my conversation with Carl. He hadn't said when he'd been drafted or when he'd gotten back. I could have asked Patty, but details really didn't matter.

We were nearly back to Pete's place when she spoke again. "Pete said you were dating someone your freshman year."

"Yeah," I said, "that's right. I didn't realize Pete knew that about me. He and I didn't know each other our freshmen year." Her question surprised me. I wondered what she was getting at and how I should have answered.

"So," she asked, "did she write you like Anna wrote Carl?" That question certainly cleared up what she was getting at.

It was my business, no one else's. I responded bluntly. "No. We split in the spring before school ended."

"She didn't write?" She seemed disappointed.

"No, of course not." I thought of the letters Olivia had written, but they weren't what Patty was talking about.

"Well," she said after a minute, "the war is hard on us girls too, even if we don't have to leave and go do the fighting."

"Yeah. Sure." I realized I'd made a poor choice of words, so I continued. "It's true, I agree." And I could understand what she was getting at, even if I hadn't experienced it.

When we got back to the apartment, Pete greeted us, but Patty was cool to him. The other couple had left, and it was nearly eleven o'clock, so I was eager to leave.

"No," Pete responded when I said I was hitting the road, "no way, man. You've got to sit down and warm up. Sit down, and I'll get you a beer."

I knew it was stupid to drink any more, but my feet were cold, so I sat down just to get them warm. As I sat on the couch drinking the beer, Patty and Pete sat in separate chairs. We talked about school and music—anything but the army or the war. Pete liked Jimi Hendrix and thought the Beatles were over the hill. Patty disagreed. Soon, it was time I left, so I stood up to go, only to have the room start swinging around me. I sat back down.

"Damn, man," Pete said. "You're tanked"

"No, no, I'm okay. Just give me a second here."

Pete was having none of that. "It would be stupid to walk back now. Put your feet up and sleep on the couch."

"No way, I'm okay," I said, but I didn't try to get up. Pete brought me another pillow, and Patty put my jacket to cover me.

"Okay," I said, rolling on my side. "I'll just clear my head a little."

That was it. I was asleep before the two of them made it to the bedroom.

I slept fitfully with disturbing dreams. I would wake myself up enough to be certain it was a dream then go back to sleep only to have another dream creep into my mind. That's the way I slept when I was in a strange and uncomfortable place. I had had dozens and dozens of nights like this in the past two years. I got up to piss once. The bathroom was upstairs, which made it spooky at night. The old landlady might mistake me for a prowler and shoot me with her grandfather's Civil War hand cannon. The lights in the kitchen area were still on, though, which made it easier to get up the stairs, which creaked no matter how carefully I stepped.

When I came back down, I noticed that Patty's coat was still draped over a chair, and one of her shoes was in the middle of the floor. Pete's door was closed. I envied him. How wonderful it must be to make love with someone you care for in a safe and comfortable place without worry about time or consequences. I didn't envy the sex. I envied the love.

I considered putting my shoes on and walking back to the apartment, but the green luminous dots and hands of my watch showed it was three thirty. It would be cold outside, so instead, I grabbed one of Pete's jackets off a hook and, with my own jacket, made myself more comfortable and went back to sleep on the couch.

WEEK 3

OCTOBER 6, 1968–OCTOBER 12, 1968

SUNDAY, OCTOBER 6, 1968

When I awoke again, it was light enough to see my watch clearly. It was eight thirty in the morning. The minute I stepped outside, the cold air woke me up with a snap. The air gave me a sharp chill, but it was clean and easy to breathe compared with the air down in the apartment. The sun was up and caught me direct in the face, making me squint. I walked quickly down the paved brick alley and turned left toward campus. It was a relief to have the sun to my right side and out of my eyes. The sun felt like a warm soft hand on my cheek.

I walked halfway down the block before the first car passed me. Thick Sunday newspapers lay on people's walks and front porches, along with the leaves that had fallen during the night and covered the sidewalks. I kept my head down, watching my feet churn the leaves. It bothered me not to be able to see what I was walking on. It was important to know what you might step on or if there was a trip wire in your path. This wasn't Vietnam, but it was still a good habit to watch where you walked.

Suddenly a movement entered my field of vision. I looked up. "Shit!" I said to myself. Two girls were walking toward me, and one of them was Natalie. A feeling of failure swept over me. I hated being surprised. How had I survived Vietnam? Luck? Thank God the girls had no weapons, or I would have been dead. They had seen me, and despite the sun in her eyes, Natalie had recognized me and smiled. They were dressed for church. I remembered there was a large Methodist church further up the street past Pete's house.

"Well, hello," Natalie said. "This is a surprise."

"Yes," I replied, "a surprise but a pleasant one. It looks like you two are off to church." I smiled at Natalie then at the other girl.

Natalie smiled back. "Yes, it gives the dorm mother a good impression."

"I don't think you've any trouble with that," I said.

I had stopped close to them but had shuffled back as far as possible without being obvious. I had not showered or changed clothes for twenty-four hours and had spent the night in a cellar filled with cigarette and pot smoke. The further away I stood, the better. Natalie's complexion was like a white rose petal, and the sun in her hair highlighted the streaks of red. Then I thought of the stubble of beard I must have.

She continued the conversation. "And you're up early for a Sunday morning."

"Well," I said, "I couldn't sleep, and taking a walk will do me good. I'm going to get breakfast downtown at a diner." I knew my story was weak. "But I can't hold you two up. You'll be late." I stepped past them and then turned briefly and looked at Natalie.

"Well," she said, "enjoy your breakfast. See you in class."

"Yeah, see you. Maybe we can get coffee after class sometime?"

She nodded. "That sounds great. Bye."

What the hell, I thought. *Had I made a date? Why had I said that?* Too often my mouth ran along without my brain. I walked on, wondering if the day had started well or ill.

MONDAY, OCTOBER 7

I got the impression that my political science professor, Mr. Diefenbaker, was enjoying the turmoil of election year. It certainly simplified his class preparations. He had only vaguely followed the course outline since the semester had begun and had taken every opportunity to talk about current events. I didn't care, except the result was a lot of talk about the war.

Monday morning's class followed this pattern. Diefenbaker was all charged up from hearing politicians interviewed on the Sunday news programs. He scanned the class and took a quick attendance then walked around his desk and jumped right in, talking about what he had seen the morning before. "Who saw Muskie on *Face the Nation?*" he asked.

I kept my head down, but I could hear hands being raised as a few of the class puppets indicated they had seen the program. "And did anyone read the newspaper, even just the headlines?" he asked. I heard about the same amount of body movement and suspected it was the same people signaling compliance. I had breezed over the paper, but I wasn't going to admit it.

"You have heard it from me a number of times already," Diefenbaker said, "and you will hear it again and again. Political science is happening right in front of you, and you don't need to read dry textbooks to understand it. More important is the fact that we are squarely in the middle of one of the most dynamic periods of American political science. You're fortunate. You're witnessing a renaissance in American political thinking. Scientifically, these changes would be equivalent to the work of Newton or Galileo." Diefenbaker leaned toward the melodramatic, but at least you didn't sleep in his class.

Another reason not to sleep was that he constantly called on students. Class participation was big. This was a problem for me because Diefenbaker had tagged me as a veteran, which I guess I didn't try to hide, but that made him consider me an authority on the details of combat. That meant I had to control my daydreaming in his class and pay enough attention to know what was being discussed. One thing that helped me concentrate was that there weren't any particularly good-looking girls in the class. One of the class stars, a girl, piped up to get the ball rolling. "Muskie's comment shocked me," she said. I was pretty sure she was a drama major, and I could tell she and Diefenbaker were going to be a predictable duet during the semester. The discussion progressed, and the professor called on a number of kids. In my mind, I visualized each name being called as an incoming artillery round landing on a map coordinate in the classroom. "Mr. Fredricks," he called, and an incoming splashed two rows to my left and three seats back. Unlike reality, Diefenbaker didn't call the same person twice during the class, so when you were hit, you could relax for the rest of the hour. I sneaked a look at my watch. Only fifteen minutes left. The risk of being called on was getting smaller. Then the topic turned to the proposed bombing halt.

"So, Mr. Collins," Diefenbaker looked at me, "would you say a bombing halt would endanger our troops?" *Wump.* I was hit. I didn't respond immediately. Diefenbaker had the habit of asking a question with the tone and inflection of a reporter, and it annoyed me. I looked at him to acknowledge the question then said, "Sure. Certainly. The NVA would be fools not to take advantage of it." I felt lucky to get such an easy question to answer.

"Why are we proposing a bombing halt?" he asked. "It sounds like a dumb thing to do. Why?" He was looking all around the room, pleading for class participation.

One of the frequent class contributors said, "We must send a signal that we are willing to negotiate. It could be the beginning of peace."

With that, Diefenbaker turned to me again. "What do you think, Mr. Collins? Is the chance for peace worth the risk to the GIs?"

Just like in real life, incoming hit me twice. I answered as quickly as possible. "Sure. I didn't say the bombing halt wasn't a good idea. You just asked if it would cost GIs' lives."

"Then you support the bombing halt?"

I felt myself slipping into an endless string of questions. "Sure. We have to wiggle our way out as soon as possible."

"Wiggle our way out?" Diefenbaker laughed. "I haven't heard it put that way before. Can't we win this war?" He was standing in the aisle, one desk away, looking at me.

I shook my head. "Oh god, no!"

Then a guy behind and to one side of me spoke up. "That's a defeatist attitude. Don't you still have friends over there? With support like that, they may not come back."

I looked straight ahead. "My support doesn't mean crap. I'm just telling it like it is."

"Well," the guy said, "we in the ROTC have military training too, and we know that, with the right support, we can win this war. Instead of a bombing halt, we should be intensifying the bombing."

"Bomb them back to the Stone Age?" Diefenbaker asked sarcastically.

"If necessary," the ROTC kid replied. "That's what brought Hitler to his knees."

I finally turned and looked at the guy. "Oh, man," I said, "they're already in the Stone Age. They were when we got there. We can't hurt them."

"B-52s can hurt them and hurt them bad," he replied. I could hear the emotion building in his voice.

I could just imagine this young butter-bar getting fragged his first week in country. I smiled at him. "You've been watching too many John Wayne movies." Then I turned back to the front of the room. He huffed and puffed and spit some reply back at me, but Diefenbaker cut him off.

"Gentlemen! Gentlemen! We get the picture. I would say there is no clear answer to this question." He went on talking and strolling around the room.

The muffled sound of the campus bell tower chiming three quarters of an hour drifted into the room, making everyone eager for the end of class. Soon, some people started shuffling papers and putting away their notebooks. Finally, Diefenbaker released us, and we evacuated the room in a rush. Many people had to hurry, since they had long walks to their next class. I didn't have a class after that, but I walked as fast as I could along the crowded sidewalks toward the student union. Thoughts of good fresh coffee and a doughnut immediately replaced all talk of political science in my mind.

I had intended to go through the cafeteria line to get the brewed coffee, but when I got there, the line was too long to wait. There was a row of vending machines along the far wall, so I walked over, fished change out of my pocket, and fed the coffee machine. People like me crowded the place as they come in from classes and others rushed out for their ten-o-clock classes. I didn't pay much attention to the crowd behind me. The coffee machine clicked and clanked, and finally, a jet of coffee pissed into a paper cup. I juggled my books and took the cup out of the slot and was turning around when a guy behind me began to speak.

"So here's the campus warrior! You know, I don't like being ridiculed in class." It was the ROTC guy. Standing close to him, I saw we were about the same height. He dressed better than me, wearing a knit shirt and slacks with a crease.

"Well then," I responded, taking a sip of my coffee, "don't say anything ridiculous."

"It's ridiculous to win the war?" he shot back. "Maybe the problem is the quality of people we have over there. If they're all like you, we probably couldn't win."

"Fuck you," I said and began to move off. Then I realized two other guys were with him. One made a move to block me, and another ROTC guy from class moved toward me too. We collided, and my coffee spilled on me and one of them. We were all swearing when a deep voice cut in.

"What's going on here? Come on, keep the aisle open. What happened here?" It was the manager of the company that ran the student union and the campus dining halls. The guy was big, bigger than any of us, and he was dressed in a sharp business suit. He was frequently in the student union because his office was there. Everyone knew who he was.

The four of us responded in chorus, "Nothing." I added that I'd spilled my coffee.

"I don't want spills or arguments in my cafeteria," he barked, "so let's clear this area."

The guy sounded like a first sergeant. I stepped around the group and found a table, and the ROTC bunch went to their fraternity table. Most of the ROTC guys belonged to the same fraternity. It took a while for me to settle down. Looking at my coffee cup as I sipped, I saw my hand was shaking slightly. "Green Tambourine Man" was playing on the jukebox, so I concentrated on the song and tried to relax. I didn't have much time to stew over the incident, though, because Robert came limping up to the table, balancing a tray, and sat down. "Hi," he said, "how long have you got?" Neither of us had bothered to figure out the other's schedule.

"Oh, a while," I said, looking at my watch. It was nearly ten thirty. "I've got speech at eleven. You have anything else?"

"Yeah. Math at eleven."

We talked about our schedules. Robert was taking more physics and math that I was. I didn't understand how he did it. He claimed he had to take the heavy stuff to get into graduate school. He hoped to get into the University of Chicago to study nuclear physics. I thought of Olivia going to graduate school.

"What?" I joked. "You want to make bombs?"

"No, no. None of that stuff," he said. "I just think the explanation for everything will be found through nuclear physics. It's exciting."

"*Everything?*"

"Everything physical," he said. "If you know . . . matter and how it's put together."

"Well, good luck. I guess I have enough trouble with the simple stuff. But I hope I can say someday that I roomed with a Nobel Prize winner."

"Fat chance of that," he answered. It wasn't imitation modesty either. Robert was just a regular guy, a real smart regular guy. I was damn lucky to have him to talk to.

After my speech class and lunch, I had forgotten about the morning's incident with the ROTC guys. That afternoon,

I went back to the union to get a snack. Those student soldiers weren't going to change my habits. From the union, I went to the library and studied for the rest of the day.

Schoolwork was going better than I'd expected, even though it was taking a great deal of effort to concentrate. I'd worried that I wouldn't be able to do schoolwork at all. The changes in pace and environment from the army were tremendous, but after four weeks, I still had my head above water. I had a constant fear, though, that I was forgetting something, that I would fall behind and never catch up. There was no alternative to being back in school. I had no skills. Combat engineering in the army might qualify me for menial construction work, but that didn't fit me. Neither of my parents nor any of my other relatives had a business or any connections that would get me a job. Of course, there was still the army. I could reenlist, maybe at the same rank as I left, but that seemed equivalent to jumping off a cliff.

During these first weeks of the semester, I also had to solve the problem of where to study. I needed nearly complete isolation to be able to concentrate, which made the apartment a lost cause. I would be constantly eating and drinking and distracted by the TV and anyone else there. That was why I had been going to the basement of the library, where desks lined the walls. There was almost no foot traffic down there. There was, however, competition for the desks. The best—most isolated—desks were taken in the late afternoon or early evening. If I missed a desk at the library, there were several classroom buildings where rooms were left open as study halls. I'd also done that number of times. That afternoon, there were still open desks when I got to the library, and I got right into my reading assignments. I was two years behind everyone else, and if I couldn't make this work, I was in deep shit.

TUESDAY, OCTOBER 8

I had suggested to Natalie Fontaine that we have coffee on Tuesday after our American literature class. The ROTC incident had intervened and made it seem like a long time since I'd met her on Sunday morning. Now I was late getting to class. I popped into the classroom just ahead of the professor and dropped into my seat behind Natalie. We didn't even look at each other, and there was no chance to repeat my invitation. During class, I kept wondering if our meeting on the sidewalk had been an illusion of my hungover mind. I figured the test of whether she cared to have coffee with me was how she acted when class let out. If she just jumped up and split, I wouldn't press the issue.

Having to drag through class before approaching her gave me more time to think about what I might be getting myself into. I didn't know anything about her. She was reasonably good-looking. She seemed intelligent. She contributed in class and spoke well. She'd seemed warm and showed a mild sense of humor when I'd talked to her after class last week. But those might be reasons to stay away from her. A charming intellectual girl had given me a cigarette burn, and I didn't need another. Besides, the possibility of getting any action off her was probably nil. I would be better off hitting up some girl over at Pete's who wasn't trying to be a scholar but was only looking for good time after high school.

I hadn't come to any conclusion when class ended. The professor went through his closing summation and made the next assignment. Instead of standing to leave with everyone else, Natalie turned around and smiled and asked, "Are we still on for coffee?"

"You bet," I responded. "If you're still game, so am I." We picked up our books and joined the flood of people pressing out of the room, down the narrow stairs, and out into the fresh air. It had warmed up considerably since I had rushed into the building an hour before. We moved along the sidewalk with what seemed like the entire student body. "Do you have an eleven-o-clock class?" I asked her.

"Yes. How about you?"

"Yeah. Art history."

"Well," she said, "that's an interesting class."

"I guess, but when the lights are dimmed to show the slides, I have a heck of a time staying awake. What's your class?"

"Journalism. They keep the lights on, so I enjoy the class."

"Well, that helps."

We walked up the steps of the student union and into the cafeteria. I looked over at the coffee machines and then at the table where the ROTC hung out. The asshole from my class wasn't there nor was any of his friends.

We went through the line and got our coffee and a doughnut to split, and then we managed to get a small table by a window. I set my coffee down without spilling it, which was a relief. Then we began a conversation to discover who the other person was. "So where're you from?" I asked her.

"Sandusky. Near Cleveland."

"Oh yeah, on the lake. That must be great in the summer." I was polite and didn't mention the snowstorms I knew blew off the lake in the winter.

"Oh, it is. My father loves to sail, so we spend a lot of time on the lake."

"So you're part of the crew?" I asked in slight amazement.

"Sure. It's fun. The boat isn't big, so it isn't hard work."

"Still," I said, "you have to do the right thing at the right time."

She turned the questioning on me. "And where are you from?"

I hesitated a moment then said. "Newburgh, New York. About seventy miles north of New York City. In the Hudson Valley."

"Gee, that must be nice too. Isn't that the area Washington Irving wrote about? *Sleepy Hollow?*"

"Right. It's fine, particularly this time of year. There are steeper mountains than here, and the fall leaves are colorful." I noticed that she had a French textbook with her. "You must like French to be taking it in college." I said, pointing to the book.

"*Oui*, I do. It's a charming language. And a challenge. I had a great teacher in high school and actually spent a month in France at a language school. The summer between my junior and senior years." She gave me a proud smile. "So I'm trying to keep it up. If I don't speak it, I'll lose it."

"The trip to France must have been great. Were you in school all the time, or did you get to see the sites?"

"We took bus trips on the weekends, and the last week was all touring. Mostly Paris."

I was impressed, and I'm sure it showed in the envious tone of my voice. "Tell me about Paris. I'd love to get there someday. Which part of the city did you stay in?"

"Paris is great! We were on the left bank but not in the Latin Quarter. The hotel was near Les Invalides. But it's so easy to get around on the Metro, we could go anywhere."

"I've looked at maps," I said. "I know places like Notre-Dame, the Eiffel Tower, and Montmartre, but I haven't heard of the Invalides. What's that?"

She explained that it was where Napoleon's tomb was. Then I asked her if French was her major.

"Oh no," she said. "I'm a journalism major."

"Journalism?" I said with mild surprise. "How come? Do you want to be a reporter?"

"Maybe, I don't know. Journalism and the news are exciting. It's fun. I work on the *Monitor*." The *Middlesex Monitor* was the student newspaper.

"Oh," I said. "Well, I guess I'd better be careful what I say."

"Don't worry," she said with a grin. "This is off the record." The Beatles were playing on the jukebox, pleading with Jude to let them into her heart. For a moment, we just sipped our coffee and watched the crowd move in an out of the cafeteria. Then I continued with the subject of journalism.

"There certainly is enough to write about . . . with the war, campus riots, student power, women's rights."

"There's a lot," she agreed, "but I don't get to do any of the hard news. I'm only a sophomore. I end up with the usual Greek news, sports, and other light school news.

"Would you rather be on a bigger campus?"

"Oh no. Middlesex is just fine. I might not have had a chance to work on a newspaper at all at a big school." She paused a moment then asked, "What do you think of the paper?"

I snapped to attention at the direct question. "It's great. I read it," I responded defensively before there was a need to be defensive.

"Oh good." She smiled. "Now do you read it thoroughly? Don't worry, you won't insult me."

I tried to be more emphatic. "I always look it over. I read the parts that interest me." In fact, I hardly ever got past the headlines.

She smiled again and checked her watch. She must have calculated the time she had left to get the information she wanted out of me because she dropped the newspaper talk immediately. "So what's your major?" she asked. She seemed a bit nervous and looked out the window as she asked the question.

"My major is survival." It was a good answer, better than I thought I would give. Then I continued. "I guess I'm undecided. Or undeclared, to use the official term."

"Well, that's fine." She faced me again. Suddenly I was self-conscious about my looks. I ran my thumb over my chin to check if I had shaved, which I had. After a moment, she continued. "You seem to like the American lit class. You make some good comments in class. Maybe that's what you should concentrate on."

I was sipping my coffee and had to pause so I wouldn't spill it. With a distinct sputter, I responded. "Me? English? Hell—I can hardly speak it. No, I'll figure out a major when I have to."

"What did you take last year at your other school?"

My mental circuits overloaded momentarily. I should have given some thought to how to tell her about the gaps in my life. Now I had to think fast. "My other school?" I responded defensively. "I've never been at any other school."

"Oh, I'm sorry." She looked apologetic. "I thought, since you're taking sophomore lit but weren't on campus last year, you must have transferred in this year."

She was trying to be a reporter and a detective, but she'd misinterpreted something. I could have just manipulated the conversation off the subject and left her wondering about my history, but she was obviously a sincere person and didn't deserve deceit. I felt I could confide in her.

"No reason to be sorry," I said. "I was a freshman here three years ago. I was drafted the summer after that. I was in the army the last two years. I should be a senior. Make sense?"

"Yes, of course. I didn't mean to be nosy."

"You're not nosy. It's an unusual situation. I understand." I didn't feel like following normal pattern of conversation, so I didn't explain what I'd done or where I'd been. She'd find out, or the details would come out in future conversations, if there were any.

We continued to talk about unimportant things, but within minutes, she said she had to leave. "I have to swing by the newspaper office before my eleven-o-clock," she said.

"I've never seen the newspaper office," I said. "Would you mind if I went with you. I'm just curious."

"Sure. It isn't much to see. We have two rooms with a bunch of desks and typewriters."

The student newspaper office was on the second floor of the student activities building. The campus bookstore was on the first floor. I'd been in bookstore many times but had never gone up the stairs to second floor. Besides the newspaper, the second floor had offices used by just about all the campus student organizations, including the student senate, although the senate held its general meetings in the game room of the student union.

As we took the short walk over to the activities building, I asked Natalie a question that had been on my mind. "How did you know I wasn't on campus last year? We might just not have seen each other."

"Oh, I . . ." The tone of her voice changed. "I just knew you weren't here. It isn't that big a school." From this, I assumed she must have looked me up somehow, as any good reporter would. *Shit*, I thought, *she probably knows what unit I was in Vietnam.*

I had a strong sensation of déjà vu when we walked into the activities building. Olivia and I had gone into the bookstore together several times. From the lobby, Natalie and I went up the side stairs to the student offices. When we got to the newspaper office, I started getting uncomfortable. The hall was a buzz of activity, with many of the campus movers and shakers milling about and going in out of offices and talking in loud voices.

When Natalie went into the newspaper office and headed for a desk, I followed her but stayed by the door. The place was busy with people typing and talking. "Hey," I said, "thanks for the look-see. See you in class."

My remark must have surprised her, but she only smiled and said, "Okay, see you Thursday." I turned and left the building. I did have another class.

FRIDAY, OCTOBER 11

Friday brought some relief from classes. I would have to study some on Sunday, but on Friday afternoon, the weekend seemed limitless. The weather was good, and no tests or papers were due the next week. The only problem was I had no plans, and I was afraid the weekend would flash past without my enjoying it.

As I was walking directly back to the apartment after my last class, a diesel truck passed me. It had a high-pitched whistle that sounded like an army deuce and a half. The whistle came from the turbo charger. But there were no bored GIs stuffed in the back flashing the peace sign. It was only a lumber delivery truck.

The apartment was empty, which was unusual. I dropped my books on my bed and hit the kitchen. The place wasn't in too bad a shape, just one day's dishes in the sink and some toast crumbs on the countertop. I opened the fridge and stared for a moment before taking out a block of cheese and a beer. I sliced some cheese and went into the living room. TV stank at that time of the day, so I stepped out on the porch and walked to the corner of the house where I could look down the hill and over toward campus. Some high school kids were walking up the hill with books under their arms. One of the girls was attractive, but naturally, she refused to look at me, an evil beer-drinking college guy. The boys seemed young and were doing the usual clowning.

I went back into my bedroom and, with nothing else to do, shuffled my books from the bed to my small desk. There was no chair to go with the desk, so I sat on the edge of the bed and thumbed through the American lit book, looking at the reading I was going to have to do over the weekend.

I hadn't intended to take a nap, and I didn't feel tired, but I lay back on the bed and pulled the corner of the bedspread over my eyes. I had slept reasonably well during the week, only having trouble getting to sleep Tuesday night. That night, I had gone to bed, but I couldn't sleep, so I'd gotten up and watched TV until 2:00 a.m. There had been the usual crazy dreams during the week but nothing extreme. Only the intense dreams forced me to get up and walk them off, and I hadn't had any of those that week. This afternoon, justifiably tired or not, I fell asleep with the late afternoon sun filtering through the bedspread covering my eyes.

It was dark when I woke up. I smelled something cooking in the kitchen. When I got up to look, I saw Robert was cooking a hamburger. "Where is everyone?" I asked.

"At the frat house. Something about getting ready for rush. Want a burger?"

"Yeah, sure. Thanks. I'll cook it."

Robert had nearly finished eating by the time my burger was done, and I sat down at the table across him. "Hey, you don't need to sit here if you're done," I said.

"What the hell, there's nothing on TV."

"I guess not. *Gomer Pyle* and the like isn't the greatest. Got much work to do over the weekend?"

"Actually, no," he said, "and it worries me. I guess I could work on my semester physics paper."

I perked up and said, "Well, what the hell. You wanna go downtown and stir up some girls?"

"Stir up girls? What kind of crude sport is that?"

"It's a fine sport," I said. "You're gonna love it. I've heard of a new hangout called the Hunt Club. You been there?"

"Yeah, I've been by it. I've heard it's classy compared to the Fargo Hotel. It's been open a couple of years"

"So I just missed the grand opening," I said. "Let's go! What do you say?" I expected excuses, but he agreed. It was still early in the month, so I figured I could blow maybe $10, which ought to be enough for a good evening. I ate quickly and finished the beer I'd started.

We both changed clothes. I put on the best shirt I had. It was a knit pullover, like the ones with the alligator, only mine didn't have the alligator. Robert looked all right too, but I knew we weren't going to sweep any girls off their feet. I had been out of uniform for months, but I still worried that I didn't wear civilian clothes right.

It was a four-block walk from the apartment to the Hunt Club. Considering Robert's leg problem, I wondered why his parents hadn't gotten him a car. I didn't know much about his parents or about Robert's background, except that he was from Silver Springs, Maryland, and was an only child. He'd said something once about his father working for the federal government, but he'd never said what he did.

Our walk took us past the end of campus. To our right and behind a manicured lawn was a new women's dorm built while I was away. On the other side of the street were older residence halls, of which two were sorority houses. It was dark by now, which made it great for watching windows, but none of the girls had forgotten to pull their shades down. We didn't even see a sensuous silhouette.

"Girls to the right of us, girls to left of us, girls in front of us at the Hunt Club," I said.

"I think I just heard Tennyson groan," Robert replied.

"Maybe, but a poet knows the beauty residing in those buildings and the desire too. They have desires. We have desires. So we should just abandon ourselves and let nature take its course."

"You're full of it."

He was right. I was full of it. The beer I'd had with dinner had loosened me up. I was surprised when we came to the block where the Hunt Club was. The city was undergoing redevelopment, and the area had changed since my freshmen year. The block was just east of the main shopping district and the riverfront street along the Chadicoin River. When I was a freshman, the area had been dilapidated, but now the old brick buildings had been sandblasted clean, small trees in planters dotted the sidewalks, and antiques stores, restaurants, and dress shops had opened. The Hunt Club was decorated like an Old English pub. There were a big multi-pane bay window and exposed timbers along the front, and the heavy wood door looked weathered, and it had black hammered wrought iron hardware on it.

"This is a school hangout?" I asked myself as we walked up. It looked too classy. I was beginning to wonder if my $10 would be enough.

"I don't know," Robert answered, "but that was too long a walk not to find out."

I felt conspicuous walking in because it was obvious from the way we stopped and looked around that we hadn't been there before. The place was deep but narrow. A large wooden bar ran partway down the left and a row of comfortable cushioned booths went down the right. Further back were tables, a small dance floor, and a platform for a band. There were brass-hunting horns and pictures of foxhunts on the wall. The place was quiet, but I noticed some girls at a table far in the back. I assumed they were students. It was early, and the first movie run of the night hadn't let out, so after our initial hesitation, I suggested that we sit at the bar.

The bar stools were fancy too, with nice thick padding. The mirror across the back of the bar gave us a good reflection of the booths behind us. There were the usual rows of liquor bottles below the mirror and glasses hung from racks at the ends of the mirror. Best of all were the bowls of popcorn on the bar. I wondered how much a lousy draft was going to cost.

We found out right away. We both ordered a draft. They were 75¢ each. So it was a quarter more than I was used to paying, but the place was pleasant, and if some girls showed up, it would be worth it. "This atmosphere should bring out the Shakespeare in you," I said to Robert.

He took a sip of his beer. "Let's see . . . 'Do not think I'm drunk. This is my right hand, and this is my left. I am not drunk. I can stand and speak well enough.'" He smiled and tipped his beer to me.

"Falstaff, I bet. One of the *Henrys?*"

"Nope. *Othello.* But I don't remember who said it."

"Well," I said, "you may be able to stand and speak well enough now, but we've just started."

We exchanged additional comments, each of us speculating on why there weren't more people in the place. A twinge of panic hit me when I realized it was possible that Olivia could walk in the door with her boyfriend. If that was a scary thought, then the possibility of Natalie coming in was a nicer thought. But that was stupid. Natalie would probably be with a date too. My beer was low, so I ordered another one and didn't think about who might come in the door.

Some people down the bar a bit were talking about the Detroit Tigers winning the World Series. So I commented to Robert, "What do you think of the Tigers winning the series?"

"Fine, I guess. I don't follow baseball."

"Well, then how about the *Apollo* launch?"

"I think I followed that. It was great. I watched it in the student lounge. I think the project is back on track now that we have men going up again."

"Lucky number 7," I replied. *Apollo 7* was the first manned mission since the crew of *Apollo 1* had died in a fire.

"It took luck and a lot of work," Robert replied.

"So you think you might get into the space game? Work for one of those contractors?"

"I doubt it. I want to stick to nuclear physics."

"Oh right."

"Anyway, moon landings will be common events by the time I get out of grad school."

"Sure," I agreed, "a few missions, but then there will still be adventure like in that space odyssey movie with big stations in orbit and on the moon."

He grinned. "I admit it's tempting when you see the launches. I'd be working as an engineer, obviously." He was referring to his leg. I made no reply and took a look around the place to see if any female prospects had come in.

Then Robert spoke up in a more serious tone than before. "Hey, I've got to ask you something. But I don't want you to get pissed or anything."

I turned back to him. "Pissed? Me, pissed? I don't know what you could ask that would get me pissed." I figured it was something about the war.

"Well, it's kind of personal."

"I don't care. Shoot."

"It's the racket you make at night." He spoke slowly. "Talking. Banging the wall. Things like that. What's up with you?"

"When I'm asleep?"

"Yeah. Sometimes it even wakes up Adam and Brice."

I suddenly felt embarrassed. "I don't know," I said with a shake of my head. "I didn't realize I was doing it. Maybe I'm dreaming I'm with some big beautiful broad. That can get noisy, you know."

"I don't think you're with any girl," he said. "You're usually angry."

"Well, I'm sorry. I don't know what to say—"

"It's not something to be sorry about," he cut in. "I'm just concerned, that's all. Maybe you should take something to relax before going to bed. Milk or something."

"Yeah. Well." I didn't know what to say. "I guess I could try something. Go ahead and wake me up if I'm making a racket. I might appreciate it if it's a bad dream." Of course, I knew nearly all of them were bad dreams. But with my luck, old Robert would wake me up from a dream where I was banging the Old Bangkok Whore.

"I might do that," he said. "It worries me more than disturbs me. You're not mad I asked, I hope."

"No, no. It's okay. Don't worry about it. You've got to get your sleep too. I know I get restless. I'll try something. Milk, maybe, like you say." My tone of voice indicated that I was ready for a change of subject.

People had been coming in, and now the place was nearly full. I got up and went to the restroom. Coming back, I checked out the crowd, trying to pick out some likely targets. This was self-flattery, of course, since I probably wouldn't put any moves on anyone. As I made my way between tables and through knots of people, one of the groups turned out to be the fraternity crowd the ROTC guy I had scrapped with in my political science class belonged to. I didn't see him, but then I wasn't looking too hard.

"Hey, this place is finally the place to be," I told Robert as I sat back on my stool and picked up my beer.

"So when are those sex-starved Amazons going to sweep us off our stools?"

"Momentarily," I answered. "As soon as we pick out some sweethearts and send the waitress over with a round of drinks."

He laughed and shook his head. "That may be the way it's done in the movies, but it costs money in real life."

I turned and looked at the tables again. That's when I saw the ROTC guy from my class and a couple of his buddies. The guy's name, I remembered, was Holden. I hadn't seen him come in, but he probably came in while I was in the men's room. Whatever the case, the guy was behind me now. I turned back to Robert and ignored the crowd.

"This is actually relaxing," he said. He was getting a little tight.

I hoped I was getting more than a little tight. Then from behind me, a voice said, "Look, it's our demoralized warrior. How fortunate." I looked up into the mirror on the back bar and saw Holden standing right behind me. "Collins," he went on, "you must do me a favor. Tell my buddies here why we can't win the war. They didn't have the privilege of hearing you in class."

"Shit," I muttered. I looked over my shoulder. "What the hell do you want?"

"Like I said, I want your experienced opinion on why we can't win the war. My buddies need to know. They're in ROTC too."

"Give it a rest," I said. I turned my head back toward the bar.

"No," he insisted. "I'm serious. They need to hear from an experienced combat veteran."

He was drunk, but so was I, and for moment, I took him seriously. I turned completely around to face them and looked right and left at the figures on either side of him, who I assumed were his buddies. "We can't win the war because the South Vietnamese don't give a shit about their country and our leadership stinks. Does that make sense to you?" As soon as I had said my piece, I turned back to the bar. It worried me that Robert would think I was starting trouble.

Holden had a quick retort. "Defeatist! Thank God the Patriots didn't take that attitude in 1776."

I let Holden have the last word and just kept sipping my beer. After a moment, Robert asked the question I knew was coming. "What was that about?" He was looking straight ahead at my reflection in the mirror.

I responded in the same way, looking at Robert in the mirror. "He's in my political science class. We got into a little debate in class. I guess he can't tolerate the facts."

After the Holden incident, it was difficult to think of anything to talk to Robert about. Finally, I tried. "So what's the plan for the apartment when Adam and Brice move out?"

"Well, the latest I've heard is it won't be before Thanksgiving. Charlie and Dave still say they will take the room over for next spring."

"Fine. But I hope Adam and Brice don't leave us holding the bag for a month or two of rent."

"Right," Robert said. "We should figure that out with them."

The band had started to play in the back, but we couldn't see anything from the bar. It was too crowded.

Robert drained his beer and looked at my glass, which had about a quarter left. "How about we get out of here? The smoke is choking me, and no campus queen is going to abduct us."

I wasn't too happy about giving up on the girls, but Robert was right. "Fine," I said. "It's because I forgot to put on my English Leather cologne."

"I wish it were that easy."

I finished my beer in two gulps, and when I stood up, three people behind me edged toward my stool. "You leaving?" one asked to make sure I wasn't just going to the restroom.

"It's all yours." I told him.

I got a surprise when I pushed the heavy door open and stepped outside. There was another dense crowd milling around the door on the sidewalk. I couldn't see Robert behind me, so I made my way to the edge of the crowd and stood on the curb to wait for him. But Holden and his buddies came out of the crowd before Robert did.

"Well, here he is again," Holden sneered, "the campus warrior that's given up on his buddies back at the front."

"Holden," I said, "this is getting old. Why don't you find some pretty little sorority girl to impress?"

"But we're enjoying talking to you," he said, "and we want to change your opinion about the war."

"Sure. And you're showing such a great example of the leadership that will be over there soon.

"I'm a damn sight better leader than you'll ever be. What were you—some pissant enlisted man?"

"You couldn't lead flies to shit." I turned my back on him.

"What'd you say?" Holden's voice was no longer artificially friendly.

I turned back to face him. "I said you couldn't lead flies to shit. Would you follow him to the restroom?" I nodded at his friends.

Holden's voice cracked. "You asshole!" He lunged forward, but Robert stepped between us.

"Come on, damn it. No trouble."

"Man," I blurted out to Holden and his friends, "you just don't know what you don't know. When you find out, you'll feel like an ass about this." I let Robert pull me away from them.

Holden's friends were trying to calm him down too. "I'm sick of your disrespect!" he yelled at me.

"Gentleman!" A deep voice cut in like a foghorn at sea. The chief of campus security, dressed in his signature faded brown business suit, looked at Holden then at me. Being the bright college lads we were, Holden and I had started a drunken argument with the campus flatfoot standing right next to us.

"Holden, isn't it?" He looked Holden in the eye then turned to me. "You're back with us again, I see. I don't recall your name. I would like to keep it that way."

"There's no problem," Holden said. "We were just having a discussion. A difference of a political opinion."

"He's right," I said. "There's no problem."

The campus cop wasn't buying it. "Sure, sure, and I'm the Lone Ranger. Now I want you two to clear out of here. Holden, you go that way." He pointed toward the center of town. "Collins—that's it, isn't it?" I nodded. "Collins, you go that way." He pointed back toward campus. "And if there's any trouble, I'll stomp on you both."

Holden muttered something under his breath and eased back into his crowd. Robert was beside me now, and he and I started walking back to the apartment. After a long silence, Robert made a glib remark about this being the closest he'd ever been to a street brawl and the evening had been entertaining, even if there had been no girls.

"Yeah," I said. "Great fun."

WEEK 4

OCTOBER 13, 1968–OCTOBER 19, 1968

TUESDAY, OCTOBER 15

Front campus presented a classic image of academia to the community. Tall stately trees, old but flawlessly maintained buildings, and well-attended lawns that rolled down to the street all contributed to the idyllic picture.

None of this mattered to the students, but there was one feature of front campus that did attract them, a secluded nook formed by honeysuckle and lilac bushes. A sidewalk to nowhere looped around the spot, and when students spoke of "front campus," this is the place they meant.

Tuesday was a warm Indian summer day. The trees were turning red and orange and stood against a cloudless pale blue sky. Nature had colored the day with pastels. After my last class of the afternoon, I succumbed to nostalgia and decided to spend some time reading on front campus. Olivia and I had gone there during the few weeks we'd been together.

I turned the corner behind the administration building and started down a wide sidewalk. Ahead of me, in front of Adams Hall, I saw a crowd blocking the way. They were listening to a speaker who was standing on the steps and using a bullhorn, which gave his voice a mechanical twang. He held papers in his free hand and waved them at the crowd. I circled the back of the crowd and went on to the secluded corner of front campus. The little I heard was enough for me to realize it was a rally to organize a chapter of Students for a Democratic Society.

At front campus, the shrubbery formed a horseshoe at the lovers' hideaway. It occurred to me that someone might be there, and I might cause an untimely interruption, but no one was there. Before sitting down, I tested the ground to be sure it was dry, which it was, then sat down on the mat of leaves.

It took about fifteen minutes of reading a class assignment before I slipped off into daydreams. I looked out past the shrubbery at the pristine lawn. The whole campus was so correct and orderly that I suddenly wished I could disturb it. Soon, I was envisioning what a mobile 105 mm howitzer battery would look like set up on the lawn. Just the prop wash from the big dual-rotor Chinook helicopter that brought the battery in would blow everything around and maybe knock out some windows. The gun crew would dig into the lawn to set the tailpieces and lay the gun. Combat boots would trample the grass into mud. Shirtless, sweating GIs would dig a slit trench for a latrine. There would be stacks of artillery shells placed by the guns. Mounds of debris would pile up, scrap from the packaging cylinders for the shells, as well as the spent casings. Trash from C rations, white plastic spoons, cardboard boxes, and empty green cans with black lettering would litter the ground. As I sat there daydreaming, it seemed to me that I would be more comfortable with the 105 battery than reading a college textbook.

I was still in a kind of trance, staring blankly and seeing things that weren't there, when Natalie walked into my field of view and waved at me.

"Hi! Am I interrupting?"

I scrambled to my feet, sending leaves flying. I was glad I hadn't been asleep when she sneaked up on me. "Hi! No, no, come on into the hideaway. How did you know I was here?" But I asked the question too fast, which made it obvious she had surprised me.

She came up beside me and looked at the ground, no doubt wondering if it was wet. "I was covering the SDS rally for the paper. I saw you walk past and disappear down here. I was just curious."

"I'm glad you were," I replied. "Sit down. It's dry, and the leaves smell great when you're sitting in them." We exchanged comments about how great the weather was and how we each liked the fall season. Then I asked her about the SDS. "So what was all that about? I thought the SDS was already on campus?"

"Oh no! Not at Middlesex. That would be too radical. This is a conservative campus."

"Right. It was when I was a freshmen, but that was two years ago. It seems like it's changing though. There's a lot of talk about change."

Natalie responded as though she'd been considering that question. "There's talk but little action," she said. "My opinion is that since Middlesex is a private school and costs more than the state colleges, the students come from the well-off upper-middle class. They're just conservative."

"No doubt," I agreed. "So what do you think the SDS's chances are?"

"Well," she began, "the crowd impressed me." She looked back up toward the buildings. "The old dictatorial way the administration runs the place irritates many kids today. It's Victorian at best. Some would say Puritanical."

"Yeah. I was surprised women's hours hadn't been extended. That was an issue when I was here before."

"Extended?" She gave me a stern look. "Hours are discriminatory. Women should be treated the same as men."

"You're right! Absolutely right!" My enthusiasm was exaggerated. "You should be in our clutches all night!" When I smiled at her, she gave me a condescending smile in return.

"There are other problems too," she said. "Academic issues the students have no say in. Like we want a few pass/ fail classes. Student evaluations of professors is another issue. We pay the money, but we can't say how satisfied we are with the product."

I told her that it was parents who mostly paid the bill, and she countered with a comment about kids taking loans.

I just let the subject drop. After a minute or so, I said, "That's a nice camera you have."

She was carrying a single-lens-reflex camera buttoned up in a brightly polished black leather case. "Oh, it is!" she responded with obvious pride. "I'm so lucky." She started to unsnap the case. "My parents got it for me last Christmas to help with my newspaper work. Here, look though it." She handed it to me.

It was a Pentax and had the delightful feel of a fine quality instrument. I brought the camera up to my eye and saw a bright but blurred image. Twisting the lens snapped the world into a bright, sharp focus. "That's a lot of light," I said as I adjusted the silky smooth focus.

"It is. I'll have to show you some pictures. Do you know photography?"

"Just a little. One of my high school science teachers helped some of us, like a club, but not well organized.

We did our own developing, which was fun. So you do photography for the paper?"

"Not officially. There are two guys that are the official photographers, but us writers give them pictures to go with our stories sometimes."

"Do you mind if I change the shutter speed?" I asked.

"No. Go ahead."

I noted what speed she had set and then just clicked the knob up to a slower speed, then back up to a higher speed, and then back down to where it had been. Then looking through the lens, I adjusted the "f" stop up and down. The camera was a jewel. I envied her.

We talked awhile about the camera's features and photography in general. She understood the value of the camera and knew the technology of photography too but was modest about her knowledge. Her modesty impressed me as much as her knowledge did.

"I had a camera in Vietnam," I told her. "It was a small 16 mm pocket camera. Like the spies use." I was trying to impress her.

"Really? Did it work well? Did you get good pictures?"

"It worked great as far a being able to carry it, which was most important. But I had to get the film sent to me by my mother, and I had to send it back to her to be developed. The pictures were mostly grainy. It was hard to guess the light in Nam."

"But that's great!" she said. "You kept a record. Anything is better than nothing. May I see some of your work sometime?"

Her remark embarrassed me. "God no! I'm not a photographer. I just take pictures."

When she didn't respond immediately, I continued. "But sure I have a few here at school. The rest are at home."

She abruptly changed the subject. "I'm sorry to hear you had to go to Vietnam." As she spoke, she looked down at a colorful leaf she was twirling in her fingers.

"Oh," I said, not knowing what to say. "It was just one of those things."

"One of those terrible things . . .," she responded, her voice trailing off.

Fortunately, she didn't press for details. I probably wouldn't have told her anything anyway. We talked for a few more minutes before she got up, and we said pleasant good-byes to each other. Our meeting had been another recognizance by each of us of the other. Now we both were going to think over what we had learned.

SATURDAY, OCTOBER 19

Robert had two close friends, Charlie Reynolds and David Sims. They were physics majors like Robert. I had met them my freshman year and had become friendly with them. Now they often came to the apartment to work with him on assignments.

Charlie was short and slightly pudgy. He was the worry-wart of the group and often scolded Robert and David about when their projects were due. When he did relax, he was quiet and enjoyed just being with the group. Dave was the most extroverted of the three. He was a joker, always cracking a comment and trying to get a laugh. Although he talked twice as much as Charlie, I didn't think he was obnoxious. He was from New Jersey, so he and I were the Easterners. Except for being smart like Robert, Charlie and Dave were normal students. There were eggheads on campus that were reclusive and unconscious of how (or if) they were dressed, and they didn't bother to shower. Robert, Dave, and

Charlie would joke about some of their fellow geniuses, and I was glad they never invited any of them around.

Saturday was laundry day. I had stuffed my old army duffel bag with my dirty clothes and spent part of the afternoon at the neighborhood Laundromat. When I got back to the apartment about three o'clock, I found Charlie in the living room, sitting on the couch and watching TV with his hand in a box of pretzels.

"Hi," I said as I swung the duffel bag off my shoulder and dropped it on the floor with a thump. "God, that thing is hot." Charlie just looked at the bag, so I continued. "I've been to the Laundromat. The clothes are still hot from the dryer."

"Yeah, I guess they would be."

I looked at the TV long enough to see that it was an Ohio State game. Then I picked up the bag up by the side grip and took it to the bedroom. Dave was in the kitchen with Robert, so I went on in with them.

Dave was sitting at the kitchen table, hunched over a newspaper laid out flat in front of him. Robert stood at the stove stirring some scrambled eggs. The eggshells were on the counter next to the stove.

We exchanged greetings that amounted to not much more than grunts, but which we accepted as adequate, and then Robert and I went on about finding lunch. Dave fooled with my radio on the table and cleared the static on a station that was playing a Beatles song. "You going over to your buddy's tonight?" he asked me. Pete had already become known as my buddy to everyone at the apartment.

"I don't know," I said. "Maybe. Why?"

"Well, we're going to have dates over, and I didn't want you to feel out of it. I mean, it doesn't matter to us, but why don't you get a date? You too, Robert. The last time

I remember you having a date was with Rose Marie last spring."

Charlie had come in while Dave was talking and stood in the doorway watching us. I had never heard about Robert and Rose Marie, but then two years leaves a big hole. So I asked who she was.

"Oh, you don't know?" Charlie replied. "Rose Marie is a really nice girl that Robert just takes for granted."

"Yeah," Dave said. "You ought to give her a call, Robert. I've seen you with her on campus. She's interested, or she wouldn't hang around you. Yeah, give her a call."

"For crying out loud," Robert said, "you guys are a bunch of jackals. Leave me alone. It's too late to call now. Hell, it wouldn't be polite."

"What's polite got to do with it?" I cut in, joining in the friendly persecution of Robert.

Robert pointed the wooden spoon he'd been stirring the eggs with at me. "Hey, you keep out of this. You don't have a date. At least I have a prospect."

"He's got you there," Dave chimed in with a big grin on his face.

I immediately sensed a setup. I wasn't going to fall for some damn trap. "Yeah, that's true," I said, "and it's going to stay that way. All I've seen on campus is a bunch of teenyboppers trying to look snotty. I'll go to Pete's place and hang out."

By this time, the soup I had put on the stove was hot. Dave had finished eating and gotten up from the table and dumped his dishes in the sink, so I poured my soup in a bowl and put it down on the open paper on the table and sat where Dave had just been. The vinyl seat of the chair was still warm. Finishing his can of soda, Dave chastised Robert and me as he went to the living room. "Well, fine," he said.

"You two sit around like a couple of monks, but don't be watching us tonight when we get a handful on the couch."

"Handful, my ass!" I yelled down the hall. I blew on the soup to cool it. Robert was shuffling between the stove and counter, adding slices of American cheese to his scrambled eggs. He came over to the table, moving extra slow so his limp wouldn't cause a spill. We both shoveled away at our lunches and didn't talk. I wanted to know about Rose Marie, but I wasn't about to ask. Robert had had only two, maybe three dates our freshman year. Each date was with a different girl. Then with no thought at all, I piped up, "If I get a date, would you?"

"Let's skip the crap," he said. He reached over and shuffled a section of newspaper out from under what I was reading then flipped it open and began to read, tipping the paper up with one hand and eating with the other.

"Well," I said, "a date wouldn't hurt either of us." Then in a foolish, dramatic move, I stood up and walked to the wall phone. During the second or two it took me to reach the phone, I realized I didn't know a single damn girl on campus other than Olivia.

The fall student directory hung on a string from the wall phone. I opened it in a deliberate manner as if I knew just what name I was looking for. As I turned the pages, I suddenly realized the only name I knew was Natalie Fontaine. I slid my finger down the F page and found Fontaine. At that moment, an icicle formed in my stomach, and I had to force myself not to pause and give myself away to Robert, who calmly went on reading the paper and ignoring me.

I began to dial the phone, and with each turn of the dial, I committed myself deeper. It was stilly to get a date just to goad Robert into getting one, but then as the phone began to ring at the other end, I decided it didn't make a damn bit of difference if I made a fool of myself. Sure this was collegiate bullshit, and I was way beyond college, but what the hell?

The dorm switchboard operator answered. "Grace Donnelly Hall, may I help you?"

"Ahh yes, Natalie Fontaine, please." My voice wasn't normal, but it wasn't too bad. I heard Robert flipping the paper behind me and clinking his fork against his plate. The operator put my call through to Natalie's floor, and the phone rang with a different tone. Almost immediately, a girl answered. "Third floor east. Who would you like?"

I paused, thinking the switchboard operator would repeat the name, but then blurted out, "Natalie Fontaine, please." I expected a delay and maybe some yelling down the hall, but the answer came back abruptly.

"She isn't here," the girl on the other end said. She made no offer to take a message.

"Oh," I responded, trying to think of what to do next.

The unknown voice cut back in and saved me. "She might be at the newspaper office. She spends a lot of time there."

"Oh. Okay. Thanks. Thanks a lot." I clicked the receiver down with my finger and stood there, looking at the phone, working myself up to continue the pursuit. Robert put the newspaper down, slid his chair back, and took his bowl to the sink and added it to the pile. He walked past me, saying, "This isn't necessary, you know," and kept on walking.

"Hey," I answered, "I want a date."

Saying the words committed me. I picked up the student directory again and looked up the newspaper office phone number. I dialed the number faster than I had dialed the dorm phone number. It rang once, rang again, rang a third time. I had decided to hang up as soon as the fourth ring started, but after a loud click, a slightly winded voice answered, *"Middlesex Monitor!"*

I had called my own bluff. Now I had to think quickly. Hearing her voice froze me momentarily. "Yes," I finally blurted out, "is this Natalie?" I knew damn well it was.

"Yes. Who is this?" She sounded suspicious.

I was gaining confidence and composure. After all, this was a girl two years younger than me and most likely was still a virgin. My voice stiffened up, and I responded, "This is Mike Collins, your coffee-conversation friend."

Men never know what women are thinking. At least I never do. I thought she would be surprised or confused. Instead, she responded as if I had called her dozens of times and she was expecting this call too.

"Oh hi, Mike," she said in a matter-of-fact tone.

This left me dead in my tracks again. I should have done some thinking about what to say, but I responded reasonably well. "Hi," I said. "What are you doing working at the paper on a Saturday afternoon?" Maybe an aggressive question would give me time to think. Then a possible answer to my own question came to mind. Hell, she probably had a boyfriend on the paper, and that's where they hung out. If that were the case, I would be a real dunce.

"Getting work done," she answered. "There's always something to do." After a pause, during which I couldn't think of anything to say, she continued. "What are you doing calling the newspaper on a Saturday afternoon? Have you got a story for me?"

"Yes. Yes, I do. There is going to be a big party tonight. Who knows, the cops might bust it up. That's a story, isn't it?"

"Oh sure, sure. That's no big news. It's like dog bites man."

"But," I said as persuasively as I could, "this is a special party, and I'd like to give you the opportunity to be there and report on it firsthand." It was easy to talk to her, and I became relaxed and started to enjoy the conversation.

"Well . . . I'm a reporter, so I'm obligated to investigate all possible stories. What are the details?"

I broke down and dropped the chatter and just asked her. "The details are I'd like to take you to our party here at the apartment. It's off campus, well, obviously. But I mean there are a bunch of us that are just having a little party." I began to ramble. I was walking around the kitchen, stretching out the phone cord.

"Tonight, I assume?"

"Yes," I said. "Tonight. About seven. I guess."

There was a short silence that made me stop walking. Then she said, "Sure. Count me in. It sounds great. So do you know what dorm I'm in?"

"Yeah. Grace. Grace Donnelly."

"Okay. I'll see you then. Do I need to bring my steno pad so I can take notes?" She sounded nonchalant, as if she had been called out on an assignment.

"Well, probably not," I admitted. "But we are a wild bunch."

"Oh, I'm sure. I'll see you later?"

"Yeah. Thanks. See you later."

We hung up at the same time. "Damn!" I said to myself. "Why does getting a date have to be so hard?"

My performance on the phone hadn't been great, but I had gotten a date. At least that answered my unasked question about whether she was hanging out with a boyfriend at the newspaper office. For a moment, I was pleased with myself, but my mood changed quickly. I had gone and committed myself. Now I had to follow through.

My simple Saturday afternoon had suddenly become complicated. I went to the living room and discovered that Charlie was the only one still here with me at the apartment.

"Where's Dave?" I asked.

"He's gone over to ask Fran if she can still make it tonight." He was still watching the football game.

"What? I've just gotten a date. What if Dave's date falls through? Have you really got a date?"

"Who knows?" He looked up at me and smiled. "Yes, I've got a date, and Dave will have a date, and there will be a party. Don't sweat it."

I walked back to the kitchen and sat down at the table. I had a lot to worry about, even if Dave and Charlie had dates. The apartment was a mess, there was no party food, and I'd forgotten just what people did at college parties. I checked the time. It was just after four o'clock. We had to clean up the kitchen first, so I immediately went back to the living room to get Charlie off his ass to help.

"The kitchen's fine," he said.

"Okay," I said, "I promise that at some point during the evening, I'll tell the girls the place would have looked, better but no one would help me. Now you know girls. They'll make a fuss over me for being so thoughtful and hardworking."

That did it. He got up, and we started working on the kitchen.

Half an hour later, Dave came back, and he got out the vacuum and did the living room and hall. By five fifteen, the place looked presentable. Then Dave and I made a list of snacks and drinks for a grocery run. "We can't wait for Robert to get back," I said. "What do you think he'll want?"

"A wedge of cheese and some crackers."

"Where the hell did he stomp off to anyway?" I asked.

"He's over talking to Rose Marie. He'll be back, and she'll come to the party. He knew that when we were ragging on him."

"So," I asked, brandishing an old T-shirt to dust with, "what's the story on Rose Marie?"

"She's a swell girl. She and Robert have been dating for years, though neither would say so. They'll marry, whether they know it or not. They're made for each other."

"Amazing! Good, good for him. I just didn't realize. He didn't get out much our freshman year. But why was he so hesitant about asking her over for tonight?" I asked.

"Homecoming's next weekend. If he asks her out this weekend, it will be awkward not to take her to homecoming. Right?" Dave looked at me like he was a lawyer questioning a witness.

"Yeah, I guess so." I sounded really dumb. "So what's the big deal about homecoming? I'd think he'd just take her."

"Come on!" Dave looked at me like I had just fumbled a strategic chess move. "The big event of homecoming is the dance. Now think . . . How well does Robert dance?"

I got it. "Yeah. Well, I don't blame him for ignoring our nagging him to get a date. This is a good example of what happens when women get involved in your life. Everything becomes a maze of complexities and implications." I really sympathized with Robert.

Dave and I finally started for the grocery store, which was a five-minute walk from the apartment. The weather was overcast, but it was reasonably warm, about fifty degrees. Saturday was shopping day in the city for the rural people of the area, and the store parking lot was full of cars, many of which had three or four kids bouncing around inside while their parents shopped. As we walked across the parking lot, I decided to ask Dave a question that had bothered me since he first mentioned homecoming. "So this weekend, I've got a date with a girl I hardly know," I said. "Does that mean she expects me to ask her out for homecoming?"

Dave was enjoying my predicament. "It will be on her mind," he said.

I scowled but said nothing, and we went on into the store. We got the usual party snacks, including cheese for Robert, and then stopped at the state store. The small state-run stores were the only place in Ohio allowed to sell hard liquor. They were more like distribution centers than stores and were very popular on Saturday afternoon. I didn't know if Natalie drank, so I decided to get sloe gin. I had gotten 7 Up and maraschino cherries at the grocery store.

Robert was at the apartment when we got back. I didn't ask about Rose Marie. "We got you some cheese," I told him as Dave and I put away what we'd bought. "If you want some booze, I guess you'll have to go to the state store yourself."

"We don't need anything," he said. "Thanks for doing the shopping." Then he changed the subject. "Say, have you taken anything from Allen and Brice's refrigerator shelves?" Although they didn't eat at the apartment, Allen and Brice had two designated shelves in refrigerator.

"No," I said, closing the refrigerator door. "What's up?"

"Bryce was here changing clothes while you were gone. When he was in the fridge, he grumbled that things disappeared awfully fast from their shelves."

"Honest," I said, "I haven't taken anything. I would if I wanted something, but then I'd tell them."

Talking about our other roommates reminded me about the possible problem if they moved out before the end of the semester. "Dave," I said, "are you and Charlie still planning on moving in next semester?"

He put a bag of potato chips in the cabinet. "Sure."

"If Allen and Brice move out early, would you consider moving in early?"

"And still be paying the school for the dorm? I don't think so."

"Not exactly," Robert said. "We agreed with them in September that if they moved out, they would pay half of the remaining rent."

"Then I'll think about it," Dave responded.

It was six fifteen by the time we had the place ready. That left getting ourselves ready. No one was in the bathroom, so I jumped into the shower. Showers meant a lot to me since coming back from Nam. It wasn't unusual for me to spend fifteen minutes in the shower, but this time, it caused a flap. A few minutes into my shower, Robert knocked on the door and told me to hurry up. I didn't ignore him, but I didn't rush either. Then he got mad and stuck his head in the door and told me he would be pissed off if there was no hot water. I shut the water off and stood in the shower performing a ritual I'd started in Vietnam. In Nam, we only had small green towels. Since you had to carry everything you owned in a duffle bag, I only had two of them. Because of this, I had gotten into the habit of running my hands over myself like a squeegee to dry myself as much as possible before using the towel. It was a habit now, even if it wasn't necessary. That evening, my habit took more time than Robert thought I needed. Since he'd heard the water stop, he yelled in the door again. "What the hell are you doing now? Hurry up!"

Then it wasn't easy finding proper clothes for the evening. I had been wearing more bits and pieces of my old uniform than I realized. Tonight, I ended up in jeans and a faded plaid cotton shirt that I had worn when I was a freshman. Part of my next VA check would have to go for some civilian clothes.

We finished our grooming at last, and Robert and I walked over to the girls' dorms together. The closer we came to the dorms, the more I tried to plan what I would talk with Natalie about. It had been a long time since I had spent an evening with a nice girl who wasn't making a living. Natalie was polite and intelligent, but she was two years younger than me and light years from me in life experience. Certainly, I had better keep my hands off her during the evening. This was a date, not a purchase.

Rose Marie was in a different dorm than Natalie, so Robert and I agreed to meet in front of Natalie's dorm and walk back as a group. He went on to the other dorm, and I went up the steps of Grace Donnelly Hall. I had never been in the dorm to pick up a date. Grace's lounge was well lit and decorated with overstuffed chairs, a couple of couches, and an old grand piano that no one played. There was also a fireplace that never had a fire. The receptionist's desk was in a side hall. After telling the girl who I wanted, I stepped back into the lounge and stood where I could see each of the several doors that Natalie might come through. The dorm had multiple wings that came together at the central hall, and I didn't know where her room was.

She came through a door on my right with a couple of other girls. She was wearing black slacks with a sharp crease in them and a brown and red wool sweater. Her hair was bright, with flecks of red in the blond. As she smiled and came toward me, I had the thought that I would remember this meeting for a long time.

We greeted each other and proceeded through the usual ritual of inquiring how the other person's day had been, and then we walked out front to meet Robert and Rose Marie.

Introductions went smoothly, and I actually remembered Natalie's last name. Rose Marie was a delight. She had a happy smile and was deliberately holding on to Robert's arm. My immediate conclusion was that she was just what Robert needed. Seeing the way she held his arm made me happy, and I wished I could congratulate Robert and tease him. I would do that later. Rose Marie wore a beret that perched on top of her curly black hair. Later, I found out she was a language major concentrating in French. All things European captivated her. She was thin too, and when I looked at her as we passed under a streetlight, I saw that her face was narrow and her eyes dark. It was difficult to see her figure, since she had on a heavy jacket with scarf. But then Robert probably wasn't that interested in getting his hands on her. Maybe what she looked like didn't matter. Her effervescent personality would certainly compensate for anything else.

We had walked about halfway back to the apartment when it became obvious that Rose Marie and Natalie were quite complementary. Natalie laughed and talked warmly with Robert and Rose Marie as though they were longtime friends. Natalie and Robert had shared one class the previous semester, so they also sort of knew each other. Also, since Natalie was taking French, she had seen Rose Marie around the language building. Natalie and Rose Marie were happy, extroverted, and confident women.

When we arrived at the apartment, we found Charlie and his date in the living room. Charlie introduced me to her. Her name was Ellen Reilly. I introduced Natalie and, fortunately, again remembered her whole name. As Dave had told me earlier, Ellen knew Rose Marie, and they greeted each other like good friends. Ellen was petite with long brown hair. She wore slacks and a blouse of what struck me as dull colors. She spoke pleasantly, though, and was more extroverted than Charlie. I felt like a rat for thinking it, but she and Charlie looked made for each other.

When we walked back to the bedroom to put our jackets away, I felt awkward showing the girls into what had been our private male environment. Then we went to the kitchen, and Robert said, "Well, this is where we do the cooking." Rose Marie said he sounded like a real estate salesman showing a house. We started to relax and talk about housekeeping and cooking.

Natalie didn't drink, so I got her a Coke and even poured it over ice in a glass rather than just giving her a can. I had a beer, and Robert made sloe gin fizzes for Rose Marie and him using my gin, 7 Up, and cherries, which was fine with me.

The conversation drifted from this to that while we just stood around in the kitchen. Natalie and Rose Marie talked about the student senate's petitioning the administration to extend women's curfew hours. Naturally, Robert and I supported the effort, but both of the girls scolded us when we admitted we'd never been to a senate meeting.

"Just being there is important," Natalie said. "One of the deans is always there, and they judge how serious students are by the turnout."

That's when Dave and his date arrived. Her name was Fran Windsor, and her distinctive eyes immediately fascinated me. They were large, but not objectionably so, and of a pale gray color. I had an urge to let her hypnotize me. She was carefully dressed with matching skirt and blouse. It was apparent after only a few minutes that she had firm personality that stood up well to Dave's mild aggressiveness.

Shortly after Dave got there, Robert started the great pizza-making operation. Weeks before, he had bought two boxed pizza kits and some extra mozzarella cheese. We were on the second round of drinks by then, and the kitchen turned into mild bedlam as we mixed and rolled dough. Natalie wasn't drinking, but she got as silly as the rest of us. She patted her cheeks with flour and convinced Rose Marie to do it too, and they looked like clowns. When the pizza was baked, we filled our plates and went into the living room.

There weren't enough places to sit, so Natalie and Rose Marie sat together on the easy chair with their legs pressed against the arms, while Robert and I sat on the floor in front of them and leaned back against the chair. Dave, Fran, Charlie, and Ellen squeezed together on the old couch. We started with my favorite album, Mason Williams's *Classical Gas*. The talk was about Graduate Record Exams and graduate school, so I didn't have much to contribute, and then Natalie asked some general questions, which Dave seemed eager to answer.

The album finished, and Rose Marie suggested turning on the TV. *The Ghost and Mrs. Muir* was on, so we watched it, and when the show ended, Ellen wanted to hear a Johnny Mathis album. That was the signal for the lights to go out. I felt conspicuous, so I suggested to Natalie that we go to the kitchen for another drink. We had only been there a moment when Robert and Rose Marie joined us. By this time, the booze was wearing off, and the mood had become more sober. The four of us sat at the kitchen table with a bowl of pretzels and sodas and played Crazy Eights. We could hear the music from the living room. It was pleasant. At one point, I went to the bathroom and returned to find the girls taking about buying shoes. Robert looked bored.

"I'm done with cards," he said. "How about watching TV?" he asked Rose Marie.

"Okay," she said, and they moved to the living room, though I had my doubts that they'd be watching TV. I wanted to spend time alone with Natalie, so I suggested another card game. "Mind playing with just me?" I asked her.

"Of course not," she said.

I dealt out a hand and continued the conversation. "So tell me more about your trip to France. What make of plane did you fly over on?"

"Gee, I don't know," she said, thinking for a moment. "It was the first time I had flown. The airline was Pan Am."

"Was it a jet or propeller?"

"A jet. It was comfortable, and the stewardesses were just great, but it was tiring."

"Where did you fly from?"

"New York, Kennedy Airport. It was a grueling experience. First, we had to get to New York and wait for the flight. Then there was the flight, and after we landed, we had to go through customs. And then finally get to the hotel. It took nearly a day and a half."

"Did you know anyone on the trip?" I asked her. "Did anyone else go from your high school?"

"One other girl from my class went and a couple of people from schools near ours, which gave us all a group of friends."

"Hey—any *guys*? Anything interesting go on?"

"No. Guys never take French. And if they did, they wouldn't go to any extra effort to learn more."

"Such an opportunity," I said with a smirk. "Lonely American girls longing for excitement."

"Well," she said with a suggestive pause, "there were French boys who were very happy to help us with our French and show us the town."

"Okay, I won't ask you any private or potentially incriminating questions."

She laughed and said, "I wish."

We continued talking about her school's facilities in France, particularly her dorm room and the bath or what the French called a bath. She described the city of Lyon as picturesque and quaint. To me, the idea of being in France for a month sounded great. Except for the language classes.

"Art history would be a breeze for you," I said, "especially after all the art you must have seen in Paris."

"I wish that were true," she replied, slapping a card on the table. "Everything was a big blur. We only had four days to tour Paris. It seemed like we were always rushing around."

"But you must have seen the big museums. What's the name of that famous one? I can't pronounce it. *Lover* or something like that?"

"Louvre." Her pronunciation sounded great to me.

"Louvre." I attempted to mimic her.

"That's good enough," she said. "Anyone would know what you said."

"So tell me about the place."

"It's a huge palace made into a museum. When I say huge, I mean *huge*. There must be miles of corridors and hundreds of rooms. It's divided into sections for the different periods of history. We just didn't have enough time, but what we saw was wonderful."

"Which part or period did you like the best?"

"I'm like most people. I like the Impressionists the best. They had a great collection there. I stood in front of a Renoir for what must have been fifteen minutes."

"Which one?"

"*The Boating Party*."

"Oh sure. That one's full of life. The painting of the garden dance is lively too."

"Have you already gotten to the Impressionists in your class?"

"No. I browse ahead."

"You like art that much?" she asked.

I had talked too much. "Well," I said, "who doesn't like art? I enjoy beauty just like anyone else." Then I tried to dumb down the conversation, which was easy for me to do. "I enjoy Greek sculpture—you know, the partially draped goddess of this or that." I leered at her and wiggled my eyebrows.

"You don't have to make excuses to me because you have a sensitivity for art," she said quietly. "I think it's wonderful."

"Sensitivity," I repeated. "You give me too much credit."

Still talking, we played several hands of cards. Sometime before eleven o'clock, Dave and Fran came in to get drinks, and he stood by the table for a time taking to us and watching us play. Fran had gone into the bathroom. Soon, Charlie and Ellen were in the kitchen too, and there were two, sometimes three, conversations going on at once. We quit playing cards, and I got Natalie another glass of soda and a beer for myself. We had run out of ice earlier, and the new ice cubes were only partially frozen, so Natalie got only scraps of ice in her drink. She was slightly disappointed, but with all the chatter going on, I didn't try to apologize.

Ellen was upset about the Russians stomping on the Czechoslovaks and soon had Natalie engaged in an intense conversation. I had been talking with Dave about the World Series, or I should say he was talking to me about it. I didn't particularly care for either the Tigers or the Cardinals, but I told him I hoped the Cardinals would win the series. Dave said that was unlikely, since not many teams were repeat World Series winners.

While this was going on, Natalie got up from the table and left the room. Ellen then came over and told me Natalie wasn't feeling well. I moved over to the door to the hall, and when she came out of the bathroom, I stepped into the hall to speak to her.

She spoke first, saying, "I'm sorry, but I'm feeling pretty queasy. I've probably eaten and drunk too much."

"I can see that," I said. "You do look a little pale. Would you like to go out on the porch for a breath of air?"

"No, I don't think so. I'm afraid I ought to get back to the dorm. I'm sorry, but I'd rather be where I can lie down and get up fast. If you know what I mean."

"Well, sure. I'll just tell them we're leaving."

I went back to the kitchen and told Robert and Dave we were leaving. Dave leaned closer to me and said in a low, concerned voice, "Natalie has a date for homecoming. She mentioned it to Rose Marie when you were in the bathroom. That's why they were talking about shoe shopping."

I stepped back and said, "Well, fine. I wasn't going to ask her anyway." I sounded a bit irritated.

"Okay. I just wanted you to know."

"Yeah, you're right, man. Thanks."

After Natalie told Rose Marie, Ellen, and Fran we were leaving, they wished her well, and we said good night and left the room.

I went into the bedroom to get my field jacket and Natalie's coat. Natalie looked in the open door. The room looked okay, so that didn't worry me. "Are those your uniforms?" I heard her ask behind me.

"What?"

"In the closet," she said. "The green shirts with the patches." She had seen my fatigue jackets hanging in the open closet. There were more of them than civilian shirts.

"Oh right," I answered. "They're so durable I couldn't just throw them away." I changed the subject by asking her if she would be warm enough. She thought she would be.

During the walk back to her dorm, she asked me what had caused Robert's limp. She was inquisitive, not rude. A journalism major was probably the right major for her. I told her that Robert had told me it was a "problem from birth" and that he never called it a "defect." We talked about other things, incidental chitchat, and then she asked if I had known Dave and Charlie my freshman year. I replied that I knew them because of rooming with Robert. It was obvious that putting the people puzzle together was important to her.

As we approached Grace Donnelly Hall, I heard the campus bell tower strike half past eleven. It was early to be returning from a date. Then I began wondering how cordial our good night should be. I certainly wasn't going to try and lay a big kiss on her. Thanks to Dave, I knew something of how important the date was to her. Her not feeling well also helped to excuse my not being romantic.

We walked up the steps of her dorm and stopped beside the door. An unusual number of lights made the porch as bright as day. "You know," she said, "I feel a lot better. I'm sure the cool air must have helped. It's early. Would you like to sit in the lounge for a while?"

I wished Robert hadn't told me about her having a homecoming date because I felt more confused than enthusiastic. We sat on half of a couch, sharing it with another couple, and had an easy conversation. I asked her if she had any brothers or sisters.

"I've got a younger sister," she said. "She's a senior in high school this year. I certainly hope she doesn't come here."

"Why not? Don't you get along?"

She described a normal cycle of rivalry and affection between them then asked me if I had a brothers or sisters. I told her I had an elder brother but didn't give any details.

More couples gathered in the lounge as it got closer to the midnight curfew. I used this as an excuse to end our conversation and to start the awkward process of saying good night. "I guess I should shove off and make room in here for other people," I said.

We stood up and walked to the hall. "I'm glad you called," she said. "It was fun."

"It was fun," I agreed, "and thanks for tolerating such short notice. Maybe we can do it again sometime." I hadn't planned to suggest that, but it fit the mood.

"Sure. But maybe call me earlier?" She said this with a disarming smile.

"Absolutely! Well, good night."

"See you in class."

"Right. Bye"

I left the girls' dorm and started to walk back to the apartment. It was still a mild evening, and there was a half moon that occasionally shone down through the clouds. *That went well*, I told myself, though her reaction was confusing. Maybe Robert was wrong, and she didn't have a homecoming date. I ran this idea backward and forward through my mind as I walked back to the apartment. Couples were running past me in the other direction to get to the girls' dorms before the curfew. I felt a strong familiarity with the whole scene. More than two years had passed since I had walked Olivia back from a date along these same sidewalks, but the sensations I was feeling were the same. The most powerful sensation was the urge to enjoy the moment. After all, it had been a successful date.

But then walking alone through the dark changed my mood. I remembered other dark nights when I'd been on guard duty and had to send up illumination flares from a mortar tube and then watch to see if any of the black-and-white images in the perimeter wire moved. School life was a fairy tale, and fairy tales don't last. I should always be ready to return to the reality.

At the apartment, Robert, Dave, and Charlie were talking in the kitchen. I only said a few words to them, just letting them know I agreed that it had been a successful evening. Then I washed up and crashed in bed. Sleep came like a heavy door slamming shut. My mind was quiet during the night. Nothing from my conscious world, past or present, disturbed my sleep. I didn't dream.

WEEK 5

OCTOBER 20, 1968–OCTOBER 26, 1968

MONDAY, OCTOBER 21

After two years of stress-filled nomadic army life, I wanted school to be a quiet and relaxing place, but it hadn't worked out that way, and I was depressed. My academic work was okay, even if it did take more time than I had hoped. My problems were with people. My problem with Olivia was my own fault. While in the army, I had thought about her and what it would be like being back on campus with her, but I hadn't been honest with myself. If I'd been honest, I'd have realized coming back was pursuing a fantasy.

But if I hadn't come back to Middlesex, I wouldn't have met Natalie, another person presenting me with a problem. If I were honest with myself this time, I'd have to admit I liked her. I spent time studying her in my mind, the way a scientist or engineer might study a problem. I thought about her personality and wondered how it could be so genuine and innocent. From what she described of her home life and high school, it seemed possible she truly was what she appeared to be. Her beauty was beyond question. It wasn't a stunning beauty but rather a beauty of balance and pleasing proportions. She had a delightful symmetry that made me want to just look at her. I was surprised that she hadn't been staked out her freshman year by some wealthy fast-talking upper classman. Obviously, other guys had seen what I had; she had a date for homecoming.

Then there was the problem with the ROTC fatheads. I had blown it there. The war was my hot button. There were marginally justifiable reasons for my assuming such a superior attitude when talking about the war; after all, I had actually experienced it. But I was going to have to learn to ignore all the talk of the war that went on around me. Doing that would be hard. The whole country was a buzzing about the war. It was on TV constantly and was the topic of too many casual conversations. There should be other things to talk about and other issues for the campus politicos to take up. I didn't want to hear about the war.

Meeting Pete had helped me get back into campus life. Sure we occasionally talked of the war, but we talked as brothers who knew intimately what the other one was talking about. Just a few words between us carried an immense amount of understanding. I was comfortable over at his apartment, and I thought his friends were honest, sincere people trying to make it. The pot smoking and hippie atmosphere was tolerable. I always got along with the heads in the army. I just let them be themselves and at the same time continued being my own self.

Getting to know Robert again had been enjoyable too. He hadn't changed since our freshman year. It was nice to find some consistency. I had a fear, though, a fear that I would lean on his friendship too much. He was going on to graduate school, and I would be here another two years—if I stuck it out.

So as homecoming week started, my disposition was mixed. The weather was staging one last Indian summer.

Monday afternoon, the temperature reached seventy-eight degrees, and it hadn't rained in a week. There had been a hard frost the week before, which finished the leaves for the season and left many trees bare. The next storm would bring all the leaves down.

TUESDAY, OCTOBER 22

I was apprehensive about seeing Natalie in our Tuesday morning American lit class. She was already seated when I came into the room, and we exchanged smiles. I hadn't planned to approach her after class, but neither did I intend to avoid her. It was a mystery why she would be warm to me when she had someone serious enough to take her to homecoming.

When class ended, I packed up my books at a slightly slower pace than usual. If she wanted to bolt and not talk to me, I would make it easy for her. But she hesitated too, and we stood up at the same time. It would have been rude not to speak to her.

"Hi," I said. "You're looking well. Were you better Sunday?"

"I was fine. I'm sure it was just something I ate. And the crowded room."

"Well . . ." I smiled at her. "It wasn't from drinking too much." I immediately qualified my sentence. "I mean, it's okay not to drink. It's smart, I mean. Then you don't have problems." I was going to continue making a fool of myself, but she interrupted me.

"I understand. I do drink sometimes, but I like the sweet fruity drinks, and it's easy to have too much of them."

Neither of us mentioned the possibility of having coffee as we walked down the stairs together and out of the building. We talked about schoolwork, and she said again the people at the apartment had been a fun group. When we reached a junction in the sidewalk, she went toward what I assumed was the newspaper office, and I went to the library. The rest of the afternoon was normal tedium. I finished classes and played pool at the student union for a while, and then back at the apartment, I had a can of pork and beans and a couple of pieces of leftover fried chicken for dinner. After dinner, I went back to the library to study. It was just a boring day until I screwed it up at the end.

I studied in the library till about nine o'clock then took a break and headed for the student union to get a Coke. As I was walking down the steps of the library, a Mustang pulled up to the curb on the other side of the street. I like cars and could see it was a nice '65 fastback. The driver got out and walked around the back of the car. When he stepped up on the sidewalk and into light from a street lamp, I saw that it was my ROTC nemesis, Alan Holden. I walked on to the student union. Fortunately, he and his friends were going somewhere else.

The library closed at ten o'clock, but I still had reading to do. At first, I wanted to forget about it, but then I decided to stick to it, so I walked from the library to one of the classroom buildings the school leaves open for study. Walking across the street in front of the library, I noticed Holden's Mustang still sitting at the curb.

About eleven fifteen, I packed it in and left the building. The campus was empty at that hour, and my route took me back past the library. Holden's Mustang was still there. It sat in a shadow just beyond the light of a street lamp. Without hesitation, I turned and walked toward it. I bent down and got an angle to see through the car windows. No one was in the car. I walked slowly past the car and close to the passenger side door and looked in to double-check. Empty.

I took a couple more paces and then turned back again, scanning the area as I did. I saw no one but knew that was no guarantee that no one was watching me from a shadow somewhere.

Then I turned and walked back and grabbed the radio antenna and twisted it flat, pulled it up, and then pushed it flat again. It wouldn't break. I left it twisted down and grabbed the rearview mirror and gave it a yank. It bent, but it didn't break either. Not having broken anything off frustrated me, but standing by the car any longer was pushing my luck.

The palm of my hand hurt, and I felt like a criminal, worse was that I knew I was as big an asshole as I considered Holden to be. I had proven what I'd always known: Assholeism brings out assholeism. This wasn't an eloquent evaluation of social behavior, but it fit many cases. It fit individuals, groups, and nations. And now me.

Walking back to the apartment, I began to sweat. Once, I stepped off the sidewalk and into a shadow and watched, but I didn't see anyone. No one was up at the apartment when I got back, so I went straight to bed. As usual, it took a while to get to sleep. I thought about the shit that had been pulled on me in the army and wondered if the people who had screwed me over had worried about it afterward. I had had a watch stolen while out on a firebase in Vietnam. The Vietnamese civilian who was the camp barber took it while I was taking a shower in a plywood stall. My clothes and watch were on a hook outside the stall. I saw the skinny old man through cracks in the wood as he walked past the shower. The watch was missing when I got out, but I couldn't prove anything. Other shit had happened too, like my footlocker being rifled, and I'd been sucker punched for a minor disagreement. Thinking about these things did nothing to ease my guilt about vandalizing Holden's Mustang. Maybe the army and the war had ruined me. Maybe I was too hard a case now to be back among these kids who had spent the last two years on this genteel campus. I consoled myself by thinking that if Holden could afford a Mustang, he could afford an antenna. It wasn't like I had screwed over some poor kid.

I had a bad dream that night. I usually do when I'm stressed out. In the dream, I was back in the army and getting an Article 15 punishment for some silly infraction of military code. Obviously, I had an overactive conscience.

THURSDAY, OCTOBER 24

On Thursday, I decided to ask Natalie about her homecoming date, but I didn't get the chance. As we left class together, she was the one who brought up the subject.

"I'm kind of in a hurry today," she said as we walked down the stairs. "I've got to get downtown and look at shoes. Maybe you've heard I'm going to homecoming?"

"Oh sure," I said. "I just assumed you were going. The guys on this campus aren't blind—crude, maybe, but not blind." My response was so quick it was obvious I knew she had a date.

She smiled and said, "See ya," and took off down the sidewalk that led downtown.

It was good to have that issue taken care of. It still didn't explain much, but at least she was open about it. I was definitely not going watch her to find out who she was going out with. That Peeping Tom crap had just made the situation with Olivia worse. I should get dates with different girls, like maybe one of the young town girls from Pete's circle of friends.

FRIDAY, OCTOBER 25

So Friday night, I went over to Pete's but not with the conscious intention of hooking up with a girl. Pete's place was like a refuge from school. Everyone at my apartment was a student. Everyone who visited the apartment was a student. All the talk was campus talk. At Pete's place, though, there was a real-world variety of people and talk. When I got there, I found him excited.

"My old man sent me two hundred bucks for my birthday!"

"Two hundred? You're kidding." The music in his cellar apartment was so loud I thought maybe I had misunderstood him.

"No shit, man," he said. "He says it's to make up for last year when I was in Nam and there was no sense sending money."

"Lucky dog."

"You're lucky too, buddy. We're going out to dinner and then to a real hoedown hootenanny. We're gonna cut the rug." He chuckled at his use of an antiquated phrase.

I backed away. "You're crazy, man. Take Patty, for crying out loud. Two guys having dinner together in this town are liable to get the crap beat out of them."

Pete grinned. "Oh, she's coming too," he said, "but we have to wait until she gets off work."

"Now wait," I said. "We're buddies, but just because I drop in, that doesn't mean you have to treat me to dinner."

"Hell, are you kidding? Your coming is the best thing that could have happened. Having dinner alone with Patty would be just too romantic. She won't care if you come."

"Like hell she won't," I protested. But it was no use. When something popped into Pete's head, it was there to stay. Pete's plan was to go to dinner and dancing at the

Big Sycamore Inn. He described the place as roadhouse hidden deep in the backwoods north of town. When I heard where he wanted to go, I thought I had a good reason the plan wouldn't work. "Hey," I said, "we'll stick out like sore thumbs. The hillbillies will know we're college for sure. Those places can get downright ugly for outsiders."

Pete made a quick and cheery response. "Patty's local. She might even know people there. Besides, if you wear your army field jacket and I wear mine, they'll think we're big heroes. Your shirt doesn't look fancy, and neither will mine. We won't be as conspicuous as you think."

"Well . . . I don't know." I was thinking about Pete's long hair. He looked like a real hippie.

"Bullshit," he said. "You don't know. This is going to be great! Patty says the place has a great western band and the food is plain good home cooking." He was so enthusiastic I couldn't help catching the spirit.

While we waited for Patty, I lay back on the couch and watched TV. Pete was puttering in the kitchen area. "Hey!" I yelled out to him. "I haven't seen you on campus lately."

"School sucks," he said. "I'll never use the crap those doddering old farts try to teach. And the kids are mostly spoiled brats hanging out at their fraternities and sororities."

"So I guess you don't like it?"

"It's a joke, I tell you. I'm going to find something else to do."

"Work?" I exclaimed in a mock shocked voice.

"Maybe. Who knows? Nothing's happening here. This town is dead."

"You're right. It's not very exciting."

"It's dead, I tell you."

I dropped the subject and went back to watching TV. Soon, Patty arrived, and we piled into Pete's GTO. I sat in the back, of course. With a deep rumble from his exhaust, the engine fired, and we knew a fun evening had begun.

Two major state routes passed through town, so there were four ways out of town, roughly the points of the compass. Instead of one of these routes, however, Patty directed us to a small county road neither Pete nor I knew about. The road wove up a steep hill. At the top, I looked back and caught a glimpse of the lights of the town below. Then the road went down the back side of the hill and began to follow a small stream. Rural roads are dark, but this one seemed like a trip up a huge empty pipe. The stream, "Goose Run," Patty told us, was on our left, and the trees on our right were so close to the road that their limbs hung out over us. We'd been driving along the twisty road about five minutes when I spoke up.

"How far is it to this place?"

"Hang on," Patty answered. "It'll be another ten miles." With that, I lost all hope of getting the special dinner Pete had described. The only people out here were the Hatfields and the McCoys, and they didn't go to restaurants.

Eventually, however, the headlights flashed on a large sign. *The Big Sycamore Inn*, it said, *just ahead!* All we had to do was follow the arrow. Soon, a glow of light appeared ahead of us, giving the impression we might be coming to a village, and then the Big Sycamore Inn appeared, all brightly lit up, right beside the steam.

The building was a rambling structure made up of additions put on as the business grew. From the looks of it, the business had started in a home. The central structure was a two-story house, but three single-level additions had been added. Each addition had different siding and a different roofline. Every window had at least two neon beer signs lighting up the night. A large partially paved parking lot filled with cars and pickup trucks stretched across in front of the building.

Pete's car left the road with a clunk as we drove on to the rutted parking lot. We splashed through a few large puddles and then parked at the one end of the inn. The place was busy, and the lot was nearly full. When we got out, we noticed a sycamore tree at the edge of the pavement that was distinctly bigger than all the other trees.

"That must be the namesake tree," Pete said as we walked up to a door marked *Restaurant*. There were two other doors further along, the bar and the dance hall.

As soon as we walked in, the hostess greeted us warmly and led us to a large round wooden table. There was no particular theme to the dining room decor. After a pleasant older waitress handed us laminated menus, Pete warned us not to consider price as we reviewed the selections.

Pete ordered before me, so I ordered the same New York steak he did, and Patty ordered pork chops. Each of us ordered a beer without the waitress asking us for proof of age. Our salads came right away, and as we were beginning to eat, Pete asked me a question. "So did you get turkey at the holidays when you were in Nam?"

I remembered turkey but had to think about which holiday we'd had it for. "Yeah," I finally said. "Actually at both Thanksgiving and Christmas. From November through January, I was working out on an LZ that had a good mess hall. They flew the turkey in. The meals were great, considering the circumstances. How about you?"

"Me too," he said. "Both holidays. It wasn't home cooking, but they made an effort. I remember I wrote letters Christmas night." As if on cue, we were both quiet for a moment. Then we talked about the food here and the restaurant for a few minutes. Our dinners came. The steaks were on small platters held in wooden trays. Our vegetables and potatoes were in side dishes. I felt quite grown-up and sophisticated.

The Big Sycamore Inn impressed me, and I felt I had to say so, since I'd been skeptical at the beginning of the trip. "Patty," I said, "this is a great place. Thanks for suggesting it."

"You're welcome. It is a ways out of town. The story is the place started as a speakeasy selling local moonshine during Prohibition."

"I'll believe that!" Pete said.

Whenever I ate with a Vietnam vet who had been outside the wire and in combat, we would eventually talk about C rations. Pete and I didn't pass up this opportunity to compare the feast we were having with eating C rations. I asked Pete the central question first. "What was your favorite C ration?"

"Ham!" he responded. "But it was hard to get, and I would probably choke on it now. How about you?"

"Ham was great, but I liked the turkey loaf too."

We laughed when we realized we each still had a P-38 can opener on us, both of them on our key rings. We reminisced some more. Each of us had at one time or another gone for more than ten days on nothing but C rations. Pete had been out on a search-and-destroy operation when he'd had to eat the Cs for a long stretch. I had been stuck with C rations for nearly two weeks because our LZ was socked in by a monsoon and the normal rations couldn't be flown in.

Finally, Patty spoke up, saying the parents of someone she knew were sitting at another table. Pete and I had been more or less ignoring her, so when she and Pete began talking, I concentrated on playing with a candle in the middle of the table. It was in an antique pewter candleholder. I pressed my finger in the warm wax that had dripped down the side of the candle.

During the lull in the conversation, I also thought about Natalie. I envied her date and allowed myself some wishful thinking that maybe she didn't care for the guy. It would have been nice if Natalie had been with us. We were sitting at a table for four, and I looked over at the empty seat, where the waitress had removed the unused table setting.

Dinner was so filling that none of us wanted desert. I had a $10 bill that I wanted to leave as a tip, but Pete insisted that he'd take care of it. "My old man's money can take care of it," he said. He discreetly put cash in the black folded wallet the waiter had left the check in.

Dinner had been an enjoyable interlude, but we didn't want to leave yet. Since I hadn't paid the tip, I insisted on buying a round of drinks in the dance hall, so we went on over.

Compared with the restaurant, the dance hall was noisy and crowed. Two distinct rooms had been joined at the point where two of the building additions came together. We walked from the restaurant into the section that had tables and a great long bar down the entire one side of the room. There must have been ten bartenders furiously working the bar, and the band hadn't started yet, but the jukebox was loud, and place was full. There were no open tables, so we stood against one wall where a shelf ran the length of the room and provided a place to put your beer. The crowd appeared dressed as if they'd come right from work. There was no pretense about anyone's appearance. Everyone seemed intent on enjoying themselves, not impressing one another. Well, that was true with the exception of the mating rituals going on.

Pete and Patty went out and danced. Pete didn't look out of place, so I stopped worrying about the locals picking a fight with a hippie. Standing alone at the wall, I realized there were many unattached girls in the crowd. Strangely, I had no urge to put moves on any of them.

After three songs, Pete and Patty came off the floor, and as soon as a table opened up, we sat down. Pete was really happy. "This is the best bar I've been in since my R & R," he said. "How about you, Mike?"

In an earlier conversation somewhere, Pete and I had discovered that we'd both been to the Patpong District of Bangkok on R & R. "It certainly smells better," I said.

That struck him funny. "Thank God for that! Oh, the smells! But you got used to it, didn't you?"

"Sure, sort of. The flush toilet in this place is a luxury compared with Bangkok." I hoped he would leave the subject. There was no way you could talk about R & R in Bangkok without talking about drinking and screwing. R & R in Bangkok was sometimes called I & I, for intoxication and intercourse.

But Pete went on. "When were you there? What month?"

"September," I said. "The second week of September."

"I was there in mid-August. We couldn't have picked hotter months. Where did you stay?"

"The Long Branch Saloon on Sukhumvit Road."

Then the conversation went right where I knew it had to go. "What was your girl's name?" Pete asked me.

I was embarrassed with Patty there and hesitated to answer. Pete picked up on that immediately and probed again. "Come on, everyone knows what GIs do on R & R. Did you rent one or just do short-timers?"

I gave up and answered him. "I had a contract for a couple of days. She called herself Susie. I never heard her real name."

"What's this renting you're talking about?" Patty asked in a matter-of-fact voice.

"Some silly paper the hotel people made you sign," Pete said. "It called the girl a *companion* or *tour guide* so they could deny prostitution." The word *prostitution* hung between us for a moment. But Pete had talked himself into the situation, so I let him talk his way out of it. "War is messy business," he said at last. "It makes you do things you never thought you would do."

"War forces you to act like a pig?" Patty asked, her voice full of sarcasm.

Pete responded immediately. "Not exactly *forces* you, but you're put into situations you didn't chose. Six months in the bush changes you in all sorts of ways."

I felt obliged to support him by now, so I spoke up. "There aren't many saints in uniform, and if you start out a saint, they just pounded it out of you." I wanted to get back to the good feelings we'd had when we were eating dinner. When the waitress came up to the table, I ordered another round. No one had spoken after my comment. Since girls always like to travel, I described Bangkok to Patty. "It was an interesting city. There are a lot of canals through the city that are used like streets. Then there's the river. What was the river's name?" I asked Pete, trying to get him back into the conversation.

"The Flower River."

I nodded and continued. "And there were lots of bald Buddhist monks shuffling around in long pink robes."

"The markets were neat too," Pete said. "They had everything—fruit, vegetables, pigs, chickens, cows, flowers, lots of flowers, and even birds in little bamboo cages. It was wonderful compared to Vietnam."

All three of us began to talk some more. The biggest city Patty had ever been to was Columbus, Ohio. Pete told her about New York City. She enjoyed his description of shopping on Fifth Avenue and walking in Central Park. He told her that when they went to New York together he would take her to breakfast and then to Tiffany's.

The band began to play at nine o'clock. It was a country band with both electric and acoustic guitars. Pete and Patty danced a lot, but I just sat and drank. Around eleven, a fight broke out in a far corner of the dance hall. There were more bouncers in the crowd than I realized, and they moved in so quickly the band didn't even stop playing. Soon after the fight, Patty asked to leave.

She hadn't drunk nearly as much as Pete and I, so she drove back to town. She managed the heavy clutch of the GTO quite well. The trip back was difficult because the twisty road made me queasy, but fortunately, I was able to hang on. At one point, Patty had to brake hard to let deer cross in front of us. I remember seeing them in the headlights as they ambled off into the dark at the side of the road.

When I got back to the apartment, Robert and Rose Marie were the only ones there. Rose Marie had worked magic on Robert during the week, and they were going to all the homecoming events, except the campus hop at the student union on Friday night. This was good because they were seniors, and this would be their last homecoming. I remembered Dave's remark about Robert not being able to dance and wondered what he would do at the formal. People were mature enough to see that he could just do the best he could, and the only one concerned would be him. If he and I were in the army, I would have kidded him about it. Being in the army gave you a thick skin.

It took me a long time to get to sleep that night. I couldn't find a comfortable memory that would put me to sleep. Eventually, I thought about the woods behind the house where I grew up. My school friends and I wore trails among the trees, played games that had no rulebooks and were not officiated by adults. We made camps and forts and camped out overnight in the forest. These memories carried me into sleep.

But the good memories ended. That night, I dreamed of being on guard duty with no perimeter lights, no moon, and no hand flares. There were other GIs in the dream, but I only heard their voices in the dark. All of us were pissed off that we had no illumination. We stayed awake instead of someone sleeping while others were on guard, which was the usual procedure. The dream was not so bad that I had to wake myself up, so eventually, I got a good night's sleep.

SATURDAY, OCTOBER 26

I did laundry after lunch on Saturday. I deserved no sympathy for being alone, since Robert and Rose Marie had asked me to join them at the football game. It would have worked too, and I probably would have been a pleasant time, but Olivia and Natalie were certain to be there.

Later in the afternoon, I joined a group of other vets playing pool in the student union game room. There were about twenty vets on campus, but this random pool game was the only activity we did as a group. We weren't exactly friendly when we played pool either. We communicated more with grunts and nods than words. When we did talk, we spoke in short often incomplete sentences, and there was no talk of the military.

Like the rest of the campus, the Hideout was deserted that afternoon. Everyone was at the football game and the halftime crowning of the queen. After the game, though, people began to show up at the Hideout, and our pool game broke up. As two of the guys were leaving, they announced they would be playing pool at a bar downtown that evening.

"Where is this place?" I asked.

A navy vet answered as he picked up his pea jacket. "It's called Mike and Sam's. It's on Third Street, down by where the railroad crosses the street."

"They serve anything to eat?"

"Great pizza."

Playing pool for the evening was better than anything else I could think of to do. I couldn't just sit around the apartment with everyone going to and from the formal. Pete's wasn't an option either. Pete, Patty, and some of their friends were going to Athens, about an hour's drive from Middlesex. There was a large state university campus there with, I suspected, more action and more pot than could be found at Middlesex.

Since I was hungry, I decided to go directly to the bar. None of us asked the others if they were going, but three of us ended up in a cluster walking downtown. No one had a car. Mike and Sam's was on the same street as the Hunt Club and just a block past Main Street. By the time we got to the bar, we had exchanged names and told one another where we were from. The navy vet was named Frank and was from a small Ohio village. The other guy, an army vet named George, was from Pittsburgh.

Mike and Sam's was in an old brick building that in years past had been used for several different commercial activities and now had apartments on the upper floors. A large green, white, and red neon sign that hung over the sidewalk read *Mike and Sam Talintino's Italian Restaurant*. Stepping inside, I got the feeling the place had been in business for a long time. All the Italian decorations looked tired and worn. A faded spotted wallpaper mural of an Italian garden, complete with an ancient stone column and grapevines, decorated one wall. The tables were covered with white-and-red checked oilcloth tablecloths, and a wine bottle with a candle decorated the center of each table. I heard Italian being spoken by customers, so I was encouraged that the food would be good. A small kitchen was through a door at the end of the bar. Two people, which were all that would fit in the kitchen, were busily kneading out pizza dough on a flour-covered wooden counter. Two big ovens poured out heat, and the cooks looked tired, even though the evening had just started. I had ten bucks with me, so I ordered a large pizza, which I knew was more than I could eat, but then I could offer some to the other guys. When I ordered the pizza, the bartender said I could pay when the pizza came out.

I followed the other two guys directly to the bar, and we each ordered a draft. "Hello, boys!" one of the bartenders greeted Frank and George. "Nice to see you. Enjoy your game."

We took our beers to the back, where there were two pool tables. Both were being played, so we stood around for a time watching other guys shoot. I looked over cues in the wall rack and found them to be in poor shape. Since they were all equally bad, though, it didn't matter.

A table opened up, and we had just racked up the balls when one of the cooks came out with two extra-large pizzas. My first thought was that my order had been misunderstood, but the cook said, "Here you go, boys. Something on the house from Sam and me."

"What's that you say?" Frank asked the cook.

"Yes, yes," he said. "It's free tonight. Sam and I sit here when there are no customers and watch all the trouble on TV. Then we remember when we were in the army. We want to give you boys our thanks. It's a little thing, really."

"No kidding!" Frank exclaimed. "Well, thanks a lot. Yeah, you told us once you and Sam were in World War II."

Mike, the cook, nodded. "Yes. We were sent to Italy, probably because we knew Italian from our parents. Sam went first, and then I went to Anzio."

George had stepped back to the bar and yelled his thanks to Sam, who waved back at him. Then George came up to Mike and thanked him too. "Hey, this is real nice," he said. "You know our VA checks get mighty thin at this time of the month."

Mike smiled at all three of us. "Well, all of you deserve a little something," he said. "We see the people on TV complain and blame the soldiers, but they don't know. Some of the guys at our VFW don't think you fight hard enough. But they weren't combat soldiers. They don't understand. You boys were away from your families and girls a long time. Your buddies that didn't come back are gone with the same honor as my friends who left us at Anzio. You're all the same as anyone in the big fights in any war, Normandy or the trenches, years ago when I was a boy."

We all thanked him again, and he went back to the bar. "Damn!" said George as he pulled out a wedge of pizza and struggled with the long strings of mozzarella and hot tomato sauce. "This is the first time anything like this has happened."

We ate, drank, and played pool until our pool playing fell apart from the drinking. Then we sat at a table where we could watch the TV at the end of the bar and drank some more. The late movie was a Bing Crosby-Bob Hope road comedy. I chuckled some at the slapstick, but neither George nor Frank saw anything funny. Their mood had remained consistent throughout the evening, no matter how much they drank. I hadn't lightened up myself either. It was wonderful to get the free pizza, but listening to Sam talk was a strain. I didn't like to be reminded I was a vet, even for a free meal.

Coming back from one of my many visits to the restroom, I staggered and grabbed the back of a chair to steady myself. Instead of sitting down when I got back to the table, I picked up my beer and drained it while I was still standing. "Okay," I announced as I set the glass down, "that's enough for me. I'll see you, guys."

George glanced up at me and said, "Yeah, take it easy. See you at the tables sometime."

"Can you make it back okay?" Frank asked.

"I may weave up the sidewalk," I assured him, "but I think I can stay out of the street." I pulled my jacket off the back of the chair and walked past the bar. "Thanks again!" I said to Mike as I went out the door.

It was cold outside, and hardly any cars passed me as I walked back to the apartment. I walked slowly at first, but as the cold penetrated my jacket, I picked up the pace. When I got back to the apartment, I made more noise than usual walking across the porch, but no one was in the front room.

Robert came in shortly after I had gotten into bed. I was nearly asleep but asked him how the formal was. He said the band had been better than he expected. That was the last thing I remember.

WEEK 6

OCTOBER 27, 1968–NOVEMBER 2, 1968

SUNDAY, OCTOBER 27

Coffee tasted better on Sunday morning—*late* Sunday morning. Even the weather was cooperative. It was gray and raining. I made pancakes for Robert and me. He was reading the Sunday paper. The election, more details of Jackie's wedding to Onassis, and the *Apollo* rocket mission were on the front page.

"You going to the concert tonight?" Robert asked. There was a concert at the field house that night to wrap up the homecoming weekend.

"No, I hadn't planned to."

"Well, it's going to be a good concert."

Since it was the Vanilla Fudge playing, I just gave a dry response. "Yeah. Right."

Midterm exams were only a few weeks away, so I spent Sunday afternoon in the library. Sunday evening, I watched *The Ed Sullivan Show* and went to bed early. That ended my homecoming weekend.

MONDAY, OCTOBER 28

Getting back to class on Monday was a relief. It seemed like I was returning from a long crazy trip and was getting back to normal. But the campus wasn't normal. The election was just a week away, and even though it was mostly the seniors who could vote, both parties had campus support clubs that put on rallies. Even candidates Wallace and Le May had vocal supporters who decorated the campus with campaign signs.

Adding to the national political activity, the campus chapter of the Students for a Democratic Society was in a frenzy trying to get the college administration to issue a condemnation of the way Berkeley was handling the riots out there. The SDS had held two rallies to show support for the Berkeley students. The turnout at the rallies had been disappointing, and the SDS told the student body they should be ashamed of not supporting our oppressed brother students.

I was thinking of anything but the political turmoil as I walked down the sidewalk after my speech class. Then I saw Officer Cooper, the campus cop who had interrupted my ruckus with Holden, walking in my direction. He was walking slowly, checking the cars parked at the curb for campus parking stickers. I was right beside him and assumed he hadn't noticed me when he turned and startled me.

"Collins! Hold on a moment, will you?" I stopped a pace or two beyond him and turned back. "I need your help on something. Have you got a second?"

"Sure, sure."

"Now as I said, we have a problem, and I hope you can help me. My night watchmen say they often see you studying late in the open classrooms. That right?"

I answered slowly, trying to figure out how to respond. My mind searched for anything I might have heard about a classroom getting trashed or something similar. "That's right," I told him. "It's quiet. I need quiet to concentrate."

"That's fine," he said. "That's why we leave the rooms open. It's when you're walking back and forth to the rooms that we need your help. You see, we have had some cars vandalized, and I was thinking you could keep your eyes open and tell a watchman if you see any problems."

It suddenly occurred to me why he was shaking me down before he mentioned the car damage. I responded with the best nonchalance I could muster and even tried to add a small touch of perplexity. "Yeah." I nodded. "I could do that."

"You're quite a thing with the guards," he said, his voice too friendly. "They say you move around campus like a shadow. They catch a glimpse of you, and then you're gone." He paused. "You learn that in the army?"

"I'm not trying to duck away or anything," I replied. "I even speak to them sometimes."

"Oh, there's no problem with that," he said, leaving the impression there might still be a problem with something. "The boys don't mind you walking around. So you'll keep your eyes open for us?"

"Sure, I'll try," I said with no inflection to my voice.

"Okay. Thanks." He walked on, checking the next car for a parking sticker.

"*The Shadow.* What bullshit," I muttered to myself as I walked on.

A moment later, I found out that I was the fool, not Officer Cooper. I'd been on my way to the campus post office to check my mailbox. In the box, I found an appointment notice to meet with the dean of men at one o'clock, forty-five minutes from now. A wave of fear passed over me, the same wave that come to me whenever I am caught screwing up. After the quick shot of fear, I began trying to expect what the dean of men would do to me. Officer Cooper would have nailed me straight away if they had positively fingered me for busting up the Mustang. I suspected the dean was just going to get in line with Cooper and twist the screws down on me. Even though I was confident of this conclusion, I was still spooked.

I didn't want to go to the student union for lunch. I didn't want to be in a crowd. Instead, I decided to go downtown and have lunch at a drugstore lunch counter. I walked down the main sidewalk that led off campus, but then I stopped at the intersection of another sidewalk. Instead of getting lunch, I just kept walking until I had looped back to the administration building. All the time I was walking, I was working on myself for being such a jerk.

Five minutes before my appointment, I walked up the steps and into the administration building, I passed the registrar's and bursar's offices with their perpetual lines of students, and I went down the hall to the dean of men's office. An old lady who reminded me of one of my elementary school teachers was guarding the dean's office from behind a desk that was as old as she was. She peered over her spectacles and told me to knock and go on into the office. I knocked. The dean said, "Come in." I had to suppress my reflex to give a salute as I walked up to his desk.

The dean's greeting was friendly. "I'm glad you could make it in such short notice," he said. "Sit down." He pointed to a chair beside a small round table. We shook hands, and he sat in another chair at the table. The dean, whose name was McNamara, was a tall middle-aged man losing his hair. He dressed in a neat but inexpensive suit, and his office was modestly decorated. It was obvious that the school didn't lavish money on its staff. Bookshelves lined a wall behind his desk, and a window gave a view of one of the main cross-campus sidewalks.

"So, Mike," the dean began, "I see you're an alumni of sorts." He had a file that I assumed was the school's equivalent of my DD 201 file. "And I take it, the draft interrupted your education?"

"Right," I said. "I was drafted the summer after my freshman year."

"That was too bad." He looked down at the file. "Your first semester grades were okay." He shifted papers that must have been my transcripts. "But they fell all off at the end of your second semester. You must have had a tough draft board." He looked up. "What did you do in the army?"

"I was a combat engineer."

He nodded, and I could tell from his slight frown he had no idea what that meant. I wasn't going to elaborate. "So what were your duties?" he asked to get me talking.

"Combat engineers are like construction crews for the army. We built roads and bridges and removed obstacles, mostly land mines." I gave him the textbook answer.

"That sounds like hard, dangerous work. Did you have Vietnam service?"

"Yes. In the northern part of the country called I Corps."

"Well," he said, "you should be very proud of your service. Very proud. Unfortunately, many of our students and alumni have to serve."

I nodded but didn't respond. The bullshit would come as soon as he was through with the courtesies.

When he realized I wasn't going to say anything else, he shifted in his chair and got to the point. "Certainly, you realize you're not here for a chat. The school wants all of its students to be successful, so if we see problems, we address them early. You understand?"

His use of the word *we* annoyed the hell out of me, but I kept my cool. I nodded and simply said, "Yes."

"Officer Cooper told me about the problem you had with Alan Holden downtown. That incident wasn't of great consequence, though we don't like our students engaging in alcohol-inspired arguments in public. It's bad for town-school relations. What is more serious is that Holden's car was damaged here on campus." He stopped and watched for my reaction. I didn't say anything and continued to look directly at him.

Finally, he continued. "I've looked at your grades so far this fall. They are acceptable. You have a good chance at successfully starting your education again. It would be a shame to let adolescent behavior disrupt that." He paused again, and this time, all I did was nod in response. Then he concluded his lecture. "It's important that we keep high standards of character on this campus. Character is as important as academics." After a minute, he added, "Do you agree, Mr. Collins?"

I kept steady eye contact and simply said, "Yes. Certainly."

He stood up, and I did the same. Then to my surprise, he put out his hand. As we shook hands, he said, "Good then. Let's make this year another step to that degree."

I could do nothing but agree. "Yes, I'll try," I said, and I left. I had admitted my guilt, but there was no choice. To have feigned innocence would have been worse. I'm a lousy actor.

TUESDAY, OCTOBER 29

Since I had not gone out of my way to see Natalie on Monday, Tuesday was the first time I saw her after homecoming. Being in class with her had advantages and disadvantages. On the plus side, I saw her regularly without obviously pursuing her. The disadvantage was that I couldn't avoid her, which could be a problem. It was another situation where I had little or no control. It's just like when, off in the distance, you hear a VC mortar pop out of the tube. You have no control over when the round is in the air. Sure you dig into the dirt and make yourself as flat as possible, but a puff of wind during the mortar's flight could it send directly on you or send it a quarter of a mile away. Being in the same class as Natalie could lead to something nice or be another punch in the face.

The critical moment arrived as we left the building after class. We greeted each other with smiles, and I asked if she had found the right shoes on her shopping trip the Thursday before.

"Yes," she said, "I was lucky. I found a pair that matched my dress perfectly, but wearing new shoes to a dance is a mistake. They hurt my feet!" She paused a moment then continued. "Could you stop over to the newspaper office this afternoon after three o'clock? I've got a favor to ask you."

"Sure," I said. "I'm out of geology lab at three. I can stop over then. What do you need?"

"Oh, I just need some help . . . or rather, the newspaper does. I'll give you the details then. I've got to run. See you later."

She stepped into the moving crowd of students on the sidewalk. When I said good-bye, she looked back and smiled. Her little mystery irritated me slightly.

That afternoon, I was walking over to the newspaper office in the student activities building when I noticed my political science professor getting into his car. The car was a small plain Chevy. My professor looked tired and had loosened his tie. He hadn't seen me, and I felt like I was violating his privacy as I watched him toss his overstuffed briefcase in the back, quickly start the car, and drive away.

I immediately realized that I had seen my professor not as a professor but as a tired worker leaving his job and going home. The college was something entirely different for him than for me. He had a life separate from the school. I had the sudden feeling that the college was an education factory, and I had seen a tired worker leaving when the whistle blew.

These thoughts depressed me, so I was in a solemn mood when I walked into the student activities building, past the bookstore, and up the side stairs. The long hall was buzzing with people just as it had been the last time I was there. The campus radio station was at the end of the hall, and a speaker mounted outside their door piped out the broadcast.

Natalie wasn't in either room of the newspaper office, but I decided to wait and drifted over to a closet where a news teletype was rattling away, printing incoming news on yellow paper. The workings of the machine fascinated me. I watched the print ball chatter, pause, and then chatter over the paper some more. The news it printed was the same old speculation about a bombing halt over North Vietnam. Also, McCarthy had endorsed Humphrey. I was still watching the teletype when Natalie came up behind me.

"Hi! I'm sorry I'm late. I had to go back to the dorm to get this."

I turned and saw she had her camera. "Hi," I said. "I just got here."

"How would you like to take some pictures for the newspaper? You can use my camera." We walked over to the desk she shared with another reporter. There wasn't a spare chair for me, so she sat on the desk rather than sit while I stood. Her skirt moved well above her knees as she sat. My mind blanked out, and I began wondering what's the color of the underwear she was wearing. Then I heard a distant voice ask me, "Interested?"

I came back into focus. "Sure," I said, "I'd love to use that camera. What do you want pictures of?"

"We want to do an issue with a page of pictures with a common theme arranged in a collage format."

"What theme?"

"We haven't decided. You could suggest a theme from what you shoot."

I hesitated, partly because I didn't know what to say and partly because I couldn't stop looking at her legs. I knew exactly what I wanted to take pictures of, but that was impossible. "Okay," I finally said. "I'll take some shots and see what you think."

We passed a few more comments about the camera back and forth, and I asked about processing the film. Natalie said the newspaper would take care of developing. I felt bad about having to ask, but I didn't have a cent to spare.

One of the other people in the office, a guy, approached and started a conversation with Natalie about the paper. It sounded like a serious discussion, so I didn't say anything. When he crossed the room to start another serious discussion with someone else, I asked Natalie, "Who is he?"

"That's Steve Brady, the editor," she said in a distinctly condescending voice, throwing an equally unflattering look across the room at him.

I nodded. "So what are you?"

"I'm campus editor," she said with no pride in her voice.

"An editor. That's good."

"I suppose. I'm only a sophomore."

We talked some more about what she did on the paper and the politics among the newspaper staff. As we talked, a shaft of bright afternoon sun came through a window behind her and set off small reflective fires in her hair.

It wasn't long before the editor came back over for another conversation, and I knew it was time for me to leave. I interrupted them with a quick comment to Natalie about the camera then said good-bye and left.

While walking back to the apartment, I stepped off the sidewalk and walked a few paces to stand as inconspicuously as possible beside a tree. I took out the camera and sighted through the viewfinder at students on the sidewalk. I had the sensation of sighting in on targets through a telescopic rifle site. A riflescope would have been worthless in Vietnam, I thought. There were never any clear targets. The camera was a wonderful piece of equipment, but I knew there was more to my having the camera than taking pictures for the campus newspaper. I wondered if I would have the camera if Natalie knew about my R & R in Bangkok.

Carrying the camera gave me a sensation of creative power. The camera was a unique time machine that froze a moment and sent it into the future. People in a photograph never aged. Trees never lost their leaves. But now this magical device presented me with the problem of what to capture for posterity.

A stroke of inspiration hit me. The older part of campus was on a ridge, and the newer buildings were at the base of the ridge. From where I stood, I was even with the upper floors of the men's dorms across an athletic field. I decided to take all my pictures from as high a vantage point as possible above the subject. This would give a unity to all the pictures.

I immediately turned around and went back to main campus. The most prominent high vantage point on the campus was the clock tower of Arnold Hall, the symbol of the college.

Arnold Hall was a three-story square brick building built in the Federal style before the Civil War. I had had an English class on the top floor my freshmen year, so I knew the interior. Since it was late afternoon, the classrooms were deserted as I made my way up the wooden stairs and down the creaky hall floors. I had no idea how to get up in the clock tower, but I figured there had to be a way so the clock and chimes could be serviced. At the far end of the hall on the top floor, I found a door with no casing that looked like a large closet door. The wear on the hinges and doorknob showed the door was being used. I tried the knob.

The door opened into a short narrow hall, the walls of which were tongue and groove plank paneling. As I hurriedly closed the door behind me, I realized it would be totally dark. I found a light switch. Turning on the light showed a flight of open-stepped wooden stairs at the end of the passage. Since I had been lucky so far, I went ahead and climbed the stairs. As I went up three flights of stairs, I realized I was climbing the inside of the tower. A trapdoor covered the top of the last flight of stairs. The door had a latch, but it wasn't locked. Why lock the doors? No one was expected to be fool enough to go up into the tower.

The wind pulled at the trapdoor as I pushed it up and open and stepped out on to the floor of a colonnaded portico. A white wooden railing connected the columns, giving some sense of security. It was exactly the view I wanted.

I was cautious and stayed close to the columns to reduce the risk of being seen. For half an hour, I waited for people to appear down on the sidewalks and took their pictures. My final shots were to the west to catch the sun setting over adjacent buildings.

THURSDAY, OCTOBER 31

Thursday was the last day of October, Halloween. After our class together, I told Natalie about my plans for the photographs but not from where I would take them.

"That sounds great!" she said, which encouraged me.

That afternoon, I tried to get onto the roofs of two classroom buildings but no luck. I did the best I could by leaning as far as I dared out windows on the top floor. Then I returned to Arnold Hall at the same time I had been there the day before so I would get similar light. All the doors were open, and I went up in the tower again. I repeated the same shots, but this time, I had black-and-white film in the camera.

Thursday night, I had another spooky dream about Vietnam. In the dream, I was out on a mine sweep and saw a Vietnamese farmer using a lawn mower on his rice paddy dike. I had never seen a lawn mower in Vietnam, but I had seen the neighbor next to the apartment mowing his lawn that afternoon. My subconscious was mixing things up again. I resented the interruption to my sleep, and on Friday morning, I woke up late.

FRIDAY, NOVEMBER 1

My day did not improve. When I got to my political science class, I learned that President Johnson had announced a bombing halt over North Vietnam in a speech the night before. That was the topic for the entire class period. The professor didn't ask for my opinion this time, but I was tense the entire hour, expecting that he would. The professor didn't call on Holden either.

A holiday atmosphere always came over the campus on Friday afternoon. After my last class, a geology lecture, I went over to the student union to get a plate of french fries.

They had just come out of the hot oil and had been dumped directly on my plate from the wire basket. I couldn't resist eating one as I waited to pay the cashier. I didn't see anyone to sit with, so I sat alone at a small table in a corner and opened a textbook, being careful not to get grease on the pages. About halfway through my plate of fries, Olivia walked in with her boyfriend. Sororities frequented specific tables as a group, but couples always went to the guy's fraternity table, which they did now, going to the DTU table. Olivia hadn't seen me when she walked in, but now they were behind me, and it would be hard for her to miss me. That was no problem for her, but I felt conspicuous.

The DTU table was the most crowded fraternity table that afternoon. Their voices stood out from the general din of the cafeteria. Olivia's laugh was even more distinct, since there were only two girls at the table. Everyone was having a good time.

I had paid good money for the fries, and I was damned if I was going to leave them. I did hurry though. The less laughter I heard, the better. I could have pledged a fraternity my freshmen year. There were enough fraternities on campus that I could have made myself compatible with one of them, but I hadn't bothered because fraternity life seemed artificial. I wanted to pick and choose my friends, not be obligated to be friends with everyone in the group. And I didn't want to be categorized either. Someone would have to get to know me personally to know who I was. I didn't want people making assumptions about me based on the fraternity I belonged to. So I was a lone wolf, and the lone wolf had ended up in the U.S. Army sleeping in mud, flying through fog-filled mountain passes with drunken daredevil chopper pilots on Christmas Eve, and always listening for the hollow pop out in the bush that came from a mortar leaving the tube.

I'd had a fraternity in Vietnam. Six of us had joined the company within a month of one another and were put in the same platoon and squad. When we were back in base camp, we went to the enlisted men's club and drank as much as our ration would allow. When there were fist fights, we stuck together. We knew the details of one another's lives and took care of one another. We didn't pledge; we shed blood to be a band of brothers.

I finished my fries, cleaned up my fingers with a napkin, and stood to go, being careful not to turn around. As I left, the happy voices from the DTU table faded into the general background noise. I stopped at a water fountain near the door and sneaked a quick look back at the group. Olivia was leaning close to the other girl, saying something in her ear. Olivia was happy.

Back at the apartment, I found a note on the kitchen table. My name was at the top, in Robert's handwriting, and the note said that Natalie had called, and she wanted me to call her back at the newspaper if I called before four or at her dorm if I called after five.

Natalie was at the newspaper office. "Thanks for calling," she said. "I know this is a little odd, calling you like this, but I didn't want you to do any more work unless you wanted to."

"What work? Do you mean the pictures?"

"Yes. You see, Bill, the editor, and the other editors have decided not to do the collage page."

"I guess that does change things." I spoke without thinking, and I knew my voice sounded disappointed.

"I'm sorry," Natalie said. "You can still use the camera. I want to develop the pictures you've already taken and show the staff." Her voice sounded genuinely sympathetic.

"You don't have to." I had firmed up my voice. "I've only taken two rolls."

"I want to." Now her voice had turned sharp.

"Okay, sure," I said in a quick submissive response.

"There's one more thing," she said, but she softened her voice. "My roommate is giving a poetry reading at the Blue Slipper Café tomorrow night, and I wondered if you would join me."

"The Blue Slipper! I remember that place. It opened when I was a freshman. Yeah, sure, I'd be glad to go." Being asked out by a girl was new for me. "What time?"

"You don't need to come to the dorm to get me," she said. "I'm going early to help her set up and rehearse, so if you just want to come down to the café, that would be okay."

"Fine, fine," I said. "Will seven be okay? When will she be on?"

"Seven's fine. She'll give two readings and play the piano but not before seven."

"Okay," I said. "I'll see you then. It sounds like fun. I enjoyed it when I was there before."

Before we said good-bye, she told me again that I should keep on taking pictures. We agreed that I would bring the film with me to the Blue Slipper.

SATURDAY, NOVEMBER 2

Saturday and Sunday mornings were the only times I ever saw Adam and Brice for any length of time. On weekday mornings, they left without breakfast and didn't appear again till late in the evening. Many nights, they didn't sleep at the apartment. At the beginning of the semester, they had occasionally had their friends over to visit, but that had tapered off and soon ended. Nonetheless, we were all congenial whenever we did meet.

During the prior week, I had suggested to Robert that he and I put our good relations with Adam and Brice to a test. Both Robert and I felt we were gradually doing more than our share of cleaning up the apartment. Even though they ate their meals at the fraternity house, they also did plenty of eating at the apartment, but they seldom cleaned up after themselves. The kitchen was a particular problem. I suggested to Robert that we confront them about the issue, and he agreed.

I opened a conversation with Brice as he was waiting for a piece of toast to pop up. "Hey, Brice, today's Saturday. Cleanup day. How about if you and Adam hang around and give Robert and me a hand with the cleaning?" I had become accustomed to people, sergeants in particular, getting directly to the point with me, and now I did the same.

"Sure, sure," he said, but he didn't look at me.

"Okay," I replied. "I'll get the bucket and sponges, and we can start after you finish breakfast."

Brice's toast had popped, and he was buttering it. "Well," he said, "I've got to talk to Adam. I don't think we have time now. We're on the pledge bid committee, and we have to review possible pledges this morning."

I had anticipated a stall. "I'll get him and Robert, and we can work out who does what." I went off to get the others.

Adam was in the bathroom, and I shouted at the door, "Hey, Adam, come out to the kitchen, would you? We're getting ready to clean up the place."

"What?" he yelled back.

"Come to the kitchen when you're done!"

Then I went to the living room. Robert, the physics scholar, was watching cartoons. "Come on out to the kitchen," I said. "We're going to talk over who does what to clean up the place."

Negotiations began when we were all assembled in the kitchen. "We'll help," Adam said, "but we've got to leave in an hour. We're on the homecoming float committee, and we have a lot to do."

Robert spoke up. "I think it would be a good idea to plan on every Saturday morning being cleanup time," he said. "That way, there won't be schedule conflicts."

Brice and Adam agreed halfheartedly. Then we had to address the problem of what task each of us would do that morning. I listed what we had to do: pick up and vacuum the living room, wash dishes, clean up the counter and table in the kitchen, mop the kitchen floor, and clean the sink and toilet in the bathroom.

"We haven't got time for all this," Brice objected, "and besides, we don't cook here."

"You eat enough to make a lot of dirty dishes."

"Not hardly."

"Okay." I nodded at him. "Robert and I will get a set of dishes that only we use, and then it will be obvious who uses what." I wanted to challenge them.

"We'll do the living room," Adam cut in, "and then we've got to leave."

"That's not enough," Robert said.

After a series of increasingly blunt exchanges, they agreed to do the bathroom, the most objectionable but quickest duty, and Robert and I would do everything else. Adam and Brice exchanged the bare minimum of words with Robert and me while they did their part of the work, and then they left in a rush. They didn't come back to the apartment until Sunday evening.

Compared with the commotion of the morning cleanup, Saturday afternoon was quiet. Robert was worried that he'd fallen behind on his schoolwork because he'd spent so much time socializing at homecoming the week before, so he went off to the physics building to work with Dave and Charlie. I took the hint and spent some time in the library. Midterms were just a couple of weeks away. All afternoon, though, I kept thinking about going to the Blue Slipper. A girl asking me out was a novelty. Equality of the sexes was moving out of the news and into real life, and it was fine by me.

Later, in the fading light and growing cold of the first Saturday of November, I began the walk across campus to the Blue Slipper. Cutting through campus gave me another reminder of Olivia. The campus was empty, and I took note of a shady place off the sidewalk where Olivia and I had kissed and I had put my hands inside her coat. I scolded myself for thinking of one girl while on the way to see other girl. Then too, I told myself it might be a healthy reminder, especially considering how it turned out with Olivia.

The Blue Slipper was two blocks from campus in an old brick commercial building on a side street. It was the only business still open in the building, which added to its funky image. When I got there, I looked closely at the pair of blue ballet slippers hanging on the inside of the glass door. They were the same pair I remembered from two years before. The slippers were faded nearly white now, and I got the impression they hadn't been dusted since I had seen them last.

The café was one large open room. The entrance was on the left side, and the stage, with an upright piano, microphones, and lighting, stood against the right wall. At the back of the room was the coffee bar with its typical large restaurant coffee urns and other brewing devices I wasn't familiar with. Display windows from when the place was a store lined the front (street) side of the room. The floor was wood, and old light fixtures hung from the plaster ceiling. Small tables were scattered throughout the room, and each table had a candle on it. The pleasant aroma of coffee filled the café.

I saw Natalie right away. She was on the stage with a girl I assumed was her roommate. The girl was tall, much taller than Natalie, and thin. She wore a long tight straight dress that accentuated her breasts but revealed no other curves. The two of them were testing the microphone when I walked up.

"Hi, Mike!" Natalie said with a smile. "You're just in time. Laura is going on sooner than we thought." She looked over at Laura and flicked the microphone cord out of the way. "Laura," she said, "this is Mike. Mike, Laura."

"Hi," I said, making a faint hand motion at her up.

"Hi," she said, returning a quick smile. She was preoccupied with a handful of papers that I assumed was the poetry she was going to read.

There were about twenty people in the place, but the tables were far from full. I sat at an empty table and felt awkward about not having gotten something to drink. After a flashing of the houselights, Natalie introduced Laura to the crowd (her last name was Estes) then came to sit with me.

"I'm glad you made it," she whispered as she sat down. "Laura was afraid no one would be here."

"Well, it seems like there's a reasonable number of people here," I replied quietly. Natalie and I sat close to each other on one side of our table so we both could see the stage.

Her perfume drifted over to me, and I had the urge to kiss her behind the ear.

Laura read four poems, each by a different poet, two women and two men. She read well, speaking at an easy pace using clear pronunciation and good vocal inflection. Her gestures and facial expressions worked well with what she was reading, which made me wonder if she had taken drama classes. The two women poets she read were Edna St. Vincent Millay and Elizabeth Barrett Browning. The two men were Robert Frost and Ezra Pound. My favorite was the Frost poem, "The Road Not Taken." It was clear and to the point, as well as applicable to everyone, especially me.

Laura finished and got a nice round of applause from the crowd. When she sat with us at our table, Natalie and I complimented her performance. I asked her if she had had drama training.

"Yes," she said. "Two drama classes. I'm an English major, and the drama classes helped me understand the plays."

I was checking her out as she spoke. Her thin figure made me think of the Old Bangkok Whore. There was a heck of a lot more to Laura though. She was probably eight inches taller than the Old Bangkok Whore.

"Sure that makes sense," I said, pulling my attention back to the conversation. "Maybe even help you write one." My remarks sounded more flattering than I intended, and I quickly turned to Natalie and said, "Like you, only you write journalism."

"I doubt that I will ever write a play," Laura said.

A long-haired girl was playing the guitar now, and she started singing at the same time as I went to the counter to get coffee for the three of us. When I got back, another guy and girl had pulled chairs up to our table. Natalie and Laura were obviously happy to see them, and the conversation was running fast. Natalie introduced them as Connie and George, though their last names weren't mentioned. I didn't know if they were seniors or not. If they were seniors, they might have recognized me from freshman year.

Connie looked around the table. "Will anybody vote Tuesday? Anyone registered locally?" They started talking about the election as I sat down. When none of us responded, she continued in a light accusative tone. "So that means everyone has gotten their absentee ballots sent back?"

"Don't look at me," Laura said. "I just turned twenty."

"Oh right," Connie said. "Some of you are sophomores. Well, my first election is a big deal to me."

I instinctively leaned back in my chair to avoid being questioned. I hadn't bothered to get an absentee ballot.

"Humphrey has to win! We've come too far to let Nixon stop the progress." Connie spoke with the anxiety of an avid sports fan on the eve of her team's playing for a championship.

"Says you," Natalie replied. "Not everyone sees it that way." Her voice was not convincing, and it was obvious she wasn't a Nixon supporter. She and I had talked enough politics for me to know she supported Humphrey. I assumed the whole group was Democrat.

"How can anyone not see it that way?" Connie responded quickly. "It's obvious that Nixon and all his communist-phobic supporters just want a chance to show they can win the war. I wouldn't put it past them to use nuclear weapons."

Now I joined in. "Maybe that threat is his 'secret plan' to get out of the war," I said. "We have to negotiate from strength. Nukes would make us strong. We can't just cut and run."

"You make it sound like a schoolyard fight," someone said.

"The same rules apply. Just on a bigger scale."

The debate continued like that. Fortunately, my military experience didn't come up. Around nine, Laura read some more poetry, and when she finished, she sat at a different table. I realized there was a guy at the table. That was her motivation for the change.

The Blue Slipper had a comfortable atmosphere. I tried their thick coffee in a small cup, as well as the kind with lots of milk in it, beaten to creamy consistency. The others at the table knew the coffees' names and what country they came from. The coffeehouse was a cheap night out, so I wasn't feeling guilty about spending money, like I did when I bought booze. The place would have been even better if they'd had some real food.

The other girl, the folksinger, finished her act shortly after ten, and we all applauded, and then talk began about going somewhere else. Separate conversations broke out, and questions passed between tables. Small groups of the girls went to the restroom only to return and begin the questioning again. "Where do you want to go?" "I don't know. Where do *you* wanna go?" That kind of talk. Laura and her friend and a few others decided to go to a place called the Hofbrau House, which was further downtown. They urged Natalie and me to come with them. It didn't matter to me were we went, but Natalie made an unsuccessful counter suggestion then agreed.

It had rained while we were in the Blue Slipper, but fortunately, since no one had an umbrella, it had stopped by now. Natalie and I were behind the others as we started up the side street toward Main Street. The rain and cold reminded me it was November and Thanksgiving was coming.

"Are you going home for Thanksgiving?" I asked her.

"Oh sure," she said. "Aren't you?"

"No," I said. "I'm going to hang out at the apartment. It'll be quiet. Maybe I'll even study."

"But won't your parents miss you?" She sounded puzzled. "You weren't home last year either, were you?"

"My mother will make a fuss," I said. "My parents got divorced when I was in high school, and they don't live near each other, so seeing both of them on a short visit is a hassle."

Natalie didn't reply. We came to the intersection, and the group ahead of us turned left. Natalie called to them to stop a second then turned to me. "Would you mind if we went to back to the dorm and maybe watched TV?" she asked me. "It might rain again, and it would be a long walk back from the Hofbrau House."

"That's fine with me," I said. "You're right, it could rain again."

Natalie called to the group and told them to go on without us. Laura told Natalie she would see her later.

We had only gotten a few yards back in the direction of the dorm when Natalie turned to the conversation to Thanksgiving again. "Wouldn't it be better to see at least one of your parents?" she asked.

"Not really," I said. "It's too late to make plans now anyway."

"You've got three weeks."

"My brother will see them, and I'll see them at Christmas. Besides, it saves money." I rattled off the reasons for staying at school so quickly that Natalie understood that the subject was closed.

"How much older is your brother?" she asked. I had mentioned having an elder brother before.

"Five years. He's out of school and will probably be getting married soon."

The conversation went quiet again, so I asked her what her Thanksgiving would be like. She was happy to respond. "It'll be just great. I love Thanksgiving. I think I like it more than Christmas. There's less rush and worry. We switch holidays between both my grandparents and my uncle, so every year, we have to be sure who is having which holiday. It's lots of fun."

"Everyone must get along. No family feuds?"

"Oh no. Well, maybe some bickering about who brought what to the dinner. We get along real well for a big family. Some dinners, we have twenty people."

The fear suddenly ran through me that she might think I was fishing for an invitation to her place for the holiday. I changed the subject. "Laura should be happy with her reading tonight. It went well."

"It did," she agreed. "She'll probably do it again. I think she likes to perform."

We went on making small talk as we walked back across campus. I thought about holding her hand, but we both had our hands in our coat pockets to keep warm. By the time we got to the dorm, I had given up any ideas of putting moves on her that evening. The lounge was a fishbowl, and I didn't know how aggressive I wanted to be anyway.

We were lucky to find an empty couch in the TV room. We watched the last part of a Robert Wagner, Jill St. John movie then some of the local news and sports. A girl had brought popcorn in from the kitchen area and sat slumped over in an easy chair, munching it. As it got closer to midnight, the girls' curfew, more people started coming in.

I realized the evening was nearly over, and without thinking, I turned to Natalie and said, "Would you help me? I've got a problem." I immediately thought she would think I needed to go to the bathroom and didn't know where it was.

If that's what she thought, she didn't say so. Instead, she said, "Sure. What is it?"

"I want to say a proper good night to you and thank you for the invitation to the Blue Slipper," I said, "but I feel awkward in here. Would you mind if we took a short walk."

She grinned. "Okay."

I was committed. I helped her on with her coat, and we stepped out on the porch. Since I hadn't dated anyone from this dorm, I didn't know any dark places nearby. I was nervous. It had been years since I'd kissed a girl I cared about.

We walked along a deserted sidewalk that looped around the back of her dorm and led to another girls' dorm. When we came to a dark spot, I paused. "I think this will do," I said and went directly to the business of putting my hands on her waist. She tensed but didn't pull away. "This has been a special evening," I murmured. "Thank you." I pulled her close and kissed her.

She accepted the kiss willingly, putting her hands on my shoulders. Her perfume was delightful, like a bouquet of flowers. We broke off the kiss after a reasonable time, and thankfully, my mind continued to function.

"There's something else," I told her, still holding her close and enjoying the feel of her hands on my shoulders. "I've enjoyed using your camera. Thank you." I pulled her in again, with no resistance at all, and kissed her a second time. Then she squeezed my shoulders, and together, we move gently to deepen the passion of the kiss. A third kiss would have stretched the boundaries of the moment, though, so I gave her a brisk bear hug and planted a good smooch on her neck.

As we walked back to the porch to say good night, we passed half a dozen other couples saying good night in the shadows. Back at the door, I said, "So thanks again for the invitation. Be sure to tell Laura I enjoyed her reading. She did a good job."

"I will." She smiled at me. "I enjoyed it too. It was fun."

I didn't know what else to say. "Okay . . . Well . . . I'll see you in class if not before . . . Good night."

"Good night." She gave me a little wave as she went in the door.

I had walked halfway back to the apartment before I stopped thinking about the kiss. As I walked along in the dark, I became concerned about not having my weapon. I felt exposed, especially walking diagonally across a parking lot. There was no cover within twenty yards. My hands felt useless and empty. I needed to be able to heft the weapon back and forth from hand to hand, checking periodically with my right thumb to see where I had left the selector, on semiautomatic or on full automatic.

Later in bed, as I was falling asleep, I reflected on the day. Everything had gone well, and I hadn't screwed up the kiss. The problem now was what to do next. There must have been some reason I kissed her. I answered myself quickly to avoid thinking any deeper. I had kissed her because I wanted to get into her pants.

WEEK 7

NOVEMBER 3, 1968–NOVEMBER 9, 1968

TUESDAY, NOVEMBER 5

Election Day finally came, the climax of a nation's pent-up anxiety. It was also the first day I would see Natalie since kissing her. We stood on the sidewalk after class and talked. Natalie was excited about the election and said she was going to spend all her free time that day at the newspaper office. "Come over anytime," she told me. "We're going to have three TVs going, one for each network."

"Yeah, maybe," I said noncommittally, "but I have some studying to do." In reality, there was no way I was going to go hang out with those know-it-alls on the newspaper staff. And I did have some work to do. After spending the afternoon and evening hitting the books, I took a break from studying about nine thirty and made a pass-through the student union. The TV room was packed, so I watched from the back of the room just long enough to hear that no winner had been declared.

Robert was watching the returns when I got back to the apartment around eleven. "So," I asked, "who's gonna win?"

"Nixon," he responded in a flat voice.

"What makes you think so?"

"If Humphrey was going to do it, he would have to have won something down South. Obviously, that's all going for Wallace and Le May."

"You disappointed?" I asked him.

"Oh, I suppose. It seems like the end of all those great changes that Kennedy started."

"Well," I said, "maybe the returns from out West will turn it around."

Robert ignored the glimmer of hope I tried to spark. "What about you?" he said. "I haven't heard you talk about the election. What do you think?"

"I don't," I responded. "I only think about things I can do something about. Like getting something to eat." I promptly got up and went out to the kitchen and dug some leftover fried chicken out of the refrigerator. I wasn't exaggerating about not thinking about politics. Why should I care about politics? I cared two and a half years before, and look what happened to me. I couldn't do anything about what happened to me then, so now I didn't need to worry. A hell of a lot of others had to worry but not me. I went to sleep quickly that night and slept without apprehension.

WEDNESDAY, NOVEMBER 6

The next morning, I woke up apprehensive, not of the election results but Natalie's reaction. The election didn't concern me, but I suspected Natalie took it seriously. Her apprehension was thus my apprehension, and from what I heard on the radio while I was getting dressed, it didn't look good for old Humphrey.

I stopped at the Hideout to get coffee and found the TV room just as crowded as the night before. Only moments after I looked in, I heard scattered cheers. The crowd, or part of the crowd, was cheering ABC's prediction that Nixon would take Illinois and that those electoral votes would give him the victory. With that announcement, a wave of sad-faced people began walking out. I joined them.

Since my first class that morning was political science, I had to spend another hour listening to talk about the election. The talk was all speculation put forward by individuals who were temporarily irrational with emotion. There were seniors in the class who spoke proudly of voting, but the majority of the class would have to wait four years to vote for a president. Holden, the ROTC future lifer, gloated about the election results and predicted Nixon would be a great president. I didn't volunteer any opinions, and there was more-than-enough discussion from everyone else to hide my silence.

After my speech class, I walked over to the student activities building to see if Natalie was there. I found another TV, this one in the lobby in front of the bookstore. As I passed it to go up the stairs to the newspaper office, I got the impression something important was to be announced. I met Natalie walking in the other direction at the top of the stairs then followed her back down the stairs.

"It's too crowded up in the office," she told me. "Maybe it'll be better down here." We stood as close as possible to the TV in the lobby. She seemed tired and drawn, and her voice had little expression. Her hair was unkempt, and she had no makeup on. "There's speculation that Humphrey is going to concede," she said.

The TV switched commentators, and the picture shifted to a hotel ballroom in Minneapolis. Natalie and I could hear the audio, but we had to keep stretching up or bobbing around the people in front of us, who were also straining to see the screen. Finally, a tired-looking Hubert Humphrey came to the lectern with a few sheets of paper in one hand.

The crowd applauded weakly, and Humphrey managed a washed-out smile. Then he held up a hand to quiet the crowd.

"It's over!" Natalie turned to push her way through the hushed crowd. "It's over." I followed her out the door. She gave quick glance back and said, "Let's get away from this."

I touched her arm gently to turn her around to go the other way. "No one will be out on front campus." I'd expected her to be disappointed but not this badly. Obviously, I had not realized how seriously she supported Humphrey. Her objectivity required by the newspaper work had disguised her personal feelings until now.

We walked back around the side of the student activities building, across the old brick street, down the side of the administration building, and out to front campus. We sat on a cold bench in the weak November sunlight, and she gave a deep sigh, leaned forward with her elbows on her knees, and dropped her chin into her cupped hands. It was the kind of situation I hated, but I tried nevertheless to console her.

"Hey, it won't be as bad as it seems. The Democrats still have both the House and the Senate."

"Everything is going to hell," she said in an empty voice as she looked down at her feet.

After a short pause, I continued. "There are lots of Democratic governors too."

"No. I'm serious," she said with the same expressionless voice. "Doomsday is unavoidable now. I'm certain of it."

"Doomsday? Nixon isn't that crazy."

"Nuclear war is unavoidable. Think about it. Remember the bomb drills in elementary school? We had a neighbor that built a bomb shelter. That looks like a smart move now."

"That was years ago," I said, "and nothing has happened." My voice was less compassionate now. "You're just upset."

"Sure I'm upset. I got upset in junior high school during the Cuban mess. And look at what the Russians just did to Czechoslovakia this summer. You should be upset! Why do I have to convince you? Who made all those 'in bombs' that fell on you?"

She meant "incoming," but I wasn't going to correct her. "Well," I kept trying, "look at Korea. That was long ago, and nothing happened after that. Vietnam will blow over."

"*Blow up*, you mean. Now that Goldwater and all the hawks have their man in office, they're gonna nuke Vietnam." She paused. I didn't try to reason with her. "Assassinations. Race riots. School riots." She finally looked at me. "Doesn't it sound like doomsday to you?"

"It looks like a normal fall day to me," I said, leaning back and looking up through the bare tree branches at a blue sky above us. She ignored me and kept staring down at the sidewalk. I went on with the usual clichés of encouragement "You're tired. You'll feel better after you've gotten some rest. Forget politics for a while. Think about art. Maybe another trip to France."

At that, she covered her face with her hands, and in a moment, I realized her shoulders were shaking slightly. I reached out and patted her on the back then moved my hand around and around in small circles. A long minute passed in silence.

Finally, when she gave a few short sniffles and straightened up, I tried to say something clever. "I'm sorry, but I don't have a handkerchief. They're out of style, and guys use their sleeve anyway."

She magically produced a Kleenex from somewhere. "Do you have a class at one?" she asked.

"No. One thirty. There's no rush. How about you?"

"The same, one thirty." She coughed. "I don't know what to do. I must look terrible." She straightened up and gave me a quick glance. The emotion had brought bright color to her face. Her eyes were full of moisture. I wanted to hug her, pat her on the back, tell her the world would be safe. Instead, I gave her hand a squeeze and said, "Everything will be okay."

It wasn't a brilliant comment, but it brought a nice response from her. "Thanks." She took a deep breath, looked away for a moment, and then turned back to me. "It's a relief to have someone to confide in."

"Anytime," I responded as I touched her hand again.

We walked quickly over to her dorm and said good-bye, and she went in to get ready for class.

I had dinner at the apartment that evening, hot dogs and a can of pork and beans. Adam and Brice came and went while I was there. The two of them were getting on my nerves. Since our Saturday cleanup party, it was an obvious strain for them to be civil. After I finished eating, I trudged back to campus to study.

That night, while trying to get to sleep, I concluded that the day had been a bust. I wasn't worried about a world calamity the way Natalie was, but I wasn't optimistic about the new administration either. My parents were Democrats and still talked about FDR with reverence. I was sure they were disappointed. I tried to be rational about politics, even when it seemed everyone else was emotional. Compared with the good accomplished, party politics wasted too much energy.

The country was in for a big change from the last eight years. I remembered how excited my eighth grade social studies teacher had been about the Nixon-Kennedy election. Now I realized either the woman hadn't known squat about reality or hadn't been allowed to teach reality to eighth graders.

THURSDAY, NOVEMBER 7

I got up late Thursday morning. A dream had woken me in the middle of the night and stolen some of my sleep time. In the dream, I was firing on an easy target out in the open but not getting any hits, no matter how carefully I aimed. The target kept disappearing into the tree line.

The weather Thursday morning was miserable too, cold and windy with low clouds and an intermittent drizzle. Still, I was eager to get to my American lit class. I wanted to see how Natalie was and ask her out for Saturday. I stoked myself up with a quick cup of coffee at the student union and rushed into the classroom one step ahead of the professor. Natalie gave me a smile as I sat down. Encouraged by the smile, I stretched my leg forward and gave her seat a nudge. She responded with an indignant shifting in her seat.

The class was reasonably interesting, and the coffee helped keep me awake. Also, I was paying close attention for any remarks about the mid-term test that was coming up the next week.

Natalie and I met on the sidewalk after class. "Feeling better today?" I asked her.

"So far." She gave me a big smile. "I went off the deep end yesterday, didn't I? It must have been a release of tension."

"You and everyone else were on edge. I'm glad it's over. How about a cup of coffee?"

"I'm sorry," she said, "but I'd rather not. I went to bed right after dinner last night, and now I'm behind. I need to do some reading before my French class. How about next time?"

"Okay, fine." I kept talking. "I'm sure getting the rest was the best thing for you." I was in a predicament now. She needed to rush off to study, but I wanted to ask her for a date. I decided to plunge ahead.

"Before you go and hit the books," I started, "well, I promised you I'd try to make plans in advance, so would you like to take in a movie Saturday night?" As soon as I blurted out the question, I wished I'd waited for a better time to ask.

Natalie frowned and took a deep breath. "I'd really like to," she said. "I really would, but next week is midterms, and I'll need all the time I can get to study. I'd rather not do anything this weekend." She gave me a bright smile. "But how about after exams?"

I nodded. "Sure. I guess I could use some extra study time too."

"Okay." She moved off toward the library. "We can talk about it later. Bye!"

I wondered when later would be. It wouldn't be tomorrow unless I looked her up or phoned her. My weekend suddenly had a big hole in it. The best way to fill the gap was to study. Just like Natalie.

Speech and political science were my problem subjects. I had to give a speech on Friday of the next week, and I hadn't picked a topic yet. Political science was a zinger, a three-page essay on the election. I was going to have to be thinking about that mess. The other subjects would be just standard tests: fill in the blank, short of paragraphs, whatever was necessary to prove you were in the class and awake during the first half of the semester.

FRIDAY, NOVEMBER 8

I had speech class on Friday, so after class, I decided to ask the professor for advice on a topic. We spoke as we left the classroom. "Well," he said, "since it has to be an informative speech, you're open on the topic." The guy was middle aged and taught some English classes too. He smelled of pipe tobacco. "I'd suggest some topic you're very familiar with," he added in a genial voice. "Maybe a hobby or some recent life experience. Don't worry so much about the topic. It's the outline and presentation skills I'm interested in."

We had walked outside and were talking on the sidewalk. I thanked him and walked across the street. As I stepped up on the curb on the other side of the street, I glanced back at the professor. He had lit his pipe and blown a puff of smoke. I wondered if I should be a teacher of some sort. How hard could it be?

SATURDAY, NOVEMBER 9

Saturday was a problem. Sure Natalie could show resolve and study while the campus partied, but I wasn't going to spend all afternoon and evening hitting the books. I had to spend the afternoon working, though, so I went to my usual place in the basement of the library and camped out at a study desk. I put the time in on the political science paper about the election. The political science paper presented nearly the same problem as the speech—what topic? What aspect of the election should I write about? After looking through a couple of newspapers, I decided to do a piece on opinion polls, with some mention of how computing machines were used. It was a productive afternoon. I wasn't alone. The library was more crowded than other Saturdays. I walked around in the library a couple of times during the afternoon, but Natalie wasn't in the crowd.

By four thirty, I was burned out, so I headed back to the apartment. As I was walking along, a car blew its horn and pulled up to the curb ahead of me. It was Pete in his GTO. I hustled up to the car, and Pete leaned over and opened the passenger side door and yelled, "Jump in! I'm on my way to pick up Patty."

I pitched my books into the backseat and got in. Pete punched it, and the rear of the car squatted down as the front rose up and the engine gulped some air with a deep *woof*.

"Where did you say you're going?" I yelled at Pete. He was slapping the gear lever forward into third as we passed through seventy-five miles per hour.

"To pick up Patty from work!" he yelled back. A traffic light brought us to a stop. "I'm a little late," he added in a lower voice.

Patty worked at a supermarket about four miles from campus. When we got there, Pete was surprised not to see her waiting outside, so he parked, and we both went in.

I followed Pete at a distance as he walked around the store and finally found Patty working at a register. They talked, and then Pete came back to me. "It seems like someone hasn't shown up for their shift," he said. "She'll be on for another hour." We talked it over and decided it wasn't worth going back to hang out at the apartment. We were both hungry, so we bought a six-pack of beer and a couple of big bags of potato chips and went back out to the car. It was getting dark.

In the car, I held the potato chip bag under my chin so that crumbs would fall back into the bag. I held my beer can between my legs. After munching away awhile, I made some small talk. "Too bad, she has to work late. Is she working full time?"

"Yeah. Pretty much. She puts in thirty to fifty hours a week."

"School sucks," I said, "but it beats working."

"I'm thinking it's the other way around," he replied. "School sucks worse. At least you get paid for working."

"Good point," I said, taking a drink. "School's no picnic. How's it going anyway?"

"I'm sick of it. I cut most of my classes."

"Yeah. I haven't seen you at all on campus."

"School's ridiculous." He drained his can. "Senile old farts teaching from the same ancient notes they've used for years, giving the same tests year after year. The world's changing, and this school is stuck back before World War II."

"It sure seems that way," I agreed. "I'll help you with what I can if you want. Proofreading, whatever I can."

"Thanks but no." He shook his head. "It's beyond that."

"You talk to anybody? Your adviser?"

"Oh sure, I had to go see the dean of men because of all the cuts."

"Oh yeah! I had to see him too!" I blurted out, not thinking I'd have to explain it to Pete.

"You? Why? You cutting class too?"

Now I had to say something, but telling Pete was no embarrassment. "Nah. I got into a shoving match with some assholes downtown."

"Cool! Over a girl?"

"No. An ROTC lifer. We'd just gotten into it over Vietnam stuff." I wanted to change the topic back to Pete. "What did the dean tell you about cutting?"

"Nothing, really. It was more of me telling him."

"Telling him what?"

"That the school wasn't teaching me shit and I learned more in the army." He paused, but when I didn't respond, he continued. "I'm thinking of leaving school. There's no sense in hanging around here. This is a jerkwater town, and the weather stinks. I'm thinking about going to San Francisco. There's a happening out there."

"Shit," I said, "you'd lose your GI Bill checks. You might have to work. That sucks too."

"There has to be something better than this."

Patty went through my mind, but I didn't say anything. She would probably go with him. It didn't seem like she was strongly attached to her family.

We each had drunk two beers and were about through with the chips when I took an inconspicuous look at my watch. We had at least twenty more minutes to wait. Muttering something about checking to see if she wouldn't be any later than she had expected, Pete got out and went back in the store. A couple of minutes later, he was back.

"She won't be much longer," he said as he squirmed back into the driver's seat. "Damn, it's cold in this car. I bet it snows tonight." He started the engine and turned on the heater.

"I guess we're both still used to the warm weather in Nam," I said.

"I never thought I'd miss that."

"I got to the USO on the beach at Chu Lai twice," I told him. "It was like a tropical paradise. Great, soft, sand beach, clear blue water, gentle surf. I could've bobbed around in that water for my whole tour."

"No women though," he said. "No round eyes."

"Right. Nothing but GIs, either bare-assed or in green underwear swimsuits." For a moment, my mind ran through the memories of that beach. Only the lucky bastards permanently assigned to Chu Lai had real bathing suits. The rest of us swam in our green camouflage underwear or just skinny-dipped.

Pete turned to me and frowned. "Combat engineer. That's almost as bad as an '11 Bushwhack' like me. How come you couldn't get some soft job in headquarters somewhere? Even with the combat engineer MOS, a smart guy could always pull something off, like company clerk or helping out in the communications shack. Anything inside the wire. Could you type?"

"Yeah," I said. "I knew the sharp guys could get something soft. And I could type. I just didn't want to kiss anyone's ass and be in debt to them."

"So you stuck your neck out. I bet you got a thrill out of it."

"Yeah. Great thrill. Like holding your helmet on with one hand while running for a hole in the ground when the incoming hits." I turned to face him. "What about you? What the hell? You could have played the angles and gotten something."

"I fucked up, I guess. I didn't give a damn. To be honest, I felt that since I'd been pushed that far, I might as well see the worst of combat." Pete looked out the side window.

"I suppose," I said. "Actually, I didn't envy those rear echelon motherfuckers. They had to keep up spit and polish somewhat anyway. The way I did my tour, nobody has anything on me. I did the worst of it. You grunts out in the bush looking for the little fuckers had it worse."

He nodded and popped open another beer. "Yeah. It got to be a game after a while. It was worth it when we finally did corner the gooks. Man, we could bring down some pee on those motherfuckers. We would just hose down the tree line, literally cut the brush. And, man, you've never lived till you've been close enough to a napalm strike that you feel the heat. That was a religious experience. It was like we called the fist of an angry God down out of those beautiful white clouds, and he laid down a river of burning hell. It made some GIs kiss the cross they wore around their neck, and everyone prayed those pilots wouldn't fuck up and dump that shit on us.

"We're both full of shit."

"But it was one hell of an experience!" Pete exclaimed with a laugh.

We were quiet for a moment. We were on our last beers, and the car had warmed up. I watched cars come in and park and families get out. "Ever think about going back? Re-upping?"

"You crazy, man?"

"Well, like you say, this place isn't the greatest. You know, some of the crap they said at separation is coming true. Did you get the re-up speech when you separated?"

"Yeah," he said, "I got it, and yeah, some things about civilian life suck, but nothing don't suck as bad as the olive drab."

I saw Patty coming out of the store. She was carrying a grocery bag. I got out and jumped into the back, and she got in and gave Pete a kiss. "I've got some more beer and pop," she said.

"Great!" Pete gave her a peck on the cheek in return. Then Pete's goat ripped out of the parking lot like a bat out of hell.

WEEK 8

NOVEMBER 10, 1968–NOVEMBER 16, 1968

MONDAY, NOVEMBER 11

My political science class was in an old brick building that had iron exterior fire escapes. My classroom had a door that opened out on to one of the fire escapes, so many students left the classroom that way. I was going down the fire escape when I caught sight of Natalie in the crowd on the sidewalk below. Seeing her surprised me, since I didn't think her schedule brought her to this part of campus at this time on Monday. By the time I had wound my way down the fire escape, though, she was well up the sidewalk and out of sight. I didn't have a class the next hour, so I tried to follow her, straining to see her among the people ahead of me. I caught a glimpse of her once, but I didn't want to run up beside her, so I just kept walking fast.

The sidewalk Natalie and I were on crossed another major campus sidewalk. Glancing to my left, I saw Olivia coming along on that sidewalk. She would probably cross in front of me in the merging of people. To avoid meeting her, I slowed my pace and stepped aside to let other people pass, but to my chagrin, she turned on to my sidewalk and began walking the same direction. Now she was between me and Natalie.

I kept following the two girls, figuring Olivia would eventually go off in a different direction. But we kept walking up the main street of the campus and eventually came to the last building before the intersection of the main street leading down into town. The number of people walking on the sidewalk thinned, and I soon realized that only girls remained. I could see both Natalie and Olivia ahead of me, walking in separate groups of friends. I decided something odd was going on and went up the steps to the biology building and paused to watch the procession.

The stream of girls continued up to the street that ran perpendicular to them, and they spread out down that sidewalk and soon were just standing at the side of the street. Seeing them standing that way reminded me that it was nearly the eleventh hour of November 11. The city's Veterans Day Parade was coming up from the town. It would pass along the edge of campus.

Rather than sit there and watch like a Peeping Tom, I decided to join Natalie, even though Olivia was certain to see me. The color guard and the high school band leading the parade were half a block down the street when I walked up to Natalie, who had a steno pad in her hand. "Hi," I said. "Nice day for a parade."

She greeted me then turned to a friend and said, "Look. We have a veteran right here."

The band was playing "Stars and Stripes Forever," and the music drowned out any further conversation. Natalie turned her attention to the parade and began taking notes. After the band, a big Pontiac Grand Prix convertible drove past with a load of old farts in their seventies dressed in wool Dough Boy uniforms. A sign on the side of the car identified them has veterans of World War I. A platoon of World War II vets from an American Legion post marched behind the convertible. The lead color guard carried M-1 rifles. The weapon reminded me of the M-14 I'd used in training.

After the American Legion came the Veterans of Foreign Wars. "What's the difference between the VFW and the American Legion?" Natalie asked me.

"I'm sorry, but I don't know." I told her. "It may have something to do with what they consider overseas service."

After the VFW came the main attraction for the line of girls on the sidewalk. The campus ROTC contingent came marching along with solemn frowns frozen on their faces. Their girlfriends cheered and called their names from the sidewalk. Olivia's boyfriend was in the first rank, and I clearly heard Olivia call his name. My nemesis, Alan Holden, was further back. The boys looked good in their crisp uniforms and gleaming polished shoes. They had the egos required of officers. The parade ended with the college band playing "Yankee Doodle."

"I wonder where the parade ends," Natalie commented. Someone in the group said there was a memorial park with old Civil War cannons at a cemetery not too far away. Natalie finished taking notes then turned to me and said, "That was great. I loved the music. Didn't it make you feel like marching?"

"Hell no!" Then I smiled, trying to compensate for my abrupt answer. "I mean, no, I've done enough marching." As Natalie and I began walking back to campus, I asked her about her notes. "Are the notes for a story?"

"Yes. It's a campus event, so the campus editor covers it." She smiled and moved closer to me as we walked.

"How did the weekend go?" I asked her. "Get enough work done?"

"I'm much better off, but there's never enough time. I'm glad you understood. How about you? Any tests today?"

"No. My first test is tomorrow. I got some studying done too, so I guess it was better for both of us." We both had eleven-o-clock classes, so we didn't have long to talk.

"Are we still on for this Saturday night?" she asked me.

"Sure, absolutely," I answered, sounding as happy as I felt.

"What did you have in mind?"

"Oh," I said, "how about the usual . . . a movie and then some live entertainment back at the apartment?"

"Sounds great!"

With that, we rushed off in different directions.

I wasn't aware of it until that night, but the parade that morning had left an imprint on my mind. I had an intense detailed dream of a Vietnam combat scene. In the dream, my squad was pinned down behind a rice paddy dike, and we were firing over the dike at a tree line. Oddly, I carried an M-14 rifle while everyone else had the usual M-16. I was afraid of running out of ammunition because my M-14 didn't use the same ammunition as the M-16s. In the dream, I didn't panic but had the presence of mind to try to find the M-60 machine gunner because my M-14 used the same caliber ammunition as the machine gun. But the squad didn't have an M-60. My anxiety grew until I woke up.

It seemed as though I unconsciously remembered events during the day. Then when I was asleep, my mind put together crazy stories from the experiences I remembered from the day. Seeing the M-1 rifles in the parade that morning that were similar to the M-14 I had used in training had no doubt caused this dream.

TUESDAY, NOVEMBER 12

The dream left me in a bad mood. My mood was in complete contrast to the ideal weather that greeted me on my walk to class. The sky was a pale blue with only high thin wisps of clouds, and the air was abnormally warm for the time of year, which made me wonder if the good weather would hold. I checked the sunrise on the eastern horizon and saw no red tinge, so I assumed the day would be a sailor's delight. There were still trees with a few stubborn leaves that hadn't fallen but which would certainly be taken down by the next storm.

"Mike!" I heard a voice behind me as I approached the classroom building. It was Natalie. "Wait just a second before we go in," she said. She was slightly out of breath and fumbled with some papers. "I have to study after class, but I want you to have a chance to read this." She gave me two typed pages that were stapled together. "It's a draft of my story on yesterday's parade. I quoted you, so I want you to read it."

I took the papers. "Okay," I said, "but I don't know how you could have quoted me." We passed a few other comments back and forth then walked into class. I put her papers on one side of my open notebook and glanced at them between listening to the professor and scribbling notes.

She had written a good descriptive piece that would hold a reader's attention, considering it was such a bland subject. Not many students would care about a parade held every November 11 to commemorate a war three quarters of a century before. The quote from me was just the remark I'd made about not wanting to march to the music. I wondered why she had thought I needed to read the entire story. After class, I got some idea of why.

"What did you think?" she asked as I gave the article back to her. We were out on the sidewalk.

"It's fine," I said. "I would think the editor would be satisfied with it."

She was nervous and fumbled at putting the pages away while balancing her other books. "Here, let me hold those," I said and took a couple of her books.

"I wish I didn't have that midterm at eleven," she said. "I put too much time in writing the article last night instead of studying." She paused and then turned to look at me as we walked. "You see, I want to expand the story from just coverage of the parade to include some of your views on the war. If you're willing to be interviewed."

"Interviewed?"

"Yes. It'll give the story an added dimension."

Since we were standing on a busy sidewalk and she was in a rush, all I said was, "Well, let's talk it over."

"How about if we meet at the Hideout later this afternoon?" she said. "I have to turn in the story tomorrow. Can you make four thirty?"

"Yeah. I'll be there." We exchanged good luck wishes on the tests we had coming up, and she went off to study French, and I went to drink a cup of coffee and shake the last of a bad dream out of my head.

I should have been flattered that someone, even from just a small campus newspaper, cared enough about my experiences to interview me. But I was skeptical. It might be nice to help Natalie out, but I had nothing to say. Or rather, I didn't want to dig through the muck of my emotions to find something to say.

Natalie was sitting at a small window table when I got to the Hideout. My art history test had gone reasonably well, so my mood was good, and I gave her an upbeat "Hi" as I stepped up to the table. "Would you like something to drink? Coke? Coffee?"

"Yes, thanks," she said. "Coke." From the tone of her voice, I judged she had done well on her French test. I returned with two large Cokes, and as I set them down, I asked about her French test. She would only admit to its not having been as bad as she had feared. I noticed a steno notepad on top of her books. "So what's up with your newspaper story?" I asked.

She was pleased I had brought up the subject and shifted the books and the article I had read earlier aside and picked up a pencil. "Well, like I said, I want to add some punch to the story. More serious content. I thought you might be a good source."

The eagerness with which she had prepared put me off. Vietnam was *good* for someone? "Not war stories," I said coldly. "I don't have any war stories." I did have stories, but I sure wasn't going to drag them up.

She shook her head. "No, I don't want that kind of story. I was thinking more of political views, general impressions. I want your reactions to three or four general questions."

"I'm not a scholar either," I demurred. "My experiences were pretty earthy—as in walking on it, sleeping on it, and getting it all over myself. I don't know anything about politics or diplomacy."

My sullen reaction had gotten to her. "Well . . . it was only an idea." She pushed back from the table. "The story's probably good enough, just talking about the sorority girls cheering their ROTC boyfriends."

Her remarks whipped me around. This was the same girl who'd been crying over an election a week ago and was now bullying me into talking.

"All right," I said. "We can talk, but I don't want my name used. Okay? Will the story be any good if you don't mention my name?"

"Oh sure. I can just say you're a source that didn't want to be identified. I have one other favor to ask though. I'll have to turn this in tomorrow, so is it all right with you if you don't read it before it's published?"

I nodded. "Yeah. I trust you. Fire away." I looked over at her pad and saw three items listed.

"Okay." She paused to check her notes. "From what you saw in Vietnam, do you think we can win the war?"

"Militarily? Sure. At the kill ratio we have going, North Vietnam will be a ghost town in ten years. And the same with the Viet Cong," I said with smug assurance.

"Militarily, you say. What else were you thinking?"

"Politically, we can't win unless we work with Vietnamese other than those in Saigon."

"Other than the Vietnamese government you mean?"

I nodded. "Right. If you want to call them a government."

"But there isn't any other political group to work with," she said as if reminding me of an error I'd made.

"So I guess we will lose," I said then quickly asked, "So is this the kind of material you want?"

She was writing and didn't look up. "It's just right."

For a moment, I gazed out the window and watched people on the sidewalk. It was twilight, and the streetlights had just come on.

Natalie looked up. "Why is the Vietnamese government at fault?"

I launched enthusiastically into my answer. "Because the average papa-san wading through a rice paddy hates those city slickers. Why else would he sneak out at night and join the VC?

"So you think it's a war between the rich and poor? Classic Marxism?"

"Absolutely. You say it better than I do. As far as the political science, I don't know."

"Can you give me some details that support that conclusion?"

"The best evidence is that the VC come from the rural population while the wealthy sit in the city, cheating, stealing, and getting rich off the war." I paused. "One thing I was always suspicious of was the Vietnamese National Police. They wore nice crisp uniforms and always carried .38 revolvers. They would strut around the villages like they owned the place. They looked like a gestapo to me. It was obvious those police weren't part of the community. People were afraid of them.

"The police were out in the rural areas as well as in the cities?"

Her using the word "rural" amused me. "Well, I was never in big cities. Those goons were in even the small towns. As far as the boondocks, I mean out in the mountains where the people lived like the Stone Age, out there, there were none of these guys. Out there, a lot of the people, maybe most of them, weren't even Vietnamese. Those people had no feelings for Saigon. They only thought as far as their village. All they wanted was to be left alone. Left alone by *everybody*. The more Saigon messed with them, the more they supported the Viet Cong. And we were an invading army brought in by Saigon."

There was another little quiet time as she wrote in her steno pad. I noticed several people in line, placing orders at the grill. I was hungry.

"What about the South Vietnamese Army?" she said. "Can they take over?"

"ARVN." I pronounced the acronym as a word. "It stands for Army of the Republic of Vietnam. They're worthless, absolutely worthless. No, they can't take over. They hardly know which end of the rifle the bullet comes out of, and they don't give a damn about finding out."

"We're told they're doing a lot of the fighting," she said. "They must care."

"Well," I said, "they're draftees too. Pulled out of the villages and ethnic groups they care about. They're stuck in a situation with no alternative. Either they do what they're told or they go to jail. Or more likely, get shot. What irritates the hell out of me is that it's their country. They should care, but they don't. I could give specific examples, but you said you didn't want war stories." I paused while she wrote down what I was saying. Then my hunger got the best of me. "Say, I'm getting hungry. How about if I order a couple of burgers at the grill for us? My treat."

She looked up and said, "Thanks, but no, thanks. Actually, I have enough here to do what I want. I think I'll go to the dining hall and then over to the newspaper office to polish this up." Then closing the steno pad, she added in a tired voice, "And then I have more studying to do."

We both stood up, and she gathered her notebook and papers. She stepped so close to me I could smell her perfume. "It was swell of you to do this for me," she said. "I can see it's no fun for you. So thank you very much. And"— her voice picked up—"I'm really looking forward to Saturday night. Whatever we do will be fun."

"Great. I'm looking forward to it too." I had melted completely.

I spent Tuesday evening in a classroom left open for people to study in. I worked on American lit and geology. I had the geology midterm the next day. I had decided to use the same topic for my speech as I had chosen for my political science paper, election polls and surveys. Using the same topic made double use of the research I had already done. The political science paper was due Friday too. Robert had helped me with a paragraph on statistics and probability. The grades I had gotten on tests, quizzes, and papers so far that semester were reasonable but not great. The exams could swing my midterm grades either way as I clearly remembered from my freshman year. It was crunch time.

THURSDAY, NOVEMBER 14

Our American literature test was Thursday, and Natalie was already seated when I walked into the room. We exchanged smiles as I walked past her desk. The room was in a commotion, with everyone getting settled, putting books away, asking each other questions, and taking last looks at notes. I leaned forward and spoke to Natalie. "Get your story done?"

She turned around. "Yes, and thanks again. It'll be in tomorrow's paper." Then she commented on the test. "Are you ready for this one?"

"I'm never ready."

The blue books were passed out with the test, which was on a mimeographed sheet and listed five topics. We were to write on two of the five. Having five to choose from should have given me good odds at finding two I knew something about. I immediately realized I was strong on one topic. But after rereading the others, I felt a cold chill of panic. I was left to choose the least worst from the remaining four.

Ideas came quickly as I wrote on the first topic, and I put two thirds of the hour in on that essay, hoping it would be strong enough to prop up what I would lose on the other essay.

In front of me, Natalie leaned over her work, writing furiously without needing to pause to compose her thoughts.

I could see a corner of one of her pages. Her penmanship was clear and graceful. My handwriting was cramped, and my blue book was full of strikeouts and inserted words.

The harder a test is for me, the faster the time goes. Time went real fast on this test. The class stars turned in their papers at about the normal end of class. Natalie finished about five minutes before the hour and left, but I struggled until the professor called in all papers.

Natalie was waiting on the steps when I came out of the building. I hadn't expected her to wait and actually wished she hadn't. She spoke to me as I came down to her. "That wasn't easy!"

"I'll say."

"Which ones did you do?" she asked. It turned out she had also written on one of the topics I had chosen. We discussed the subject for a moment, still standing on the steps. We hadn't been to coffee in a while, but I didn't feel like it now. Then I remembered I wouldn't necessarily see her the next day.

"About Saturday night," I said. "Will the early show be okay?"

"Sure. What's showing?"

"*The Parent Trap*. It's a Disney movie."

We agreed it would be a good flick. "So I'll stop by at six thirty?" I asked to confirm the time.

"Fine," she said. We briefly talked about our remaining tests, and then she took the sidewalk in the direction of the newspaper office, and I went to the library.

The library was a busy place during test week, even in the morning. None of the study tables were open, so I just slumped into a soft chair in the periodicals section and did some reading. Three quarters of an hour later, I left for my art history class.

A steady rain began on Thursday afternoon, and the campus blossomed with umbrellas that bobbed along the sidewalks, hiding people's faces from view. That evening, I was in the basement of the library, finishing a reading assignment for political science and looking over the outline of the speech I had to give the next day. Around nine o'clock, I took a break to get some coffee at the Hideout. Leaving the library, I paused under the portico at the top of the steps to look out at the rain and wondered how wet I would get. I didn't have an umbrella. Was a cup of coffee worth getting wet for? Just then, Pete came walking past on the sidewalk looking like a drowned rat. He didn't have an umbrella either but was wearing his army field jacket with the hood pulled over his head.

"Pete!" I yelled, "Get out of the rain! You'll drown!"

He turned then bounded up the steps.

"How come you're out in the rain when you could be driving that great car? No gas money?" I was kidding him.

"I'm out walking because it's raining," he said. "It's good to walk in the rain. What about you? You're nice and dry. You must have been in the library studying." He was wiping rain off his face.

"Yeah," I said. "I've got a paper due and a speech to give tomorrow."

"I actually took my tests," he said as if to surprise me. "I don't know why, but I did."

"What the hell?" I responded. "You may as well take a swing at it."

"Absolutely."

"Well, I'm going for coffee. Wanna come along?"

"Nah. You go ahead. I've got to get back to the apartment before Patty thinks I've drowned."

"Take it easy and good luck on the tests," I said as I started down the steps and into the rain.

"Hey!" he yelled after me. "You coming over Saturday?"

The rain was heavy, but I didn't want to show that it bothered me, so I turned and walked back up the steps at a normal pace. "I've got a date," I answered. "We're planning on a movie."

"Well, bring her over after the show," he said. "We're having a party. Patty wants you to come over. You'll be there, okay?"

The cafeteria would be closing pretty soon, so I didn't want to drag out the conversation. Besides, it would be nice to hang out again at Pete's. "Okay," I said. "The show's over around nine. We'll come over for a while."

"Great!"

"See you then." I went back down the steps and into the rain.

FRIDAY, NOVEMBER 15

The rain had stopped by Friday morning, but the low heavy gray clouds still hung overhead. It felt like snow, and I watched for flurries as I walked to class.

It was the last day of midterms, but instead of being happy and relieved, I felt anxious. There was still the wait to see what my grades would be. The political science paper would be marked down, I knew. I had tried to type it, but it still looked terrible, so I just wrote the paper out as neatly as I could, which wasn't very neat. The speech went reasonably well, though I skipped around some and found myself putting in extemporaneous material. There was a surprise in my geology class. The test had been Wednesday, and the professor had done the unexpected and already gotten them graded. I got a number grade equivalent to a C. At first, I felt neutral about the grade, but that feeling deteriorated into worry. A C left me hanging on the edge. There would be no room for slacking off during the second half of the semester.

After the geology class, I walked over to the Hideout to have a late lunch. As I passed the library, I noticed students setting up a microphone on the top step in front of the main entrance. They were wiring in a portable amplifier too. Since some of them were the SDS promoters from the rally I had seen weeks before, I assumed it was another push for SDS members. There was a city cop car at the curb across the street.

The Hideout was always crowded on Friday afternoon, but it was exceptionally so that day, probably because tests were over. The Beatles were taking a long and winding road on the jukebox as I picked up a copy of the *Middlesex Monitor* off a rack, looked through it, and ordered my burger. Natalie's article was on the inside, second page. "Students Commemorate Veterans Day." I didn't read the story until I sat down.

I recognized many of the lines in the story from the original draft she'd showed me in class last Tuesday. She described the bands, the honor guards, and the uniforms very well and gave compliments to the ROTC platoon. Then Natalie admonished the general student body for not turning out for the parade, saying only a small crowd had been present as the parade passed the school. She said only friends of students in the band or ROTC had bothered to show support for the old veterans.

Then she wrote there was one exception, a student who was a returned Vietnam veteran.

From that lead-in, she wrote that she had interviewed a person who had requested anonymity. She summarized our entire conversation in two paragraphs. One paragraph covered my skepticism regarding the survival of South Vietnam and opinion that we would lose the war. She also clearly and succinctly described my feelings about the class divisions in the country. The other paragraph passed on my disdain for the Army of the Republic of Vietnam. I was impressed with how she summarized but still accurately expressed my views.

Natalie had written a good piece of journalism, but seeing my opinions in print left me feeling guilty. I looked at the two paragraphs and wondered if I had abandoned my platoon. Were comments like mine comfort to the North Vietnamese and the Viet Cong as Holden had said? I knew my comments alone wouldn't be significant, but maybe they were raindrops contributing to a flood. Maybe I should have kept my mouth shut. The guilty feeling didn't make me reconsider my opinion, though, but it did make me wonder why I'd given Natalie the interview.

I continued thinking about the interview as I walked back to the apartment and finally concluded it was foolish to feel guilty. What I'd done in the army and what I said now about the war were completely inconsequential.

I was completely inconsequential.

SATURDAY, NOVEMBER 16

The weekly apartment cleanup had gone well the previous Saturday. Adam and Brice had run the vacuum, and Robert and I had done the bathroom, the most despised task, and other chores. We hadn't formally agreed to swapping chores each week, but Robert and I assumed we would do the kitchen and vacuuming this week. So when I saw Adam starting on the kitchen about ten thirty, I spoke up.

"Damn! I guess its cleanup day already. I'll get the mop and bucket." Adam didn't say anything as I went to the closet and came back with the mob and bucket. "Are you guys planning on doing both the kitchen and the bathroom?" I asked as I started filling the bucket with hot water.

"No." He kept working on the counter and didn't look at me. "We're doing what we did last week, and then we're getting out of here."

"I thought it was understood we would swap off each week," I said. "We did last week." Robert wasn't there, and I knew I didn't have any backup.

"I never heard we agreed to anything like that," Adam said. "The best way is who ever starts a job first does that job."

"Well," I said, putting bucket on the floor, "maybe we'd better talk it over again when everyone's here." I didn't want a repeat of the confrontation of two weeks before. I started mopping the kitchen floor. A couple of minutes later, I heard the vacuum running in the living room.

Before Brice and Adam finished, three of their fraternity brothers came in. It seemed that the five of them were taking a road trip up to Columbus to visit the DAD chapter at Ohio State, supposedly on fraternity business. I stayed out of their way, and after much loud talking, they all took off. At least Brice had put the vacuum away.

Saturday evening was clear and cold when I walked over to Natalie's dorm. The sun was setting earlier and earlier as fall turned into winter, and it had been dark for an hour already. During the walk, I realized Natalie hadn't met Pete and so knew nothing about him. I would have to give her some explanation, maybe even a warning, when I spoke to her about going over there before the show.

Cars were parked at odd angles in front of the dorm as guys were picking up their dates. It passed through my mind that I might have a car too if I had re-upped and gotten a reenlistment bonus. But if I had reenlisted, I wouldn't be picking up a college girl in the car.

Boys crowded the lobby while the switchboard operator rang their dates and other couples greeted each other and went out the door. I only had a short wait until Natalie came down the hallway. She was wearing a burgundy-colored sweater and black, crisply pressed slacks, which disappointed me. But seeing her come from a distance and in good lighting reminded me that she dressed with care and had good taste with colors. She knew how to use fashion accessories effectively and was also wearing a silk scarf and an attractive bracelet. Her clothes were not expensive, but she gave an impression of casual class. My own clothes were clean but not coordinated. I had been making an effort to wear less of my old uniform parts, and tonight the only government-issue clothing I had on were my dress uniform shoes and my green camouflage underwear. I was wearing jeans, a plaid shirt, and a jacket with the college logo that I had bought at the bookstore.

"Hi," I said when she was close enough to hear me in all the noise.

She smiled and said hi and went over to the sign-out sheet at the switchboard operator's desk.

There were couples ahead of us and behind us on the sidewalk as we crossed campus heading downtown. Middlesex had only two theaters, and the one we (and everyone else) were headed for was the only one within walking distance of the campus.

After we had talked about what we expected from the movie, I mentioned her newspaper story. "I read your story," I told her. "It was good. I hope the editor liked it."

"He did, but he didn't say much."

"Why's that?" I asked.

"Oh, there's a little personal thing between us."

"Personal?" Then I realized I should probably have used that as a clue to change the subject.

"Who do you think I went to homecoming with?" She said this so quickly I realized I was supposed to have asked her.

"That doesn't sound like a problem," I said, not knowing what else to say.

"Let's say we didn't get along. He's a collector, and I don't want to be collected along with the other girls on the newspaper."

I took two steps before responding. "Well, I didn't mean to be nosy."

"No, you weren't. I didn't have to mention it."

I let the question of why she mentioned it drop immediately and instead asked her about going over to Pete's after the show. "Hey," I began, "a buddy of mine asked us to stop over to his apartment after the show. It's a block up Fifth Street from campus. Would that be okay with you?"

"Sure," she said. "Would I know him?"

"I doubt it. His name is Peter Henning. He was in my freshman class and was drafted that summer, same as I was. He doesn't hang out much on campus though."

She thought a minute then said, "I haven't heard the name."

We arrived at the theater with the rest of the campus crowd. There was already a line in front of the ticket window. I didn't know any of the students standing ahead of us and took a quick look at the people getting in line behind us. There was always the danger of running into Olivia.

After I got our tickets, we walked across the red carpet of the lobby, and I offered to get popcorn or snacks. Natalie didn't want anything, though, so we went in and settled into our seats just as lights went down and the coming attractions began. Steve McQueen had a great movie coming. *Bullitt*. The preview showed a Mustang sending billows of white smoke off its rear tires. The sound of the engine was terrific.

My mind blinked back to reality, and another preview came on. Now the issue of holding Natalie's hand had to be resolved. I decided I wouldn't bother. Holding hands seemed juvenile to me. It wasn't stimulating unless the hand-holding was in one or the other's lap, and that would take a few more dates.

The Parent Trap began, and I let myself become absorbed in the movie. The scenes where both of Haley Mills's characters appeared together intrigued me, and I wondered how the photography was done. There were also mountain scenes filmed in California, which reminded me of the remark Pete made about going to San Francisco. I felt relaxed sitting next to Natalie. She relaxed too, and soon, we were laughing and whispering comments to each other.

After the movie, we discussed it as we left the theater and agreed it was an entertaining escape from reality. Then we talked about other Disney movies. Natalie's favorite was *101 Dalmatians*, and I remembered liking *Peter Pan*. It was pleasant to talk about our good memories from childhood.

Before we had walked very far, I mentioned Pete again. "I should explain something before we get all the way over to Pete's," I said. "He's a student, but he hangs out with local . . . kids." The word I didn't say was the slightly derogatory term, "townie." "I'm mentioning this," I continued, "because there probably will be some goings-on that are . . ." I paused and then started again. "That are a little further out than you may be used to."

"Such as?"

I slowed and then stopped under a streetlamp. The naked limb of a tree under the streetlamp waved in the wind and shadows flickered around us. "Pot," I said flatly. "We don't have to go. We could go back to my place."

"Pot," she said. After a moment, she asked, "Would they—or you—be insulted if I don't join in?"

I relaxed. "No. They don't mind me, and I just hang out there sometimes. You see, I'm a juicer. I drink. Instead of smoking. Pete's fun," I continued, "and we have the army in common. Other things, like the pot, we don't have in common. I let him and his friends do their thing, and they respect what I do." I looked at her and said, "And as far as you insulting me, there's no chance of that."

She smiled. "Then I'll go. It will be an evening of discovery." She turned and started walking again. "And let's get going. It's cold out here!"

We walked up the alley to Pete's door. I knocked and, without waiting for a response, went ahead and opened it. "Oh, by the way," I said to Natalie, "Pete's place is actually in the cellar." I led her in and down the steps.

"Hey!" Pete shouted to us, "He made it!" He and Patty were to our right in the kitchen area. They were fussing with something on the counter. The living room area to the left was dark, but I could see a couple on the couch. The stereo was playing The Doors, who were trying to break on through. The penetrating odor of pot already filled the apartment. I led Natalie over to Pete and Patty.

"Sure we made it," I said. "Wouldn't miss it for the world." Then I introduced Natalie informally, using only first names. I had forgotten Patty's last name. "Natalie, this is Pete, a fellow survivor of the great conflict, and this is Patty, who is an angel for putting up with guys like him and me." We continued exchanging joking comments.

"Help yourselves to whatever you drink," Pete told Natalie. "There's no formality here. We just relax and enjoy each other." He and Patty continued working. They were making cookies.

"We should have brought something," Natalie quietly told me as I opened the refrigerator.

"It's okay," I responded without looking at her. "I've brought beer and snacks other times. It's communal here, like Pete said." I took a beer and a Coke and then made Natalie a rum and Coke.

As I handed Natalie her drink, Carl and Anna came into the kitchen area. I introduced Natalie, and then we milled around the kitchen, talking about the cookies and whatever else came into our heads.

Patty put the cookie sheet dotted with mounds of cookie dough into the oven, and we went into the living room. She and Pete and Carl and Anna sat crowded together on the couch, while Natalie sat in a big old easy chair, and I sat on the floor by her legs and leaned back against the chair.

Almost immediately, though, Pete got up again and went back to the kitchen. He brought back a coffee can that I knew he had his stash in. He took out the fixings and expertly rolled a joint then lit it and took a drag, squinting and smiling. As the joint was passed around, both Natalie and I passed up our turn to the joint.

"You're still gonna get high," Carl said. "The mice get high down here."

The smell of baking cookies gradually wafted into the living room area and blended with the smell of pot. The bell on the stove rang, and the three girls and Pete went out to the kitchen. Pete was overeager and yelled as he burned his fingers slightly when he grabbed a hot cookie off the sheet.

The cookies were chocolate chip, which the girls brought in on two plates. We gobbled them down in minutes. Then I started craving for a cup of coffee, though I knew no one else would want coffee. Soon, a mellow atmosphere came over us all. The roach had been burned out for a while when Pete and Patty went to the kitchen. They talked for a moment and then slipped into his bedroom and quietly closed the door. Meanwhile, Carl and Anna were snuggling down on the couch again. That's when Natalie nudged me and motioned to the kitchen then got up. In the kitchen she whispered to me, "We had better go."

"Right," I said. "Sure, but just a second." I was hoping there might be some cookies left and went over to the stove. There weren't any. As I turned back to Natalie, we heard Carl and Anna going up the stairs to leave. This took me by surprise, and I said, "Well, they're in a hurry."

"And they didn't even say good-bye," Natalie responded with a false insulted tone. We both laughed.

Fortune had smiled on us so suddenly I was speechless. Natalie said, "Well, we may as well get comfortable."

"Yes. Comfortable." We walked back to the couch. There was no time to be subtle. I sat at one end of the couch, and Natalie sat right next to me. She was closer than I'd expected.

"So where were we last week?" I said.

"Well," she murmured, "we certainly weren't here, but I know where we left off." She turned to me in obvious submission, and I slid my left arm around her and took her shoulder in my right hand. We fell into a delightful kiss. After a long minute, I moved my lips up to her ear and gave her earlobe a noisy kiss. She squirmed, mildly protesting, "I'm not a cookie."

"Fooled me," I whispered. "You're delicious." I kissed her behind the ear, and then we moved apart and sat quietly for a moment. Natalie spoke first, saying, "At first, I thought it was odd to have an apartment in the cellar, but now I find it quite cozy."

"It is," I agreed. "It is. I have the feeling of being safely hidden away."

We soon developed a rhythm. We'd kiss then came moments of silence, followed by inconsequential talk, and then more passion. Rather than getting myself into trouble, I set a limit on myself. I would be a gentleman, though an aggressive gentleman, and keep my hands away from any controversial places. If it turned out that my conservative limits were beyond her limits, I would back off.

"Natalie," I said, pronouncing her name very slowly. "That's happy name."

"And Michael can be biblical," she answered back. I promptly cut off the conversation with a kiss.

I had my right hand on her back and slipped it under her sweater. This elicited a quiver and a sharp sigh. I was careful to consolidate my position before moving forward, so I let my fingers just barely touch her skin and then started moving them in lazy circles in the small of her back.

"Oh, that feels so good." Her voice was so soft I could hardly hear her. My hand slowly progressed until I eventually had my handful on her back. I was still gently kneading her skin. But she gave me a friendly warning when I moved up and touched her bra strap.

"Don't mess with the suspension."

"Oh, but I had no intention!" I said in mock seriousness.

After a minute or two, we started talking about Natalie's trip to France. She spoke so enthusiastically about the food and different customs that I asked her, "Have you thought of studying over there? Aren't there programs where you can transfer credit?"

"There are," she said, "but it's expensive. And I wouldn't know anyone. In high school, I had a couple of friends with me."

"Maybe someone else on campus would be interested," I said.

"Maybe. How about you? Would you like to go to France and learn the language?"

I couldn't help but laugh. "I can hardly speak English. No, I'm not going anywhere, maybe back in the army, but no place else." The words had come suddenly and without thought. I was startled. Was I expressing some repressed desire? As quickly as possible, I added, "Well, that too is extremely unlikely."

Natalie paused then murmured, "I would hope so." A minute later, she sat up straighter and said, "Pardon me, but where's the bathroom down here?" She looked at the kitchen area.

"Oh, I'm sorry," I said. "It's upstairs. Here, let me show you." We got up, and I took her to the door between the kitchen and Pete's bedroom. We tried to walk quietly, as Pete and Patty might really be asleep. I opened the door and showed her the stairs then turned on the light for her. "It's across the hall at the top. The light switch is on the left as you go in. The landlady went to bed a long time ago."

Natalie looked apprehensively up the bare wood stairs and gave a little laugh. "This is the first time that going to the bathroom is a mystery trip."

"Would you feel better if I went up with you and stood outside?"

"Don't be silly! I'm a big girl."

When she came back down, she asked, "What's Pete's landlady like?"

"I've never met her," I said. "I've only seen glimpses of her. She's old. She must be deaf because she never complains about the racket down here."

I took my turn upstairs, and when I came back down, I found Natalie in the kitchen area. The wall clock over the sink showed eleven thirty. Since the romantic mood was already broken, I suggested we hike on back to her dorm and beat the midnight curfew.

"I suppose that's best," she agreed.

It had gotten considerably colder. It was still clear, though, and as we walked, we remarked on how pleasant it was to see the sky alive with stars. "Do you think we're high?" Natalie asked as we walked along, being careful of ice on the sidewalk.

"Probably. A little."

"Is there as much drug use in Vietnam as some say?"

"Oh sure. Lots."

"Doesn't that make it even more dangerous?"

"If you are out in the bush on patrol," I said, "it does. But it doesn't matter much if you're doing support work in one of the big bases. It worried me when I shared guard duty with smokers. I never slept, even when it wasn't my turn to be on guard." She asked me some other questions, and I described a typical sandbag and timber bunker with its crude bunks and how three of us would divide a night's guard duty. I didn't tell her how the place stank from us walking a couple of feet from the bunker to take a piss, and I didn't tell her about the rats that lived off the crumbs of C ration snacks everyone ate while on guard. I also didn't tell her about staring into the night trying to decide if what you saw was a bush moving in the wind or a sapper about to throw a satchel charge in your lap.

"Can't the drugs be stopped?" she asked.

"No, not really." I changed the subject. "God, it's cold."

It was about ten minutes before midnight when we walked up to Natalie's dorm. As usual, there were couples holding on to each other, desperate to make the most of the evening. I felt like a chaperone intruding at a high school prom.

We paused out on the sidewalk at the foot of the big steps, and Natalie smiled at me. "Thanks for taking me over to Pete's," she said. "They're nice people."

"They are," I agreed. "They aren't typical campus people, but I enjoy their company. I hope you didn't mind the goings-on."

"Oh no. If anything, it's helpful to know the real side of things I've only heard about. It is risky though. You know what I mean?"

"Yeah, right. I understand." I gave her a quick kiss on the cheek and then took off.

The walk back to the apartment from Natalie's dorm was becoming routine. As usual, I felt vulnerable without my weapon at night. Being around pot that evening and talking to Natalie about drugs in Vietnam combined to trigger a dream that night. The dream was another variation on my being the last GI in Vietnam. As in the other dreams, I was struggling to get back to the coast, to the South China Sea, where I thought the navy could pick me up. In this dream, I was wading down a shallow river that I hopped would flow to the coast. I was worried I couldn't be seen from the shore, but there were no roads or trails. The dream ended as I struggled forward in ever-deeper water.

WEEK 9

NOVEMBER 17, 1968–NOVEMBER 23, 1968

MONDAY, NOVEMBER 18

My enjoyment of Mason Williams's album, *Classical Gas*, ended on Monday. It was sunny and warm that afternoon, nearly fifty degrees. The weather alone had me feeling good, and I came back to the apartment around three thirty. As usual, no one was there. My mood was just right for listening to *Classical Gas*. When I went to Brice's stereo, however, I found a note under the plastic dustcover of the turntable. My name was written in large letters at the top. The note was from Brice. He asked me to please not play any albums because they were being scratched and the needle was being damaged. The note went on to say that it was okay to play the FM radio. It was signed formally, Adam and Brice, as if the stereo belonged to both of them. For some reason, this didn't make me blow my cork. Well, I told myself, he had said "please," and I had known I shouldn't use the stereo so much. I thought Robert would analyze my actions and say I was using the stereo because I didn't like Brice. I hadn't deliberately damaged the records, although it occurred to me to do that after I read his note.

So I put the album away and went to the kitchen, where I turned on my radio. It was a good AM/FM radio and sat on the kitchen table. I had bought it through the PX catalog before I was discharged. The radio station was playing an oldie, with Elvis calling his girl a devil in disguise. I needed to do something to take my mind off Brice's note, so I washed a sink full of dishes, wiped down the countertop, and mopped the floor.

Robert came back in around six o'clock. I was watching TV and followed him into the kitchen. After some small talk, I said, "What's with Adam and Brice? What makes people like them tick?"

Robert gave me a glance as he shuffled between the refrigerator and the stove. "They ask the same question about us," he said.

I glanced back at him. "Oh, and next, you're going to tell me it takes all kinds," I sat down at the table. "Well, I could do with fewer of their kind. Brice left me a note on his turntable. He says he doesn't want me playing his albums anymore. He claims I scratch them up." When Robert didn't immediately respond, I added, "It's bullshit. I'm careful. He just wants to be a pain in the ass."

Robert nodded. "Could be. But don't you be a jerk because he's a jerk."

"So it's my fault?"

Robert turned from the stove. "No, you're not at fault. I shouldn't have said it that way. But you haven't done much to be friendly with them."

"I'm not going to kiss some pompous fraternity kid's ass so I can use his stereo. In Nam, everybody in the squad shared."

Robert turned back to the pork chops he was frying. "You know it isn't that simple."

I was quiet for a moment. "That's a common excuse," I said. "A cop-out. Some things *are* simple. I don't like them. And I doubt they like me." Then I added, "You'd think they'd be anxious to share the stereo to make up for not doing their part of the cleanup work around here. Well, I'm going to accommodate His Highness. I won't touch his property."

"That's best."

"I'm still going to make sure they clean the damn toilet though," I growled. "If they piss in it, they can clean it."

"Don't frustrate yourself," Robert cautioned me. "They'll just use Daddy's money to hire someone to do the dirty work."

I didn't have a chance to confront Brice that evening because I spent the evening studying on campus and playing pool in the student union game room. Then instead of going back to the apartment, I took a long walk. When I got back after midnight, all the normal people were in bed. I sat at the kitchen table for an hour listening to the radio, reading, and thinking.

TUESDAY, NOVEMBER 19

Tuesday, I deliberately hung around the apartment so I could talk to Brice. When he and Adam came in the door as *Gilligan's Island* was starting, I was sitting on the couch and didn't greet them. They didn't even look my way but went directly into their room and dropped their books. Later, I heard them in the kitchen. It didn't bother me that both of them were there because what I had to say was for both of them.

When I ambled into the kitchen, Brice had his head in the refrigerator, and Adam was sitting at the table with a Coke, reading the paper. I leaned back against the counter and spoke in Brice's direction. "I got your note. Don't worry, I won't be using your stereo anymore."

Brice didn't respond immediately. He turned, closed the refrigerator, and walked past me. "I appreciate that," he said, his voice calm and quiet. "If they were your records, I think you would understand."

I shifted away from the counter to put more space between us. "None of the records are scratched. If you find any damaged ones, I'll replace them, even if I never played them."

"Look," he said, finally facing me, "the needle gets worn, and then the albums get worn."

"Sure. Well, now there'll be four or five fewer plays per week. That will make a big difference."

Neither of them said anything. It was obvious I would have to leave the kitchen. We were fundamentally different people and shouldn't be sharing space. I had no claim to the kitchen at that moment, and it would have been wrong to annoy them with the pretense of starting my dinner. As I left the kitchen, however, I gave Brice one last comment. "Next time you have a beef with me, talk to me directly. Skip the juvenile note writing."

So that was that with those two. Why should I get along with them any better than anyone else on campus? Like the ROTC guys? They were all assholes. Why was the campus populated with assholes? This Joe College thing was getting tougher and tougher.

The day had just one social bright spot. Natalie and I had coffee after class. With Simon and Garfunkel singing "Scarborough Fair" on the jukebox, we talked about our date. Natalie wanted more details about Patty and Anna, but I didn't know much about them. She didn't mention the pot smoking, and neither did I, but she did take interest in the fact that I, Pete, and Pete's other friends had all been in Vietnam. "None of you were in the same unit, were you?" she asked.

"No," I told her. "Pete was an infantryman in the First Division, the Big Red One. I was a combat engineer in the Americal Division. Carl was an artilleryman, but I don't know what unit."

"I guess you still have a lot in common," she said quietly. She frowned, looking as if she were trying to remember something. "All of you outlived the day and came safe home, so now you can stand on tiptoe with pride when the war is named."

I gave her a sharper look than I intended. "Whatever you say. But I doubt that you'll see any of us on tiptoe."

She smiled as though knowing a secret and then said "What about . . . politically . . . your political views on the war? Do you all agree on what the war's about? How to end it?"

"Political views?" I couldn't keep the sarcasm out of my voice. "We never talk politics. I don't suppose any of us really care about how the war goes on or doesn't go on."

"That's hard to believe," she said. "But I can understand why you wouldn't want to think about the war."

That's when we changed the subject to schoolwork. She had gotten a couple of grades back and expressed mild disappointment over just getting Bs in both classes. This brought back memories of Olivia. Olivia had taken her schoolwork seriously too—more seriously than she took me.

It was only Tuesday, but I was already thinking about how to ask Natalie out again. But I had no bright ideas other than a movie and then getting her back to the apartment and into my bedroom. That sequence was too obvious a repeat of the previous weekend, though, so I put off any mention of a date. We finished our coffee and went our separate ways.

WEDNESDAY, NOVEMBER 19

Wednesday afternoon, Robert solved my quandary about what Natalie and I might do for a date on Saturday. He was in our bedroom folding and putting his wash away when I came in from my last class. I hadn't seen him since my talk with Adam and Brice and wanted to tell him I hadn't made a big deal of the incident. At least, I didn't think I had. After describing the Tuesday's confrontation to him, I said, "Well, what do you think? Did I take your advice?

"You did, you did," he answered. "And it's better than trashing his stereo." Then he changed the subject immediately and asked about my plans for Thanksgiving. "You're staying in town, right?"

"Yeah," I said casually. "I assumed you were too, since I haven't heard you talk about going home."

"Right." He nodded. "What about Natalie?"

His mention of Natalie surprised me. Obviously, he thought we were really thick. "She's going home," I told him. "She's got a ride, and it's only a four-hour trip." Then I prodded him. "And is Rose Marie going to share your holiday?"

"Yes, yes, she is, actually."

I could hear the pride in his voice. I smiled and thought about how romantic he'd become in less than a semester. But then I remembered that I didn't know how close he and Rose Marie had become while I was in the army. Maybe they'd just had an understanding and not dated until now.

Robert continued. "Well, I was thinking of having something like a faux Thanksgiving dinner on Saturday night. Would you and Natalie like to join us?"

The word *faux* was pretty unusual, but I knew what he meant. "I would guess Natalie would be interested," I replied. "What do you have in mind?"

"Well, Rose Marie suggested just roasting a chicken in the oven and having canned vegetables and maybe some easy trimmings. Nothing fancy or hard to make."

"Okay. I'll ask Natalie, but you know she doesn't hold her social calendar for me. Would it change your plans if she can't make it?"

"No. No problem. You can still join us."

I didn't answer, but I thought it would be awkward with just three of us. Then it occurred to me that he was talking about cooking the Saturday *before* Thanksgiving, not the Saturday after Thanksgiving when everyone who went home would still be away.

"How come you're planning it for Saturday and not Thanksgiving?" I asked.

"John Winters and his girlfriend are planning a real Thanksgiving dinner at his apartment. You're invited too," he said. "You've met Winters, haven't you?"

I thought for a minute. "No, not that I remember."

"Well, plan on it anyway," Robert said. "The more, the merrier. There'll be plenty to eat."

"I don't know," I replied. "I'll get back to you. Maybe Pete'll be doing something." I wasn't sure about all this social activity. "I don't really know your buddies."

When I called Natalie that evening, she wasn't at the dorm. I called again later, and she still wasn't in. Rather than just call the newspaper office, I decided to walk over there and, if she was there, ask her to dinner on Saturday. It was slightly past eight thirty when I cut across campus. The bookstore was closed, but people were coming and going from the building, and the lights were on in all the student offices on the second floor. I passed a couple of student senate members as I walked up the stairs. I took a careful look into the newspaper office before entering, since I didn't want to interrupt any serious business. Natalie was sitting at her typewriter next to another person who was also typing.

"Hi," I said from a good distance behind her so I wouldn't startle her.

She turned and smiled at me. "What a surprise!"

"You're working late again," I said. "Another deadline?"

"Every week is a deadline."

She was working on an article about National Turn In Your Draft Card Day, which had been the previous Friday. She said she would love to talk but that she had about fifteen minutes of typing to do, so I said I'd take a walk to kill time and come back.

The hall outside the newspaper office was abuzz with people. The radio station was broadcasting a student call-in show, which was coming over a speaker in the hall and adding the amplified voices of angry students to the chaos. I left the building and took a long slow walk in the dark.

When I got back, Natalie was shuffling papers. I asked her right away about Saturday. "If you're available," I said, "I have an interesting dining experience I'd like to offer."

She turned in her chair and smiled up at me. "Before I commit, maybe I should get the details."

"I was worried you'd say that," I said, "but actually, I'm sure you'll like it. Two experienced and highly recommended chefs have agreed to make a small Thanksgiving-style dinner at the apartment this Saturday. I promise you a culinary delight."

Natalie didn't get a chance to respond. As I was finishing my pitch, her friend Laura was walking up behind me and greeted us with an enthusiastic, "Hi! Am I interrupting?"

Natalie had seen her coming and was happy to see her. "A moment ago you might have been," she said, "but I've just accepted a generous offer for dinner Saturday."

"You're sure I'm not interrupting anything?" Laura asked, looking at both of us. I nodded, and the two of them immediately began a conversation about a student senate committee meeting. Evidently, Natalie had been expecting to hear what had gone on in the meeting. I stepped aside and leaned back against a desk, hoping they wouldn't talk too long.

"No one is certain," Laura said. The tone of her voice made me tune back into the conversation. "Everyone saw the police car, but no one can say the FBI was there."

"The FBI?" I blurted out. "What is this all about?"

They both looked at me, and then Natalie said, "Some people claim there were FBI agents on campus last week at the draft card burning."

"Draft card burning? Was that what was going on at the library Friday?"

"It was National Turn In Your Draft Card Day," Natalie said. "Didn't you see it?"

I shook my head. "No, not really. I was walking past the library while they were setting up, but I didn't stick around. What did you call it?"

"National Turn in Your Draft Card Day," she answered. "It was a national protest. Only it didn't turn out very big."

"It fizzled," Laura added. "Just like ours, it fizzled out on campuses all over the country."

"It sure wasn't promoted very well," I said. "I walked right past them, and I didn't see any signs saying what was going on. Were either of you there?"

"I was there," Laura responded. "And you're right about the lack of promotion. That's what the student senate committee meeting was about. The campus has to be better organized. We have to be coordinated to voice an opinion and have an impact. You should come to the meetings. Maybe you could suggest techniques from your army training."

"Oh no." I fought back a grimace. "Not me! I'm not an organizer."

"There are more and more vets who are openly protesting the war," Natalie said. "They're quite effective." Her voice was suddenly cool.

"I suppose they would be," I answered in an equally cool voice. Fortunately, neither Natalie nor Laura pressed the idea of Vietnam vets against the war any further.

Laura talked about the FBI. "What would FBI agents look like?"

"Businessmen," Natalie answered. "They wear suits and ties like businessmen."

"I doubt there were any FBI on campus," I said. "But there are a number of students who would get a kick out of squealing to the Feds."

Natalie gave me a glance, and I realized she was thinking of the pot smoking over at Pete's.

Laura responded with a skeptical look, as if she was sure there were Feds on campus. Then she went on to another subject. "Do you think a resolution of solidarity would be worth the effort, even if the senate seriously considers it?" she asked Natalie.

"It would be nice, even if it's only symbolic," Natalie said, "but I think it should be a student body referendum, not just a vote by the student senate."

"Solidarity referendum," I said. "Sounds commie to me."

Laura took offense. "Well, it's not," she said. "Students all over the world are fighting for peace, opportunity, and equality. We should stand up and give them as much support as possible."

"Hey." I raised my hands as if to ward off an attack. "I wasn't serious. Really."

"Mike's just teasing," Natalie whispered to Laura.

"What's this resolution about anyway?" I asked.

"Well, if you'd read the school paper you'd know," Natalie scolded me as she picked up a copy of the paper off the desk and shook it at me.

"If you don't write it, I don't read it," I said, hoping flattery would cover my ignorance. "So just what should I know?"

Natalie put the paper down and turned back to the desk and started shuffling papers again. "As Laura said, many of us think the school—both the administration and the student body—should resolve to support the students in France, Mexico, and now Madrid. Certainly, the San Francisco State students who are getting their heads knocked in."

I suppressed my urge to tell them that I thought student protests were doomed. I knew Natalie and Laura would have strong arguments, with lots of examples of social changes made by weak minorities. "Well," I said after seeming to give the idea some real thought, "their chances would be a lot better if they had some money or power of some kind. They look like a bunch of spoiled children—ungrateful that they can study and don't have to work or be in the service." The mention of work launched Laura on to the subject of the labor union strikes in Europe and how the students and unions should work together. By now, I was expecting her to whip out her *Little Red Book* and quote from the chairman.

After a few more minutes of what I saw as only pointless talk, Natalie said she was through with her newspaper work for the evening. She put her typing away, pulled a dustcover over the typewriter, gathered up her textbooks, and the three of us walked out into the hall. Two people remained in the office, and I heard the clatter of typewriters as we left. The newspaper office always seemed stuffy and claustrophobic to me. It was a relief to leave the room. Laura went on down the hall to talk with student senate members who were still hanging around. Natalie and I walked out into the dark toward her dorm. As we walked past the field house, we could hear shouting and the tweeting of whistles from an intramural basketball game. Our conversation hadn't been too lively at this point, so I spoke up. "Don't be disappointed about the draft card protest."

"I'm more bewildered than worried," she replied. "I can't understand why more people aren't concerned enough to do something."

"Think of it this way," I said, "if you think you're not going to be drafted, why worry? Obviously, that includes the girls, and the underclass men are just hoping the war will be over before they graduate, and a lot of the senior men who are hoping they can get some deferment or a slot in the National Guard." After a pause, I added, "There just aren't very many sincere humanitarians like you."

"You're one, aren't you?"

I was on the hot seat again. "Me? Obviously, I know war sucks." I could hear the slightly exhausted and irritated tone in my voice. I decided not to say any more. I didn't need to explain myself to her. She couldn't understand what I said about war. Hell, sex can't be truly explained to a virgin, can it?

"Well," she said, "I'm going to do something about it. However insignificant my effort is, at least it clears my conscience conscious."

Her comment made me want to encourage her and cheer her on. She had spunk. But in this situation, my feelings for her conflicted with what I knew about the war. All I could say was, "You're okay, you know that? You're okay. You'll make a fine journalist."

The happy feelings we'd had while we were talking about dinner that coming Saturday were another casualty of the war. We walked on in somber silence.

When we got to her dorm, we stopped to say good night, and she asked me, "Are you sure I can't help Saturday? Not that I don't trust you and Robert's cooking"—she smiled here—"but it would make it easier."

"No," I said. "Robert and I have talked over the details. We can take care of everything. Robert and I want to cook the meal for you and Rose Marie."

"I think that would be great. Like I told you, I enjoy Thanksgiving a lot, and this makes it even better." I offered to come over to her dorm on Saturday and escort her back to the apartment, but she said she would get with Rose Marie and walk over about five thirty.

We said good night, and I walked back to the apartment, hoping this dinner idea of Robert's would pan out because Natalie was anticipating it so much. I passed a group of students merrily singing, "Over the river and through the woods . . ." The campus was getting psyched for the holiday.

FRIDAY, NOVEMBER 22

I got all my midterm test results at the end of the week. Friday afternoon after my geology class, I sat at a table in the Hideout and listened to John Fogerty proclaim his love for Suzie Q, while I calculated a possible grade for each of my classes. Then I converted the letter grades to points and figured my grade point average. Using worst-case scenarios, or what I hoped would be the worst case, I came up with about a 2.5 GPA. Grades were only important because I needed them to stay in school and draw my GI Bill benefits. School was less and less a means to something larger, such as a career.

SATURDAY, NOVEMBER 23

Robert was more organized than I was but not as well organized as his academic success would imply. Saturday morning, I found him sitting at the kitchen table working on the grocery list for that night's dinner. I hadn't even thought about making a list, but it surprised me when he started asking about what we should serve.

"Cranberries," I said. "We can get it in a can. I think." I was boiling water for my oatmeal.

We talked on and agreed on just what the menu would be. Robert slid the list over to me, and I looked at it. My first urge was to pull out my wallet and see how much money I had. Everything on the list might cost $15–$20. I knew I would be able to cover half of that, but I was also wondering how much I would have left until the next VA check.

As the day passed, Robert gained speed from a slower-than-expected start. First, he made out a rough schedule for the cooking and divided up our chores for preparing the meal.

The trip to the grocery store was businesslike. The store was busy with other people shopping for their Thanksgiving dinners, and it occurred to me as I pushed the rattling grocery cart down the aisle that my mother was probably shopping too. I didn't dwell on that thought.

As we shopped, Robert gave each selection a discriminating look before putting it in the cart and checking the item off his list. I added a small tin of cinnamon to the cart and got a questioning glance because cinnamon wasn't on the list. "It's for something special next week," I remarked. Other than that small contribution to the grocery cart, I performed only one another duty: watching for girls. The store was the closest grocery to campus.

After hauling the groceries back to the apartment, we began the preparations for dinner. It was too rigid an operation to be called cooking. We started at three in the afternoon with a target of serving at six o'clock. I was peeling potatoes. After stripping each tuber into a slippery white ball, I dropped it into a pot of water and took a swig of a beer.

"You're going to cut yourself," Robert warned me. He was cutting a butternut squash in half. The work was going well, and we were both feeling contentedly domestic.

"With this thing?" I shook the peeler gadget at him. "If this were a knife, I might be in danger, but with this damn thing, I'm surprised I get the skin off the potato."

Robert was considering his next comment. "Hey," he said a minute later, "it's been weeks since you woke me with mumbling and talking in your sleep. Are you taking some sleeping pills?"

That was out of the blue. I shrugged and gave him a bewildered look. "Hell, I don't know," I said. "I'm not taking anything. Maybe your delicate sensibilities have gotten accustomed to sleeping in the same room with me." I teased him as I continued peeling potatoes.

"Yeah," Robert said. "Any civilized person would seem delicate compared to a mug like you."

Robert was putting butter on the squash halves and didn't speak for a moment, so I thought the subject was closed until he said, "I suspect that I wouldn't see your scars, even if you stripped your sleeve."

A few minutes later, with the bird in the oven with the squash wedged in beside it, Robert and I left the kitchen to shower and change clothes. While I was taking my turn in the shower, I began to think about Robert's remark. While I was glad I wasn't disturbing him, nothing had really changed for me. In fact, the dreams were getting on my nerves. I wasn't superstitious, but they were straining my reasoning. Were my dreams a premonition, like the witches and soothsayers in Shakespeare?

I was determined to find a rational explanation for my dreams. There was a cause-and-effect relationship that sometimes—but only sometimes—explained what had stimulated a dream. What I saw and heard during the day was often in my dream that night. Because of that connection, I had long since stopped watching TV news because the news always had some story about Vietnam. Too often during the day, there'd be an unavoidable experience, like seeing the M-14s during the Veterans Day Parade, that would trigger dreams. The most disturbing characteristic of my dreams was that they weren't just a random jumble of images played back from my memory while I slept. The dreams were scripted, just like a screenplay. A skilled playwright was deliberately crafting my dreams, giving them a setting, conflict, rising action, and a climax. It seemed as if I had a separate and independent consciousness constantly seeing what I saw during the day and writing the dreams for playback at night. Robert would call it my subconscious. I had begun thinking of it as my shadow self.

Rose Marie and Natalie arrived early, at five thirty, with a pumpkin pie, an apple pie, and a carton of vanilla ice cream. It was only then that I realized Robert and I hadn't bought anything for desert.

"Hey," I said, "this is wonderful!" I told the girls to put the pies and ice cream on the kitchen table. "Robert and I forgot all about desert."

"I beg your pardon," Robert said with artificial indignation. "A great chef never forgets. The ladies insisted on bringing something. It was all arranged."

The girls were amazed when we said that dinner was nearly ready. "What about the squash?" Rose Marie asked.

"In here," Robert answered and opened the stove.

"And cranberries?" she asked, still skeptical.

"Over here," I answered proudly, showing her the cranberries I had dumped out of the can on to a plate. The glob still held the shape of the can.

"You can't serve it like that!" Rose Marie scolded me, rushing to make it look more pleasing. Both girls puttered around the kitchen, finding this or that to give the dinner a feminine touch.

As soon as all the food was on the table and everyone was seated, Robert and I reached out to begin filling our plates. Natalie cut us short by saying sternly, "Grace!"

I withdrew my hand and asked, "Grace who?"

Natalie gave me a pinched smile and then said grace for us all.

Talk during dinner was easy and fast, with three of us occasionally speaking at once. The girls each took a turn describing their holidays at home, and Natalie repeated how much she liked Thanksgiving. When Rose Marie finished, she asked Robert what his holidays at home were like. I knew I would have to complete the circle and talk about my holiday, so as Robert was describing his family dinner, I thought about what I could say when it was my turn. As soon as Robert finished, Natalie looked at me and asked, "Are you ready?"

I nodded. "I thought I'd tell a story about my GI Christmas last year in Vietnam. The story isn't about my family though. Is that okay?"

Everyone encouraged me to continue, so I started my story.

"Last Christmas, I was out on an artillery firebase helping to repair the runway. There were four of us engineers, and we shared a hooch with other non-artillery people temporarily on the fire support base. We were in a typical hooch. It looked like a chicken coop with a corrugated metal roof. There was a continuous row of windows around the entire building to keep us cool. The windows had no glass, of course, just screening and shutters propped open unless it started to rain. The hooch was set close to the runway.

"Anyway," I continued, "one of the guys got a two-foot artificial Christmas tree from home, and we put it up on a makeshift shelf. The guy's folks had sent some decorations too, and the tree looked swell until the first helicopter set down out on the runway. The rotor blast blew through the hooch windows, sending the tree flying and scattering the decorations. We fixed up the tree, but the same thing happened again the next day."

I felt I was telling the story poorly. I'd been hoping the story would be comical, but the others were listing with concerned looks on their faces.

"After the second blowdown, I had an idea." I paused, thinking I might finally get a smile of anticipation, but everyone was still serious. "I took a string and tied one end to the top of the tree and the other to a two-by-four rafter above it. Then when the choppers blew the tree off the shelf, it just swung out and then settled back down after the blow." I smiled and signaled the end of my story.

"Well, that was a good idea!" Robert said.

"It was nice you guys had some kind of decorations," Natalie added.

Their responses were polite, but I felt like I'd just dumped cold water on the festivities. No one spoke for a moment as we exchanged glances. It was then that the realization came to us that we would all clearly remember this evening long after other memories were blurred and forgotten.

Natalie ended the introspective silence at the table when she looked over at the clutter on the counter and stove and said, "Oh boy, we have our work cut out for us."

"Oh no!" I objected. "You're our guests. Robert and I can take care of it tomorrow."

"Tomorrow?" Rose Marie protested. "By tomorrow, everything will be dried solid, and the dishes and pots will be twice as hard to clean."

So we agreed to rinse the worst pots and pans right away and then to reevaluate the situation after a game of Parcheesi. The game was a tame way to pass the time, but Rose Marie and Natalie were happy to play. We shook the dice and talked for nearly an hour. At the end of a game, Rose Marie took a bathroom break, and Robert got up to make her a drink. Natalie was across me, with the game board between us.

"How many cousins will be at your Thanksgiving?" I asked her. We had talked before about her large family.

"Probably six," she said. We were still taking about her family's Thanksgiving when Rose Marie came back to the kitchen. She went up to Robert and suggested they go to the living where it was more comfortable. I smiled at Natalie and said, "That gives them dibs on the couch."

"Yes," she said as she set her glass down and left her hand on it. "That's fine." I reached out and touched her hand. She looked at me, and then our fingers intertwined.

"How would you like to see a picture of that Christmas tree I talked about?" I was looking down at our hands.

"I've wanted to see your pictures."

"Good," I said, "but I'd rather not bring them out here in the kitchen with all the food around. They might get smudged." I stood up, held out my hand, and said. "So will you join me?"

"My pleasure." We walked to the bedroom.

The two beds suddenly looked enormous. I struggled to look nonchalant as I gently closed the door behind us.

My bed was against the left wall, and Robert's against the right. His dresser was to the left of the door and mine was opposite the door under the window. As we stood at my dresser between the two beds, I pulled out my pictures out of the top drawer.

After a minute, it seemed awkward to be standing, so we sat down on my bed. I had sorted through the pictures that afternoon, so Natalie was looking through a select set. No pictures of blown-up trucks or blast holes made by incoming rockets. I gave her a commentary to go with each picture as she leafed through them. There was one group picture of my squad. In the picture, we were each loaded down with helmet, flack jacket, bandoliers of extra ammunition, two canteens, an extra belt of M-60 ammunition, and our weapons—a rifle, grenade launcher, or M-60 machine gun. I was radio telephone operator that day, so the radio antenna stuck up behind me. I told her the guys' names, where they were from, and whatever anecdotes I could remember about them.

Several pictures later, Natalie paused, looking more closely at a picture of me.

"That was after a mine sweep," I said.

"It was that hot?" she asked. It was a candid picture of me in my sweat-soaked jungle fatigues. I had just taken off my flak jacket and had my helmet in my hand. My hair was soaked, sweat was running down my arms, and I was giving the camera an angry side-glance.

"Hot and humid," I said. "I don't know why the guy took that picture. It was months before he got it developed. He left before I did. He gave me the picture as he was packing to leave."

She finished the stack of photographs, and as I took them from her, I said, "I don't have any more pictures, but that doesn't mean we have to leave." Then I lay back across the bed, leaving my feet on the floor, and lifted my hand so I could rub her back. She shivered slightly and then turned to me, also falling back. She settled next to me. "It seems we are falling into this position more often."

"Not often enough," I murmured.

We fell into the essence of the sublime, our minds clear and filled with the awareness of each other. My hand stroked her shoulder then down her back. I alternated pressing my fingertips, stirring and then smoothly stroking her skin.

We struggled for comfortable positions and finally gave up the pretense of just lying across the bed. We swung our legs up. We were in bed together. There was a momentary reluctance on her part, and I suspected she had just crossed a threshold. She had never been in such a venerable position before.

During an excited movement, I flicked open the top button of her blouse, though I didn't immediately capitalize on the advantage. "Shall I turn out the light?" I asked her.

She smiled and said, "Better not. The light might keep the temperatures down."

Within a few minutes, I managed a second button and then gave her earlobe a pinch.

"Now that's the last one," she said, looking at her chest and my hand's proximity to the next button. I would have to make do with the progress I'd made.

And the progress was satisfactory. I used what room the two buttons provided to lightly stroke as deep in her bra as possible. My exploration prompted a satisfied murmur. But we could only sustain the tempo for so long, and since we weren't going to go to the next level, we fell back after a time. We lay apart from each other, holding hands now, and exchanged smiles. The light was still on. She buttoned the lower of the two undone buttons of her blouse then touched my hand again and said, "Experienced fingers, I would say."

"I'll never tell."

She smiled again. "That was silly of me." She did up the top button.

The serious passion was over, so we passed some time with silly talk and horseplay on the bed. Eventually, we went back out to the kitchen. I needed a glass of ice water.

Robert and Rose Marie joined us in the kitchen. They were both flushed, and their clothes were rumpled. "Let's have a toast," Rose Marie suggested as Robert got them drinks too. When all four of us had a glass, we stood in a small circle, and Rose Marie proclaimed the toast. "To Thanksgiving 1968 and to the chefs of tonight's dinner!" She raised her glass.

"To Thanksgiving 1968!" we said in unison and clicked our glasses.

The evening ended in the shadows in front of Natalie's dorm. We hadn't spoiled the walk back with serious talk, as we had the weekend before, so we were both still feeling romantic. "You and Robert did a swell job with the dinner," she said, and I kissed her. "It was great," she added when she could take a breath. It was cold, and we could see our breath.

That night, I paid the price for showing Natalie my pictures. I had an unusually disturbing dream of being inducted into the army again. The scene was an induction center full of the controlled chaos and gloom that I remembered from my real-life induction. Lines of silent and scared teenage boys were being scolded, intimidated, and bullied from place to place. I kept trying to explain to a stony-faced sergeant that I had already been in the army and was discharged. He demanded to see my discharge papers. I stuttered in confusion that I shouldn't have to prove I was discharged, that I didn't know where my discharge papers were. Then we were standing in ranks in a large room with patriotic posters on the walls. An officer at a lectern was preparing to swear us in when I started yelling and creating a commotion. My anxiety reached a peak, and I woke up.

Sunday morning, I dug though my bureau and found the green plastic binder with the seal of the United States War Office on the cover that contained my DD214 form. I looked at the document carefully as if to reassure myself that it was real.

WEEK 10

NOVEMBER 24, 1968–NOVEMBER 30, 1968

TUESDAY, NOVEMBER 26

Tuesday, after our American lit class, Natalie and I were walking along the sidewalk when I asked her about her trip home. "What time are you leaving tomorrow?"

"Right after everyone in the car is finished with classes. Three o'clock, I would guess."

"Isn't anyone willing to cut class so you can leave early?"

"No. Some professors can be a real pain. Some of them like to give a quiz on the afternoon before a holiday."

"Would you mind if I came over for a few minutes tonight?" I asked her, startling myself with the question.

"Sure." She looked mildly surprised, as if she hadn't expected me to ask the question any more than I had expected to ask it.

That evening, I walked over to Natalie's dorm just after seven. It seemed much darker out than it should for that time of day, but I still hadn't adjusted to the time change back in October. The shorter days just seemed to accelerate the slide down into winter. In Vietnam, I recalled, the days had not varied so greatly from summer to winter.

While I was waiting for Natalie to come down to the lounge, it occurred to me that we might go over to the Hideout for ice cream.

"No, I'd rather not," she said. "I'd have to go back up and get a jacket, and I do have packing to do. Why don't we just sit here for a few minutes?"

I hid my disappointment, and we found an open couch. "I keep expecting you to say you've changed your mind and you're going home," she said.

I shook my head and tried to make a joke. "I couldn't leave Robert alone."

"He has Rose Marie."

"And I'll be there to protect him," I said in a voice as serious as possible.

"He will be *so* appreciative."

I couldn't help but grin. "Yeah. I guess I better know when to disappear."

I figured it was up to me to keep the conversation going, so I came up with great original line. "Tell me about Cleveland. What's the town like?"

"Pretty normal, I guess," she said seriously. "It's very much what you would probably call Midwestern. The factory parts of town are rough, but it has some very nice sections with museums and the like."

"An art museum?"

"Yes, even an art museum. A good one. There's a park called the University Cultural Circle, and it has a large art museum along with a natural history museum and botanical gardens." She seemed slightly defensive as she described her hometown.

"Well," I said, "I may live relatively near New York, but I'm not a New Yorker, so I wasn't making any comparison." I went on to describe what I meant to be from upstate. "Some people in the city consider everything above the city limit to be the wilderness populated by hillbillies."

"So what does that make Ohioans?"

"Goodness! The Hudson River marks the end of the civilized world. We may as well be in China out here," I said with exaggeration, hoping to make her smile, which she did.

Our conversation then turned to art. She liked Andrew Wyeth, and we both thought Salvador Dali fascinating, but neither of us would decorate with his works. We talked easily for about fifteen minutes, and then I saw her look over my shoulder at the wall clock behind me. "I'm sorry," she said, "but I had better get back upstairs and start packing."

We stood up in unison, and I came up with another dynamic subject for our parting comments. "The forecast is for warm weather tomorrow, maybe the mid-fifties, and no rain. You should have a good trip."

"I hope so. Last year, we had sloppy weather at both Thanksgiving and Christmas. It was lousy driving."

We stood for an awkward moment, and then I stepped back and said, "Okay . . . well . . . then . . . have a safe trip and enjoy the festivities."

"Thanks," she said. "I hope you, Robert, and Rose Marie do something together . . . and don't forget to call your parents!" She walked back toward the hallway leading to the girls' rooms.

"Bye!" I called to her.

"Bye!"

As I walked back to the apartment, I had the feeling I was the one leaving, not Natalie, only this time I didn't have my heavy duffel bag and I wasn't wearing a uniform. I had that same cold, hollow feeling I'd felt so many times in the past two years. It was a fear of the unknown, along with the certain knowledge that what and who you left behind would not be the same when or if you returned.

THURSDAY, NOVEMBER 28

I was full of regret on Thanksgiving Day. I should have gone home. This Thanksgiving wasn't going to be like Thanksgiving the year before in Vietnam, I didn't have the camaraderie of my bodies. There was Robert, of course, but he was only one person, and his attention was on Rose Marie, as it should be. But when he had asked me a second time to join him and Rose Marie for Thanksgiving dinner at their friends' house, this time, I used the excuse that the group would be all seniors that I didn't know. Pete was going to spend the holiday with Patty and her family, so I was going to be odd man out everywhere for the weekend. As usual, when I got to feeling sorry for myself, I had no one but myself to blame.

Thanksgiving morning, I deliberately got up before Robert. The weather report was typical for Thanksgiving: temperature in the mid-forties, overcast with occasional rain. I was in the kitchen making coffee when Robert came in with the morning paper. "How about some French toast?" I asked. "That's why I got the cinnamon the other day."

"Swell!"

While I cracked eggs and mixed the batter, I confessed to Robert that French toast was the height of my culinary abilities. "My mother taught my brother and me how to make French toast. She hoped we'd make it for her on the weekends," I told him.

Luckily, I got the recipe just right, and the French toast was a big hit. "You're going to have to show me how to make it," he said. We each had three pieces.

Then we sat at the table for an hour, drinking coffee and reading the newspaper. Occasionally, I looked out the window and watched the sparrows flitting on and off a neighbor's bird feeder. Despite the gray overcast, I thought it was a good Thanksgiving morning.

After Robert and I had cleaned up the kitchen, I decided to make phone calls to my parents. I called my father first, since that would be the easier conversation.

"Hi, Dad, this is Mike," I announced when he answered the phone.

"Good to hear from you!" he said. "How are you?"

"Fine. Fine. Happy Thanksgiving." Our conversation continued along those lines for ten minutes until he asked me, "How's your money holding out? Are the VA checks enough?"

"Yeah," I said. "I'm fine."

He didn't press for details, which told me he'd forgotten what it's like to be a student. No student ever had enough money. Now that two years had passed since I had been drafted, my father and I were on reasonable terms. Initially, he'd had trouble understanding how I could let my grades get so bad that I was put on probation and got snatched up by the draft board. My mother had suspected girl trouble, but she never inquired. Eventually, my old man admitted being proud of my military service.

After my father and I hung up, I didn't immediately call my mother. I needed time to think about what to say to her because I knew I'd hurt her by not coming home for Thanksgiving. I went to the living room to find a football game on TV. I was standing in front of the TV turning the channels when the phone rang in the kitchen. Robert was in the shower, so I hustled down the hall to pick it up. My immediate thought was the call would be Rose Marie to talk with Robert. Then the silly notion hit me that it might be Natalie.

"Michael!" the voice on the other end of the phone said. "It's Mom. How are you?"

I didn't need to feign surprise. "I was just about to call you. I called Dad. We just hung up."

"I'm glad you called him." She paused for a second. "Are you going to be doing anything special for the day? Are you going to have a dinner?"

"Yes," I told her. "Robert and I are cooking up a dinner. We're doing a chicken instead of a turkey though." This was nearly true, only off by a few days, and it made her feel better. We continued talking about the weather, my grandparents, what I was eating, what clothes I had, and how my schoolwork was going. She also quizzed me on what day I was coming home for Christmas and told me what the family plans were for the holiday.

It was easy talking to my mother. I sat down at the kitchen table, stretching the long coiled phone cord almost to its full length. As we talked, I watched the birds again. My mother had written me nearly every week while I was in the army, even as busy as she was with work. The conversation ended with my mother scolding me for not coming home.

"But it's such a long drive for just three days," I told her, "and besides, I'm getting some studying done."

I could tell from her voice she thought I'd made a poor choice. But she only reconfirmed what day I would get home for Christmas, and then we said good-bye.

Despite my earlier regrets, now I was glad I hadn't gone home. If I'd gone home, I would only have had to leave again, and I was sick of leaving.

Later, as I lay on the couch watching the Kansas-City-versus-Houston football game, Robert came into the living room. He was ready to leave to get Rose Marie and go to dinner.

"Last chance," he said. "Come on. Have a good dinner. Come as you are."

I got up from the couch and turned the TV down. "Hey," I told him, "I appreciate the invitation, really, but I'll just hang around here. I don't know any of your friends."

He shook his head. "Suit yourself. But if you take the part of the loner, people will start leaving you alone."

Robert's remark didn't bother me. He was right, but I didn't want to change. I went to my bedroom, pulled a blanket off the bed, and went back to the couch to watch football. I fell asleep before halftime with the blanket wrapped around me.

FRIDAY, NOVEMBER 29

When we were small, my mother used to take my brother and me shopping the day after Thanksgiving. So this year, I decided to make an effort at getting into the holiday spirit by going downtown on Friday. Shoppers crowded Middlesex's four-block shopping district. Tinseled declarations were hanging from light poles and a Salvation Army bell ringer was stationed in front of every major store. Main Street had a Woolworth's, a JC Penney store, a small Sears store (mainly for catalog orders), and one large department store, Stuart's of Middlesex. Stuart's was a five-floor department store that resembled, in every way except size, a big city department store. It even had an escalator at the rear of the cosmetics department that ran up to a mezzanine level and a small café. Santa Clause was stationed on the mezzanine too, but I didn't bother to stop and chat.

Instead, I just walked around each floor looking at all merchandise for sale. I had been back from Nam eight months, but I still enjoyed window shopping. I had gone a year without being in a typical American store of any kind. I hadn't missed shopping while I was over there, but after getting back, I realized how enjoyable it was to shop.

That day, I looked at transistor radios in particular. I lifted each radio to see how much it weighed. For a year, I'd had to carry everything I owned in a duffel bag because we were constantly on the move from one project to another, one road to another, working out of different landing zones and fire support bases. I didn't accumulate possessions. I stayed light so I could pack quickly and throw everything on a truck or chopper and be gone. If I couldn't hump it, I didn't want it.

Now I was looking at hundreds of different things I could buy. I had a reasonably permanent place to put them. After some deliberation, I bought a paperback book, one of C. S. Forrester's *Hornblower* series. The book was light and compact and only cost a buck and a quarter.

It occurred to me as I walked past of the perfume counter that I might get Natalie a Christmas present. I stopped, picked up a sample of Prince Matchabelli Golden Autumn, and passed it under my nose. The perfume had the fragrance of an angel in a rose garden. I put the bottle back down on a silver tray with other sparkling bottles. Before I bought Natalie a Christmas present, I'd have to resolve a quandary: What did Natalie mean to me? And what did I want Natalie to feel about me?

The magnitude of these questions chased me out of the department store to the crowded sidewalk. As I came through the revolving door, a young female Salvation Army bell ringer smiled at me as she rang her brass bell. She wore a bonnet tied with red ribbon and had a red and black cape over her shoulders. I quickly dug in my pocket, scooped out all my change, and dropped it in the kettle. She smiled and said, "Thank you," and I felt better. My salvation needed all the help it could get.

Robert and Rose Marie were spending the day with the friends they'd had Thanksgiving dinner with. One of them had a car, so the four of them were taking a shopping trip all the way to Cincinnati. I spent the rest of the afternoon back at the apartment reading *Hornblower and the Hotspur*. Around six, I got bored and called Pete.

"Mike, old man," Pete answered with great enthusiasm, "where have you been?"

"Oh, just hanging out."

"Well, why don't you hang out over here? It's like you've been avoiding us. Come on over!"

"Yesterday was a holiday."

"But today isn't."

I let myself be persuaded. "I'll be around in a bit."

"Good," he said, "and don't eat. We've got tons of leftovers from yesterday."

As I started my walk over to Pete's, I saw that a fog had risen from the damp ground. Car headlights looked like white shafts angled down in front of the vehicles. Although it wasn't wise to walk the same routes consistently, I took my usual route and cut diagonally across campus. Even if there was no danger of an ambush, it was better to be unpredictable. The campus seemed like an amusement park filled with haunted buildings. The darkness and fog accentuated the feeling. I stopped in front of the administration building just to prolong the feeling of being haunted.

When I came up to Pete's door, I noticed electric Christmas candles in the two narrow cellar windows. I knocked and went in without waiting for a reply.

Patty called a cheery hi up to me as I carefully stepped down the stairs. My glasses had fogged up.

"Hi," I responded as soon as I could see. "Looks like you're getting an early start on Christmas."

"If the stores can do it, so can we."

"Mike, old man!" Pete called out. He was closing the refrigerator door. "You're just in time to eat."

"Are you sure you have enough?" Even though I was hungry, I tried to be polite.

"Enough? We've got loads. Thanks to Patty's parents."

"So how was your Thanksgiving?" Patty asked me.

"Fine, fine," I said. Pete was eating a large chunky turkey sandwich, and Patty was holding a plate, eating a piece of pumpkin pie.

"Well," she said, "help yourself. The turkey's in the fridge, and bread and mayonnaise are on the counter."

Patty had a knee-length skirt on but no hose, and she was wearing Pete's bedroom slippers. I concentrated on making a sandwich so I wouldn't look at her.

"Hey," Pete said, "Carl called just after you did. We're going to meet him and Anna for the seven-o-clock show. How about coming along?"

It was about six o'clock. To decline their offer and leave after stuffing my face would be rude, but the idea of riding in the back of Pete's GTO and being the fifth person at the show didn't thrill me. Besides, it was the end of the month, and I was short on money.

"I don't know," I said. "How about if I just hang out here and eat your food and drink your beer?" I said, making a joke of it.

"I don't mind a bit," Pete replied. "We'll never eat all that food anyway. You're sure you don't want to see the flick?"

"No," I told him. "I'll just watch the tube and see you when you get back."

"Okay. Have it your way."

Patty had gone into the bedroom to put on something warm, I presumed, so Pete and I went into the living room area. We were watching the dark TV screen slowly brighten as the set warmed up when Patty came back dressed in slacks. When the TV finally came to life, a news broadcast was doing its annual Thanksgiving in Vietnam story. The story featured a chow line of GIs getting turkey slopped on the familiar stainless steel trays from green insulated food cases.

"Shit!" Pete said as he jumped up and changed the channel. "I don't want to see those poor bastards."

"You don't have to call them bastards," Patty scolded him.

"I'm not knocking them," he said. "Actually, they're lucky to be getting hot chow. I feel sorry for them. Their luck ran out, and now they're in country. Right, Mike?"

"Yeah. And some of them will have their luck get even worse. A lot worse."

"Well," Pete said, "that's behind us. They can't draft us twice."

Remembering my dream, I flinched at Pete's remark and, as inconspicuously as possible, reached over and tapped the wooden arm of the couch.

Pete changed the conversation abruptly. "Say, was all that studying you did worth it? How did your midterms turn out anyway?"

The question startled me. "All right, I guess." I didn't know what else to say, which didn't matter, since Pete didn't really want to hear about my grades.

"Well," he said, "I'm on probation again."

"It would help if you went to class." I spoke more quickly and more sharply than I might have.

"I suppose it would," Pete came back, his voice quiet. "It would help to sit in those stuffy classrooms listening to old farts talk about things they've never experienced."

"Have you talked to your adviser?" I asked him. "Maybe you can change your major or something."

"The dean insisted I talk to my adviser, but that doesn't do any good. Having an advisor is a charade. The advisors are professors. They have no interest in a student's trials and tribulations. Nobody in the school is responsible for a student's success or failure. Assigning a student to an advisor is just a ploy to be able to add counseling to the school catalog."

I nodded. "That's too true. It's a business really. Collect the tuition, pay the staff and expenses, and move the students through."

"The school is running a scam." Pete was sounding more and more angry. "They act like a sacred institution beyond accountability."

I thought for a minute. "Maybe a trade school would be an option. You're a sharp guy. If you learned a trade, you could start a business and hire other people to do the dirty work."

He ignored me. "The school could have helped us some way during our freshman year. They knew we'd be drafted. They could have had a tutoring program or done some kind of flimflam like they do for athletes. You can bet the coach wouldn't have let a star football player get drafted. And look what they do for vets now." He was stuttering with anger. "I'm asking you," he said a loud voice. "What are they doing for us?"

"Nothing, man, nothing. Nothing at all like they did for the old World War II vets."

"Fucking nothing . . .," Pete said, his voice trailing off. Patty had gone to the kitchen. When she came back, Pete was starting to cool off.

"What time is it?" she asked.

Pete responded that it was six forty. "We've got to go," he said, "or Carl and Betty will be pissed. You want to change your mind?" he asked me.

"No, I'm cool here," I said as I moved to the couch.

"Lazy bum. How come Natalie went home? Your old animal magnetism not strong enough?"

"I didn't turn it on," I told him. "I'm still playing the field."

"Bullshit. She's having fun with Old Jody while you sit here on your butt."

The reference to the all-purpose military name for guy who made time with your girl while you were gone didn't faze me. After they left, I got up and down a few times, changing the channel trying to find something to watch. A stupid commercial came on, and I jumped up again and turned the damn thing off, only to stand there in silence looking at the blank TV screen.

"Shit!" I said aloud to myself. Finally, I started thinking about how screwed up I was. My best friend invites me to a holiday dinner, but I blow him off because his friends intimidate me. Then I ignore another good friend's offer to at least do something entertaining. It seemed like all I wanted to do was a mope around.

I sat back down on the couch and looked around for something to read. Nothing. Not a book in sight. Above me, the floor boards creaked as the old landlady moved around. I had visions of her shuffling around a cluttered kitchen that she couldn't keep clean. I had never been at Pete's place when it was so quiet. I looked around and tried to imagine what the basement must have looked like before it was made into an apartment. I noticed one of the windows had an odd casement around it and concluded a coal chute might have been put through that window. That part of the room would have been the coal bin.

When I heard the old lady upstairs coughing, I decided to leave, but first, I had to write Pete a note of explanation. I couldn't be so damn rude as to eat Pete's food and then just split without giving an explanation. So I pulled a page out of a spiral notebook and wrote a note saying I had drunk too much and was going back to the apartment to crash. I couldn't think of a better excuse. I left the note on the table, turned out all but one light, and left. There was no need to lock the door, since Pete never did.

The ground fog had thickened, but when I looked up, I could see the clouds breaking up. I caught a glimpse of a waxing third-quarter moon. Wet matted leaves made the sidewalk slippery in spots as I walked up the left side of the street toward campus. A car came up behind me, crossed to my side of the street, and pulled up beside me, facing traffic. It was a cop car with flashing blue and red lights and a spot light that was trained on me.

"What the hell?" I held up a hand to block the beam of light.

"Hold it, buddy! We want to talk to you," yelled a voice from behind the spotlight. Two dark silhouettes came out of the car. I heard the car doors slam. "Let's see some ID!" the cop closest to me shouted. He carried a large flashlight, and he flashed the beam of light up and down me.

I was irritated and nervous as I fumbled to get my driver's license and student ID out. "What's the problem, officer? Was I speeding?"

"Oh! A wise-ass hippie!" the second cop said as he stepped closer and shone his flashlight on my face. Both cops were the same height, slightly shorter than me. The cop that had asked me for my ID acted like the ranking officer, though I didn't recognize any insignias on their uniforms.

"New York," the first officer said, handing my license and ID back to me. "What dorm are you in?"

"I'm in an apartment over on Quincy Street."

"What are you doing over here?" demanded the other cop.

"Hanging out with a friend."

"A party? Step over to the car and empty your pockets on the hood. Jacket pockets too."

I went over to the car and scooped out my pockets and deliberately dropped the loose change on the hood to make a clatter, only to see some of it roll off the hood. The junior cop flashed his light over what I had put down.

"Where are your cigarettes?"

"I don't smoke."

"Take off your jacket," the first cop demanded. "Check the jacket," he told the other cop.

The wind came up suddenly, and I began to shiver. "Look," I said in a voice strained by the cold, "I'm not drunk. I live here, I'm not a bum. So what gives? I've got rights." My voice didn't sound very convincing.

The junior cop examined my jacket, feeling for anything I hadn't taken out of it. Then he tossed it on the hood of the cop car.

"Turn around and hold your arms up!" he said, and when I did so, he patted my pockets and down my legs, though he didn't make a thorough search.

"Okay," the first cop said, "pick up your crap."

I had noticed he was older than the other cop by maybe ten years. As I quickly picked up my wallet, change, and other paraphernalia from the car, the younger cop demanded to know why I was wearing an army jacket.

"I was in the army!" I shot back, trying to sound tough but hearing my words come out with a strange singsong tone. I put the jacket on and pointed to my embroidered name tag. "See? My name's on it."

"That's where you learned how to smoke those funny cigarettes?" the younger cop asked. "We've heard about you guys. That's why we're losing the war."

I didn't say anything.

The older cop came up to me and shone his light in my face again. "Okay," he said, "now get out of here and don't hang around this part of town." He turned to the car and said to the other officer "Let's get out of here."

They turned off their blinking lights, pulled away from the curb, crossed back to the other side of the street, and sped away. As I walked away as fast as I could, I then noticed people looking out the windows of the house I was in front of. I wanted to stick my tongue out at them or give them the bird.

I felt a mixture of humiliation and anger that nearly made me cry. I'd never even had a traffic ticket. The worst disciplinary action I'd ever had in two years in the army was a chewing out because I forgot to salute an officer.

As I crossed campus again, it occurred to me the campus cops traded information with the city dicks. A feeling of great resentment came over me. This group of dark empty buildings was not a friendly place. Not a happy place. Not, as Pete had said earlier, what it presented itself to be. The school had a reputation to protect. Any scandal would impact the budget.

With this in mind, I took a quick detour off the sidewalk and through the low shrubs beside the administration building and took a piss against the bricks and the ivy.

I got my thoughts back under control as I walked from campus to the apartment. I was wondering why the cops would randomly shaken down a person walking in a nice neighborhood. And why did they call me a hippie when I didn't fit the hippie image? Then the realization flashed into my mind—the cops hadn't picked me out on impulse. They had stopped me because I'd come out of Pete's apartment. That meant they were watching Pete and very likely were going to bust him. I had to tell Pete. I began to walk faster then trotted.

Robert and Rose Marie were on the couch watching TV when I walked into the apartment. Even though I was slightly winded from the fast walk, I asked how the shopping trip had gone.

"Shopping was great!" Rose Marie answered. "The city was wonderfully crowded. The crowds and decorations make the holiday atmosphere."

"So did you get all your shopping done?" I asked as I crossed the room to go to the kitchen and the phone.

"Not even close," she answered. Robert continued watching the TV without saying anything.

"I was downtown today," I said. "The stores had great sales."

They both smiled, and I went out to the kitchen to call Pete and tell him about the cops. But as I dialed the number, I realized they would still be at the movie. I let it ring anyway. No one answered, and now I felt foolish for rushing. I dropped into one of the kitchen chairs, crossed my arms on the table in front of me, and put my head down.

There was no answer when I called again at nine thirty. At ten o'clock, Pete answered.

Speaking faster than normal, I immediately launched into my news. "The cops are watching your place. You'd better clean out your stash. They frisked me when I left your place tonight."

"Hey, hold on, man. Say that again so I can understand."

"The cops stopped me on the sidewalk after I left your place tonight. They frisked me and made me unload my pockets. They were looking for pot."

As I should have expected, Pete refused to be alarmed. "Well, you do look like a damn hophead," he said with a laugh. "How can you blame them?"

"Look," I said, my voice still strained, "they knew I came out of your place. You're the only college guy on that street. They called me a hippie. I sure as hell don't look like one."

"Oh. So I'm the hippie."

I paused a moment then continued. "I think it would be smart to clean out your place. Get the grass out of the house for a few days. What the hell, it wouldn't be a big inconvenience. You know other school kids have been raided. Even dorm rooms searched." That was my argument. I wasn't going to say any more.

"Okay, okay," Pete finally said. "I know you're thinking about me. I'll watch the street and do what I think best." Then he asked me about the cops. "They rough you up?"

"Nah. They were more like Mayberry's finest."

"Well, then just forget about it." The phone call ended without him thanking me for the tip. I suspected I'd caught them in bed.

I picked up my C. S. Forrester book and sat in the kitchen reading the rest of the evening. Buying the book was one of the few smart things I'd done that day. Still, the cops had no reason to shake me down. It was the end of the day, and I'd forgotten the Christmas declarations and the festive atmosphere of my morning trip into town.

WEEK 11

DECEMBER 1, 1968–DECEMBER 7, 1968

SUNDAY, DECEMBER 1

Sunday evening, Robert and I were watching Ed Sullivan on TV when the phone rang in the kitchen. We looked at each other and each raised a fist. We played paper-rock-scissors to see who gets up to answer the phone. I chose rock, and Robert had flattened his hand for paper, so I hurried down the hall and answered the call. It was Pete.

"Mike, old man!" Pete exclaimed in a loud voice. "You were right! The cops hit me last night. They had a search warrant and everything. It was just like on TV." I wanted to cut in and ask questions, but he rushed on. "And, man, they didn't find a thing, nothing, and all thanks to you, old man, my point man, my cover man, you saved my ass, ol' buddy, you saved my ass." He paused briefly then continued, speaking just as fast but in a lower tone. "Patty and I cleaned the place out completely Saturday morning. She even wiped out all the ashtrays and deodorized the place."

"Great," I said when I could finally get a word in. "That's great, I'm glad to hear it. So you're not calling from the city drunk tank."

"No," he said, "I'm calling from Patty's parents. I wouldn't risk talking like this over my phone. The cops might have a tap on it.

"Good thought. What time did they hit you?"

"About six thirty last night. Patty and I had just gotten back from getting a burger, and they swooped in on us."

I heard voices in the background, and he quickly ended the conversation. "You've got to stop by tomorrow, and I'll tell you all about it."

"Yeah, sure," I answered, but I must not have sounded convincing.

"Stop over after class," he said. "We've got a lot going on. Big news."

I assured him I would. As I went back into the living room, I decided to mention it to Robert, if only casually. I was bound to talk about the raid sometime, but I wouldn't mention my part in the incident.

"The cops searched Pete's place last night." I told him as I plopped back down on the couch.

"They find anything?"

"No. His girlfriend had made him clean the place out yesterday morning."

"Lucky."

"Very." After a pause, I continued. "I think the school's security cops are working with the town cops. The students might even be squealing on one another."

"Ugly." He obviously wasn't interested in carrying on a conversation, so I didn't say any more, and we just watched the show.

After Sullivan was over, the door swung open with a thump, and Adam and Brice came in laughing, talking, and carrying shopping bags and duffel bags. We exchanged greetings, and they went on to their room. They made a second trip through to unload clothes, and this time through, they asked how our holiday had been.

"Fine," Robert answered. "Quiet but fine."

"I'd guess it was quiet with everyone gone," Brice responded as they headed for the kitchen and rummaged around for something to eat.

While they were in the kitchen, I decided it was time to bring up the subject of getting someone to replace them. "Have you talked to Charlie or Dave lately about moving in early if Brice and Adam move out?"

"Yeah, I did," Robert said. "Charlie says he can swing it for December if they leave that soon."

"Great. That makes me feel better."

The rest of the evening passed with increasing gloom. Every Sunday evening was depressing, as it marked the end of the weekend, but the end of a holiday weekend was considerably worse. I was apprehensive about classes starting again. I had done some studying on Saturday and Sunday afternoon, but I never felt like I'd studied enough. I was looking forward to seeing Natalie and hearing about her big family holiday. It wasn't wise, though, to depend on Natalie to lift my spirits.

MONDAY, DECEMBER 2

Cars had streamed back on to campus on Sunday afternoon and evening, and by Monday morning, the campus became alive again. When my political science class let out, I considered making a dash across campus to say hello to Natalie, but I dropped the idea when I realized meeting her would have made me late for my next class.

At noon, I checked my campus mailbox in the basement of the administration building, which seemed no worse for my having pissed on it. The box held no invitation to talk to the dean of men about getting stopped by the cops. Neither Officer Cooper nor anyone else from campus security stopped me as I walked across campus that morning, so by noon, I was assuming that the city cops hadn't made trouble for me on campus.

After my afternoon geology lecture, I again considered seeing Natalie, this time at the newspaper office, but again, I decided not to see her. Instead, I went to see Pete.

Since the cops were likely to still be watching Pete's place from the street, I approached the house from the back. There was a common alley that ran behind the houses on Pete's block. I took a different street from campus then went up this alley, which was a narrow one-lane drive bordered by tool sheds, fences, and garages, all perfect cover for an ambush. I hurried along, and when I came up behind Pete's house, I went down the driveway in the opposite direction from usual to Pete's door.

The door was slightly ajar. I could hear Pete's voice, along with other clatter, as I called out, "Hi! Anyone home?" I stepped in the door.

"Mike!" Pete called the out as I went down the steps. "My point man! You really saved my ass. Come on down and have a beer."

Boxes covered the floor, and I wove my way to the kitchen area, where Pete and Patty were sorting kitchen utensils. Pete went on extolling my virtues as I got a beer from the fridge. "Honest, man, I *do* appreciate you taking care of me. I owe you, and believe me, I won't forget it."

"We're cool," I replied "It was nothing you wouldn't have done for me." I looked around and continued. "Gee, the cops did make a mess, didn't they?" Some of Pete's clothes were draped over the back of the couch.

"They did," he said, "but that's not what's going on now. We're leaving. Packing up and blowing this town, California, here we come! For once, we're going to do what we want to do."

"No shit?"

"No shit!"

I looked around at the boxes, bags, and suitcases. "When? Right away?"

"Damn straight," he said. "We can't leave fast enough."

"Ditching the semester?"

"As if that matters."

"I bet this'll piss off your parents."

"I told them," he said. "They're not upset. I called and talked to my old man—he's a lawyer, you know—about the cops. I didn't ask him if I could leave, I *told* him I was leaving, and Patty is going with me!"

I looked at Patty and just said, "Wow!"

She smiled and said, "Wow is right. It's going to be great. California's got mountains and the ocean, and all kinds of things are going on out there."

"What about your parents?"

"Oh well, they're not thrilled, but my elder sister's in Chicago, and she's doing all right, so I guess they knew I'd leave sooner or later."

I looked around again, shook my head, said it again. "Wow!"

"Hey, man, why don't you come out too?" Pete asked me as he stuffed some forks and knives into a box. "Really, man, I mean it. It would be great to have you around. The car's full, but you could catch a bus or train or something." Pete had turned to face me directly. I could hear the sincerity in his voice. "Come on, man."

I looked at him and then looked away. "I can't see it. Not now anyway. Maybe someday but not now."

"Well," he said with a shrug, "I guess you are serious about school, but they have great schools out there too. And it doesn't snow in San Francisco."

"I'm always thinking about what to do," I said. "Who knows? Let me know how it goes. You may see me. We've got to stay in touch."

"Right, man. We've got to, we've got to." He grabbed my shoulder and shook me.

They went back to packing, and I wandered into the living room area intending to turn on the TV, but I didn't. The atmosphere wasn't right for doing the same old things. Instead, I walked back into the kitchen area. "Well, is there anything I can help with?" I asked lamely.

"Relax," Pete said. "Talk to us and make us feel good. Tell us everything is going to be okay."

"Well, hell," I said, "everything is going to be okay. You guys can make it fine and have a good time too. You're off to the adventure of a lifetime."

"Did you know that blue jeans are made in San Francisco?" Pete said. "Back in the gold-rush days, this guy made pants out of canvas, and that's where Levis came from. Well, the San Francisco street people have their own style, and I was thinking we could sew up a few things and peddle them on the street. Since we'll be part of the scene, we'll know what people want, and Patty knows something about sewing. It could be a business!"

"Sounds like a good idea to me," I answered with almost equal enthusiasm. We talked until a knock came at the door, and Carl and Anna came down the stairs, both of them talking at once.

"My god!" Carl shouted. "They're packing. They're really going to do it. When are you leaving?"

"The way things are going," Pete said, "it won't be until sometime tomorrow. All of a sudden, there's one million things to do."

Then both Carl and Anna began to quiz him about how wise it was to leave. "California is going to be a hell of a long way from either of your relatives," Carl said. "Do you even know anyone out there?"

"Sure," Pete said, his tone totally positive. "There are thousands of people like us that want to enjoy this beautiful world and get away from all the bullshit. We'll have a huge family."

"Sounds good now," Anna said in a distinctly jealous tone, "but when the money runs out, things will be different."

Patty cut in to support Pete and give her full commitment to the adventure. "We'll be just fine. And anyway, what future do we have here?" There was a pause, during which no one had anything to say, and then Patty continued. This time, she tried to remove any insult from her voice. "Look, we each want something different from life. We're all in different situations. Pete and I want to try this. It might not be a good idea for anyone else, but we're going to try."

This triggered a round of reasons why everyone was doing what they were with their lives. Anna spoke first, saying, "I'm an only child. Being that far away would upset my parents terribly."

Carl claimed it would be hard to find a job as good as the one he had here.

I only contributed nods of acknowledgment and short comments of understanding and support, and pretty soon,

I saw that my hanging around was accomplishing nothing. Pete was leaving town, and I was staying in school, and the sooner I said good-bye, the better.

At a reasonably polite point, I cut into the conversation. "Well, buddy," I said to Pete, "I've got to be shoving off. Since you're shoving off too, I guess it will be a while before we see each other again."

Pete seemed a bit surprised, but he didn't protest or urge me to stay longer. We stepped away from the others, and Pete gave me a serious look. I got the feeling I was the first one to actually say good-bye to them since they had decided to leave.

"When does your last morning class let out tomorrow?" he asked me.

"Eleven."

"Good, that'll work. Meet me tomorrow in the administration building at eleven. I've got to a mess of loose ends to take care of, sort of like clearing post. Check for me at the bursar's office or at the registrar."

So Pete and I postponed our final farewell, but I had to say something to Patty. She had seen Pete and me talking, so she knew why I came up close to her. I leaned toward her and whispered in her ear. "Run away with me, not him." I made sure I was whispering loud enough for everyone to hear. "We can get rich gambling in Monte Carlo and live forever on the French Riviera." She laughed, and I continued in a normal voice. "You're sweet, and Pete's a lucky guy. I promise we will all be together again." Then I gave her a kiss on the cheek.

"You've been a good friend for Pete," she said. "He needed you around. We'll miss you." And she gave me a kiss on the cheek in return.

I made polite comments to Carl and Anna, saying I would keep in touch with them so we could trade news about the new Californians, and then I said to Pete, "I'll see the tomorrow at eleven."

"Right. I'll be there."

Just before I stepped through the door, I glanced back down and gave the group a wave. I had first seen them together at the party eight weeks before, and now I doubted that I would ever see the four of them together again.

"Shit," I muttered to myself as I walked down the drive beside the house. This was the last time I would visit this house. I was angry because Pete was taking off, escaping free. I wanted to be free too, but I didn't want to do what he was doing. That left a question as to what I *did* want to do. It was nearly dark by now, and all the cars had their headlights on. I walked past the place where I had been frisked by the cops the Friday before. Tonight, I didn't give a damn if the cops saw me back in that part of town.

My anger mellowed while I was walking across campus, and I concluded that Pete and Patty had made the right decision. Pete was sure to succeed, if he watched how much pot he smoked, no matter where he was. He was intelligent, extroverted, slightly taller than average, and usually happy. He enjoyed people and remembered names well. All this predicted a bright future for him.

I would just have to find another friend.

It was five fifteen by now, so I thought Natalie would be at her dorm getting ready for dinner. I wanted her to know Pete and Patty were leaving, even though she had only met them once, and telling someone else would make me feel better.

No one was in the lounge at her dorm. Suppertime was an unusual time for men to visit. The girl on the switchboard was reading a textbook and seemed irritated that I'd interrupted her studying to ring for Natalie. After she told me Natalie was coming down, I walked in circles in the lounge then sat down and watched groups of girls leaving for dinner. When I was a freshman, the food in the dinning hall was a major point of ridicule. After being in the army and eating their so-called food, I knew how good these people walking to dinner had it. They didn't have to stand in ranks in front of the mess hall or have to go hand over hand through a set of overhead bars before eating.

I was so lost in my daydreams about army mess halls that I didn't hear Natalie as she walked up. When she said hi, I jumped up out of the chair.

"Hi," I said, feeling slightly embarrassed. "Did I catch you on your way to dinner?"

"Oh no. I was planning on going a little later anyway. So what's up?"

It would have been impolite just to launch into telling her about Pete, so I asked her how her holiday had been.

"Great, really great." Then in a less-than-enthusiastic voice, she asked, "How was yours?"

"It was fine. Quiet, obviously, but okay." My words weren't convincing, but before she could ask for details, I went ahead and said what I'd come to tell her. "Hey, I just came from Pete's. Get this—he and Patty are leaving town tomorrow, driving to San Francisco."

"Leaving town? You mean for good?"

"Right. Packing up, pulling out, gone like the wind."

"Is he dropping out? In the middle of the semester?"

"Yeah. He wasn't serious anyway and hardly ever went to class."

"I wonder what her parents think."

"Well," I said, "she's not a little girl. She must be over twenty-one."

A long line of girls was passing by the lounge on their way to supper, giggling and talking. There was no privacy in the lounge. "Would you mind taking a walk?" I asked Natalie.

"I guess not. I've got a sweater on."

"Oh right, it's late. Well, if it gets cold, we can cut it short. I just feel like I'm in a fish bowl in here."

As we started down the front steps of the dorm, Natalie suggested we go to the fine arts building, which was only a short walk from the dorm. "Laura has some artwork on display," she said and then added, "So what made them leave so suddenly? Are they getting married?"

It was only then that my slow wit managed to comprehend the whole situation. If the police raid had been a week earlier, Natalie and I would have been involved. It would have been silly to try to avoid the truth of what was going on, and besides, my brain was only just beginning to move. There was no hope of cooking up a story, so I just told her what had happened.

"The cops raided Pete's apartment Saturday night with a search warrant. They turned the place upside down looking for drugs. But they didn't find anything. Pete was clean." I spoke rapidly. "Pete was clean," I repeated so she'd get the point.

She turned to me. "Raided him! You mean with guns? Were you there?"

"No, no, I wasn't there." I felt defensive and backed off a step or two, but I couldn't say much since I'd taken her there the week before. Rather than wait for her to mention our having been there, I plunged ahead with an apology. "And I'm sorry for having put you in such a risky situation last week."

"Gee, that's right. That was close."

Fortunately, it was a short walk to the fine arts building. As we walked up the steps, Natalie asked for more details about Pete. "If nothing was found, then why are they leaving? I don't think the police can make someone leave town like in the old western movies."

I shook my head. "Pete's just disgusted with the town," I said. "Mainly with school. Having been drafted. Everything. He just wants to try something new." I opened the door for her, and we walked into the large lobby in front of the doors to the college theater. No one else was there, and the place was silent. We walked down the hall to standing panel displays hung with student artwork. Not saying much, we checked the small white identification tags and found one of Laura's oil paintings. The picture was a landscape, and we looked at it in silence for moment. The scene was of a pasture, with a veil of mist blurring all the images and giving the feeling of a cool summer morning just after dawn. Stepping back and viewing the work from a distance increased the mystical impression of the scene.

"That's lovely," I said.

"Yes, it is. She's talented."

"That's what it takes," I responded. "Either you have it or don't."

We made a quick loop around the rest of the display, and then I looked at my watch and asked Natalie if she still had time to get to dinner.

"There's time, but I'd better hurry. I have to get ready for the senate meeting at seven o'clock. They're considering the solidarity resolution tonight."

"So," I asked, "is there student support for the resolution?"

"Yes, quite a bit. There's a petition circulating urging the senate to support it. I'm surprised."

I was surprised too, but I didn't say anything. The wind laid a cold hand on my cheek as we stepped out of the building. We hadn't said much about Pete and Patty, but as we started down the steps, Natalie asked, "What are they going to do out there? Do either of them have relatives or friends out there?"

"No, they don't. But Pete's clever and motivated when he wants something. He talked of starting a business, making clothes for the other, what would you call them, escapees from the normal life?" I tried to sound optimistic.

"San Francisco is a pretty city, but I've heard it rains a lot." She hesitated and then continued. "I can't imagine just leaving, just getting up and going without anything to go to."

Now the conversation demanded that I make a remark agreeing with or disagreeing with what Pete was doing. "I can't see living the way they will be," I said after a moment's thought. "I like regularity and stability. I guess I'm dull."

"I wouldn't say so."

"They'll have an adventure." I emphasized "adventure."

"You should stay in touch with them," she said. "They're nice people."

"I will."

As we approached Natalie's dorm, we could hear talking and music and giggling coming from a number of partially open windows. Natalie looked up at the windows. "The heat is so goofed up. We have to open windows in the winter."

"My freshmen dorm was the same way," I said.

We walked up to the steps and stopped, and Natalie turned and looked at me. "Don't worry about having taken me to Pete's the other Saturday," she said. "You told me what was going on, and I decided to go."

I let the situation stand at that and made no comment. We parted, saying, "See you in class" and "See you tomorrow."

Robert was not at the apartment when I got back. Adam and Brice were there, however, and we exchanged civil greetings in the hall between the living room and kitchen. Other than that, they just talked to each other as usual.

I went into the kitchen, opened the fridge, and just stared at the shelves. I was hungry but not hungry enough to cook anything, so I finally made an extra-large peanut-butter-and-jelly sandwich with four slices of bread. The morning paper was still on the kitchen table where Robert had left it. I read the front page as I ate, dripping grape jelly on the headline about Pakistan having granted concessions after student riots. A headline in the sports section said the Jets had beaten the Dolphins on Sunday. I still found it odd to name a football team Dolphins.

TUESDAY, DECEMBER 3

The professor's droning monotone finally ended, and my American literature class was over. The sleepers in the class were startled awake by the slapping of books being closed and squeaking chairs as people got up to leave. As soon as I had shuffled out into the hall, I stepped aside out of the stream of traffic and waited for Natalie.

"Here we are, back at it again," I said when she came out of the room.

"Right," she responded, and we started for the stairs. We didn't attempt to carry on a conversation as we went slowly down the wooden stairs of the old building with the mass of other students.

It was still unusual for us to have coffee together after class, but the possibility that we might do so created a slight tension between us until we knew the other's plan. The problem was who would say what first. When we were back out in the fresh, chill air and moving along the sidewalk, I spoke up. "How was the senate meeting? Was there any agreement on the solidarity issue?" I was deliberately delaying any comment about having coffee.

"I think a majority of the senators want a senate vote rather than a campus referendum," she said. "Would you believe it—one senator doesn't want a resolution at all?"

"You should run for a seat next spring."

"Not a chance. I can't be manipulative, and I hate compromising my principles."

We were nearing the juncture in the sidewalks where I had to turn to go to the administration building and meet Pete. "Well, I'm off to say good-bye to Pete. He's over at the bursar's office or somewhere tying up some loose ends."

She smiled. "Okay. Tell him I wish them good luck."

"I will. See ya."

She waved and turned in the direction of the newspaper office.

I had only taken a step or two when the thought came back to me that I probably wouldn't see Natalie again until class on Thursday, and I had to either ask her out now for Saturday or skip it. Asking for a date was never easy, but I turned and bolted off the sidewalk and cut across the triangle of grass between us, slipping on the wet grass and mud as I went.

"Natalie!" I called as I caught up to her. It seemed odd to hear myself call her name so loud in public.

She turned, surprised, and said, "That was quick!"

"Yeah, right," I said, walking beside her but not really looking at her. I didn't have time to think of what to say or how to say it properly, so I just blurted it out, though I did turn to look at her. "Say, would you like to do something Saturday night? I can't promise a visit to a bizarre friend, but we could find something fun."

"I've got an idea!" she said cheerfully. "It wouldn't be roaring fun, but it's something to do."

"Sure. What?"

"Laura's singing with the Oratorio Chorus in the *Messiah* Saturday night. We could go to the concert and then do something afterward too. Sound tolerable?" We had walked a ways and were about to cross the main street of campus.

"Absolutely!" I said with a grin. "A little religious music would do me good. How about if I check the start time and get back to you." I was edging away in the direction I had to go to get to the administration building to meet Pete.

"Fine," she said as she started across the street. "And," she called back to me, "if it's no fun, I'll make it up to you afterward."

"In that case," I called back through a crowd of students on the sidewalk, "I can tell you right now I'm not going to like it."

The Westminster chimes in the campus bell tower were ringing out eleven o'clock as I took the steps two at a time up to the lobby of the administration building. The bursar's office had a service window in the main lobby, but I didn't see Pete there. The registrar was around a corner and down a hall. As I went toward that office, I took a glance at the dean of men's office. No student came into this building for the fun of it.

I finally found Pete standing looking out the back entrance, the way I would have come in if I hadn't talked with Natalie. "Hey, short-timer," I called out to him.

He turned, grinned, and held up his hand, making a small gap between his thumb and forefinger. "So short I could walk under that door," he said cheerfully.

"You're all set then?" I asked him. "They're letting you go?"

"Damn straight!"

Some important-looking people wearing business suits and talking loudly came down the main staircase from either the dean's or president's office. Their footsteps echoed on the marble floor. Pete and I stopped talking till they'd walked past and out the back door.

"Let's go out the front," Pete said. "My car's on the street."

We crossed the lobby, pushed opened the heavy glass doors, and stepped out on to the top step. Pete didn't go down the steps right away, however, but walked to the side facing down the street toward the library and the student union. He put both hands on the heavy decorative railing and leaned forward. Being on the top step gave a view down campus. I stood next to him. "I'm not going to miss this place," Pete said as we gazed at people loaded with books walking between buildings. When I didn't reply, he continued. "This time, *I* decided what would happen to me. No one made the decision for me, and I feel good about it."

"You should," I said. "You've taken control."

Pete turned his head and looked at me. "Still no interest in going out West?"

"Not now, but who knows?"

He turned again and looked back down the street. Random gusts of wind tossed at the bare branches of the trees lining the street. Everyone on the sidewalks was bundled up against the wind. I was getting cold too.

"Those people don't know what's going on," Pete said, his voice quieter and more serious than I'd ever heard him. "They don't know the real shit, and worse is they don't know how lucky they are."

"They are lucky," I agreed, "and what's worse is too many of them are snooty despite their ignorance."

"Hey, what am I saying!" he said in a louder deliberately cheerful voice. "We're lucky too. We didn't come home in a bag, maybe a little nuts, but, man, we've got all our body parts."

"Right on!"

Pete's stuck out his hand, and I shook it.

"It's been great having you to talk to," he said, "someone who knows about burning shit in a tub of diesel fuel."

"It won't be the same around here without you and Patty. You've both been damn nice to me."

"Bullshit." He grinned, and we walked down the steps side by side and stopped on the sidewalk.

"Okay," he said with great finality, "I'm out of here." We simultaneously put out our hands again and shook.

"You've got to get in touch when you're settled," I told him. "I won't know where you'll be." We were stepping apart now. He was going up the street to his car, and I was going someplace but not the same direction.

"Patty will be talking to the gang," he said over his shoulder. "You'll know where we are." We were many paces apart now.

"Be cool!" I yelled.

"Take it easy, soldier!" he yelled back, and as if on cue, we raised the peace sign to each other.

I walked down toward the student union and, a moment later, heard the sharp rap of Pete's GTO as it started. The sound mellowed back down and then fluctuated as he worked the clutch, getting out of his parking space. He drove up the street, and the purr of the engine faded as he passed through the intersection where I had seen Olivia back in September.

The student union was always busiest just before noon, so when I saw the line for grill orders, I decided on a cold sandwich from a vending machine. All the tables were taken. The fraternities were at their usual tables, building pyramids out of dirty dishes and catapulting food at one another with forks.

I got a bologna sandwich with wilted lettuce and a paper cup of Coke from the machines and went into the game room. None of the guys I played pool with were there. I set the Coke on a windowsill and ate the sandwich while I stood and watched some guys shoot pool.

As I looked back into the cafeteria, it occurred to me that I didn't know where Robert ate lunch. He wasn't back at the apartment for lunch with any consistency, and though I did see him eating at the union sometimes, it wasn't at normal lunchtimes.

I went to the library after my afternoon class, not to study but to check the national weather in the *New York Times*. The periodicals section of the library was a comfortable escape from the seriousness of the rest of the library, though I felt guilty when I sat in the comfortable chairs and read magazines for pleasure.

I took Monday's *Times* from the rack where it hung on a blond birch rod. The rod annoyed me, since it made it awkward to sit and read the paper. Reading a day-old paper also annoyed me but not enough to put it back and look at the thin local paper. The weather map showed clear weather behind the front that was at that moment dumping rain on us. With luck, Pete, heading west, would be out of the rain in five to six hours. The map showed clear weather across the plains and all the way to the West Coast. I was encouraged and happy for them. They had hit a seam in the weather, and if they hurried, they would have an easy trip.

A front page headline read *U.S. Study Scores Chicago Violence as a "Police Riot."* The story discussed investigation of the riots at the Democratic convention in August. But it didn't generate any sympathy in me for the kids that had gotten their heads busted. They wanted the war to end so they wouldn't have their comfy lives upset.

The usual Vietnam story described a firefight close to Saigon. Supposedly, forty-eight VC were whacked. I highly doubted that they had been able to neatly line up forty-eight dead gooks for an accurate count. The paper made war sound so orderly and accurate. Shit, probably no one knew anything for sure. And the reporter sure as hell wasn't there. The time we were ambushed, it was all a confused mess. The Paris peace talks were also in the headlines.

After I put the paper back, I managed a couple of hours of reasonably concentrated study at the library and then walked back to the apartment. The rain had stopped for the moment.

Robert got back to the apartment just after nine that evening. *The Mod Squad* had just started, and I was sprawled out on the couch. We exchanged greetings as he walked through to dump his books in the bedroom and go to the kitchen. A commercial break came on, so I joined him and got a bowl of cornflakes. "Say," I said to him, "where do you eat lunch? I don't see you here or at the Hideout."

"Lunch? I hardly ever eat lunch. This is lunch and dinner both." He was busy filling a pot with water to boil for spaghetti. "Did I tell you Charlie and Dave want to have another party here Saturday night?" He opened a can of tomato paste to make sauce for his spaghetti. "Ellen and Fran will be coming too."

"Fine," I said. "But Natalie and I won't be here until later. Natalie wants to go to the *Messiah* concert."

"Oh yeah!" He turned from the stove to look at me. "Rose Marie and I are going too."

"Do you think it's a conspiracy?" I asked, making a false scowl. "Girls trying to get some culture into us?"

"Maybe," he said, "but what the hell, it's a good program. I went one year, my sophomore year, and it was worth the time."

"What about Charlie and Dave?"

"I told them to come anytime. We can just leave the lights on and the door unlocked."

I didn't listen to what Robert said after that because I was thinking about his casual remark about having gone to the *Messiah* when he was a sophomore. When he was a sophomore, I was a stinking private in the army, the lowest scum on earth. The night he had gone to the *Messiah*, I was probably getting shit-faced at some bar just outside the gate at Fort Leonard Wood, if I were lucky and not sitting broke in the barracks.

But now I was a big-time sophomore myself. I snapped out of my trance. "So who did you take to the *Messiah* that time?"

"There was just a bunch of us, and yes, Rose Marie was with us." He sounded slightly sarcastic, his response to my implication that he had liked Rose Marie for years.

WEDNESDAY, DECEMBER 4

It was Wednesday, and I was still depressed by Pete's leaving. Another major irritant was a political science test I got back that morning. Getting a test back was like waiting for an electric shock. Some professors were real asses about it and posted names with grades outside their office or put the grade on the front of the blue book and left them in a pile for everyone to sort through and see other people's grade. This professor at least put the grade on the inside cover, giving us some privacy, but he still left us dig through a pile of blue books after class.

I didn't open my book until I was outside. Then I flicked it open as I walked along. It was a C-. A cold chill passed through me. I thought I had done better. A string of comments was scribbled next to the grade, but I didn't want to read them right now. Normally, I went directly from political science to the Hideout for coffee. I needed the coffee today, but I was in no mood for the Hideout's happy atmosphere. Instead, I went to the front of the library, where there were heavy benches set behind the columns that lined the front portico. The benches were set far enough back to be out of the weather, and so I had a private place to look at my test and read all the comments.

The bench was cold on my butt, so I wouldn't be there long. I opened the blue book again and read the comments beside the grade. In handwriting not much better than mine, the professor complained about my handwriting. He went on to chastise me for poor spelling and punctuation, all of which made it hard for him to understand the ideas in my essay. Reading such criticism like reading someone's description of you naked, it was that intensely private. This description of me had shown me to be inferior.

But I must have communicated something in the test because the final scrawl acknowledged that I had established a position on the subject at issue and supported it with discernible, although weak, arguments. I had heard these comments before. I was getting tired of the routine.

A C- was no improvement over my midterm grade. But what did it matter? Even if I had improved to a 4.0 grade average, what good would it do me? None of the classes I was taking were preparing me for a job. Yeah, I thought, Pete had made some good points about school being a waste.

And I had to be thinking about a major soon. Theoretically, I should have a career in mind before I chose a major. The army had been a start to a career. I had learned the organization and performed well. The army wasn't ideal, but I had been a success, even if I hadn't enjoyed it. Who enjoyed work anyway? My butt was numb by now from sitting on the cold bench, so I got up and went to the student union for coffee.

Even though the union was just as crowded and noisy as the day before, I needed coffee. Rather than get a quick cup from the machine, today I waited in line for the brewed coffee. Then a doughnut covered in powdered sugar called my name as I slid my tray along the cafeteria line, so I put it on my tray.

By a stroke of luck, a small table by the window became empty just as I was looking for someplace to sit. I sat down. Gazing around the cafeteria, I was struck by how different it was from an army mess hall. There had been times in training when the company was behind schedule and we didn't have time to eat. Drill sergeants herded us through the mess line and told us to go directly to the garbage cans and scrape our trays into them. We ate what we could between having the food slopped on the tray and dumping what we couldn't eat. It turned into fun for a couple of minutes. We made barnyard noises at each other until a drill sergeant hollered at us to shut up.

In many ways, Vietnam had been much more tolerable than being in training. Life in a combat zone wasn't nearly as bad is it might have been. I never had to salute an officer, polish boots, or do KP. Maybe I'd been lucky, but everyone too got along reasonably well, no matter what rank you were. Being a combat engineer was like working on a big construction job with the added excitement that you might be blown away any moment, day or night. There was also the bonus of having a weapon with you at all times. I had carried my weapon constantly while on a mine sweep and kept it close at hand when doing manual work on a road. At night, my rifle was within arm's reach along with a bandolier of extra magazines.

I ate the doughnut without tasting it and drank the coffee. Finally, I gave up daydreaming and left the cafeteria, stopping in front of the activities bulletin board before I left the building. A large poster promoted the *Messiah*. The performance would begin at 7:30 p.m. The poster also gave a brief description of the Oratorio Chorus and Orchestra. Both college students and local singers and musicians participated in the production, which was staged by the music department. The college and civic groups had been presenting the *Messiah* together for years, I saw; this was the forty-second presentation. Two soloists who had significant professional opera experience were to perform. It occurred to me that I should drink some coffee before the concert so I'd stay awake.

With the *Messiah* starting at seven thirty and hopefully ending about ten, I figured I might have two hours with Natalie at the apartment. That would be enough time to collect on her challenge about enjoying the performance. While walking back to the apartment, I gave some thought to somehow taking Natalie to dinner before the performance. Money wasn't a problem at that point in the month, but it was so awkward to get places without a car that I dropped the idea.

THURSDAY, DECEMBER 5

Thursday morning, I woke up mad as hell. Twice during the night, I had been yanked awake by intense dreams about the army and Vietnam. I was angry because I had deliberately avoided anything like news broadcasts or war stories that might tweak my mind and stimulate a dream. The worst thing I'd done all day was comparing mess halls to the college cafeteria. Then I remembered I'd read a newspaper story about Vietnam too. But still, that shouldn't have set me off. The dreams weren't my fault.

Being angry wasn't enough. I had to find out what was causing the dreams. I had thought about my subconscious, what I called my shadow self, but hadn't done any research. Maybe the library and campus bookstore had books on psychology that would give me some answers.

The weather that morning was cold and clear. The winter solstice, the shortest day of the year, was only a few weeks away, so the sun had only just risen above the horizon. The chill air and sunshine brightened my mood as I walked to class, and I was able to think about my dreams analytically.

One of the dreams from the night before had been another repeat of the one where I was lost or left behind in Vietnam. The details were different, but the feeling was the same. In this dream, I was in a helicopter as it made a hard landing against the side of a steep hill. The rotor dug in and thrashed the rack until it stopped. I got out of the wreck and stood in deep grass looking across a foggy valley, and I knew I was alone. Panic built as I tried to think how to find other

GIs. Still dreaming, I began to deny the situation and told myself to wake up, which I did.

It was strange that I'd had such a clear and powerful dream about a situation and fear I had never experienced. It occurred to me that the dreams might be some sort of crossover from another GI, like extrasensory perception. I even wondered if I were having a spiritual or religious experience. Maybe I was taking a trip to my own *Twilight Zone*.

The TV program was one of my favorites, but I didn't take seriously the premise of phenomena beyond rational explanation. However, I could not ignore the possibility if I were going to research the cause of my dreams thoroughly.

I had worked myself back into a fret by the time I reached the English department building. Rather than go directly up the steps to my American lit class, I loitered around in front of the building to wait for Natalie. The thin wisps of clouds on the eastern horizon were painted pink and red by the rising sun. Seeing this reminded me of the saying, "Red sky in the morning, sailor take warning."

While I was looking at the sky, Natalie came out of the crowd and said, "Have you decided to go in or not?"

I turned quickly to the sound of her happy voice. Seeing her reminded me of the time I'd met her on her way to church the first week of October. The morning light brought out streaks of fire in her strawberry blond hair. No makeup spoiled her pale cheeks or masked the expression of her eyes. Just moments before, I had been thinking of mystical powers, and suddenly, I was presented with the most mystical of powers.

"Hi," was all I said. I fell into step beside her and walked up the steps, and we went into class.

My battle to stay awake began as soon as I sat down. My struggle gave me an appreciation of sleep deprivation as an effective torture technique. My eyes fluttered, but I didn't dare blink because once my eyes closed, they wouldn't open again. To stay awake, I repeatedly shifted around in my chair and tapped my hand with the point of my pen, giving myself some mild discomfort. Then, as if in slow motion, the professor walked to the big wood-framed windows, opened one a few inches, and then moved to the next and opened it too. Then he turned to the class and said, "If anyone is cold or is having trouble staying awake, please stand at the back of the room." As the room cooled, the fog lifted from my mind, and I was able to understand the lecture.

The professor, Dr. Fisher—or The Fish, as the students had nicknamed him—was a short balding man in his mid-fifties. He consistently wore a tweed jacket and a bowtie. The jackets varied, but the tie was always the same. I suspected the tie represented his school colors. Thankfully, Dr. Fisher talked with a lively enthusiasm that wasn't consistent with his stodgy appearance. Students liked him.

Today he was going on about how the characters in *Moby-Dick* were bound by superstition and myth. He paced back and forth in front of the class, reciting a list of the prophetic omens used by Melville to build tension and anticipation in the story. "Ms. Lane," he called out, facing the blackboard, "which of these premonitions did you find the most effective?"

Ms. Lane was an English major and Fisher's favorite person to call on for a response. "Ahab's dream about a hearse and Fedallah's interpretation," she responded. "The dream teases the reader by giving some clues but not enough to ruin the story."

Dr. Fisher went on to elaborate on Ahab's dream, but I shut my mind to the discussion. I didn't want to hear about prophetic dreams. Literature was a wonderful escape, like a window into other times and into an author's mind, but it was fiction. It occurred to me that Natalie might have studied psychology or another subject that would give a factual explanation to dreams. I decided it was reason enough to ask her to have coffee.

"I had a terrible time staying awake in there," I told her as soon as we had cleared the building. "How would you like to join me for a wake-up cup of coffee?" Foolishly, I took even the simplest invitation to her as a test of myself. As soon as I asked her, I was afraid she would say no.

She didn't say no but didn't say yes either. "How about coming over to the newspaper office?" she replied. "We have a coffeemaker there. It's drinkable if it's fresh."

My answer came quickly. "No, I'd rather not." I tried not to sound too insistent. "I have a question to ask you, but it can wait."

"Oh well, in that case, sure," she said. "The coffee is better at the Hideout anyway."

I quickly realized I had better qualify my mystery question.

"Thanks," I said politely. "I want to know how psychic you are."

"Psychic? Well, not very. I didn't know you wanted to know."

We exchanged smiles and talked about other things as we made our way to the student union. At the Hideout, Natalie stood watching for a table to open up while I got the coffee. When she spotted a table in the middle of the room, we sat there. It wasn't a prime table, but then the conversation wouldn't be serious.

"Well, as I said," Natalie reopened the conversation, "I'm not very psychic."

"That's fine," I responded. "'Psychic' isn't the right word anyway. Have you ever studied psychology?"

"Psychology? You mean like psychiatrists and lying on the couch and all that?"

"Right, but not the abnormal stuff. Just general psychology."

"I had a class in sociology in high school, but that's different, so . . . no, I've never studied it. I've read articles here and there though. What did you want to know?"

I was wondering how much I wanted to reveal. "Oh . . . whatever I could find out about what stimulates people's dreams."

"I've read magazine articles. Mostly about Freud and Jung." It was obvious from the expression on her face and her cautious tone of voice that the conversation wasn't going well. It was a silly idea to think she would be able to help me. If I kept asking questions, she'd think I was nuts.

"Well," I said, "I might dig into the subject some. People's behavior must be predictable to a degree if you know what to look for. Like the omens in *Moby-Dick*."

"You're talking science. *Moby-Dick* dealt with superstition."

"Right, but sometimes superstitions originate in fact." It was time to change the subject. "How long do you think it will take Pete and Patty to get to San Francisco?"

"A week, I bet. My family took a vacation to Mount Rushmore when I was in sixth grade, and that took forever."

As if her mentioning family was cue, the jukebox began playing Bing Crosby's "I'm Dreaming of a White Christmas."

"Oh, listen to that! That's the first I've heard that song this year. Isn't it wonderful?" She hummed along softly.

A strange feeling came over me as I listened to the song. For a moment, I dreaded the thought of Christmas coming. It was as if being in Vietnam the previous Christmas made me unworthy of this Christmas. Christmas had lost its magic.

As we left the student union, we passed the activities bulletin board, just as I had the day before. "Shall I stop by at seven on Saturday?" I asked her. "I'm assuming you still want to go to the *Messiah*." I put a negative inflection to my voice.

She gave me a funny look.

"Well, it won't be very good, you know. But we can still go."

That's when she caught on to my negative tone. "I know you don't care for singing, and most likely, you won't like it. But as I said, I'll make it up to you." We exchanged smiles and went our separate ways.

That afternoon, after class, I followed through on my plan to do some psychological research. My urgency to explain my dreams had dissipated some, but I had to follow through. It was easy to find books on the subject in the library, but it was much harder to make any sense out of them. The first two books I tried were obviously textbooks for medical students. The authors plunged right into the subject without a warm-up.

I pushed the second book to the center of the library table. Leaving my hand on the book, I looked up at the ceiling and said in a soft voice, "Dope." I should have started with an encyclopedia.

Finding what I wanted in the encyclopedia was an unexpected trip through a maze. There wasn't a consolidated entry for "psychology" in the *Encyclopedia Britannica* but rather a list of disciplines. Eventually, I had four volumes open and stacked in front of me as I followed all the references. There were many ways to describe being crazy.

I was distracted by the discussion of sex and the libido until a reference to a Greek king came up. My only sex problem was a lack of sex. Eventually, I found a reference to a book by Freud on interpreting dreams. Thinking I had hit the mother lode, I ran off to the card catalog, but then I discovered that the library didn't have the volume. This discouraged me. Returning to the *Britannica*, I eventually found a discussion of Freud's psychology of dreams.

Freud thought dreams were about releasing thoughts repressed while awake. That made sense and fit with my experience. Hell, why would I want to think about the war when I was awake and could control what I was thinking? The *Britannica* entry went on to say that conscious desires are played out in dreams, like having sex. Again, I thought this to be glaringly obvious. The encyclopedia lost me, though, when it discussed interpreting the meanings of dreams. Free association sounded like a bunch of mumbo-jumbo. If I dreamed about shooting gooks with a rifle, the rifle was a rifle, and I was shooting them because they were shooting at me.

I read a few paragraphs about a psychiatrist named Jung and then quit. I had burned up more than an hour and hadn't learned anything more than was common sense. It was a relief, though, that I hadn't read anything about clinical proof of dreams being prophetic.

After putting the encyclopedias back in the shelves, I went down to the periodicals section and again checked the weather for San Francisco in the *New York Times*. This time, I laid the paper open on a table. The temperatures in San Francisco were in the mid-fifties, and it was partly cloudy but no rain. The weather was clear from the Rockies to the

West Coast. Pete was having an easy trip, considering it was winter.

The *Times* had front page stories that made me think universities were falling apart all over the world, not that this was anything new. Black students had taken over the dean's office at Fordham. New York University students had demonstrated against the Vietnamese ambassador to the United Nations. An AWOL GI was holed up, seeking sanctuary, at Brandeis, and in Brussels, Belgian students were rioting and demanding a more influential student government and no campus visit by the king.

I couldn't help seeing the headlines about a fire fight the First Air Cavalry had gotten into near Cambodia. My eyes picked the numbers out of the print as I deliberately did not read the story. They had taken seventy-eight KIA, twenty-four out of one company alone. "Well," I muttered, "they stuck their peckers in a hornet's nest."

The library basement was warm and quiet in the late afternoon. No one had walked by me in five minutes. I folded my arms on the paper and laid my head on them. I was instantly asleep.

I woke up, feeling embarrassed. I looked around to see if anyone was watching me. No one was in sight, though I could hear coughing and throat clearing back in the stacks. I had slept about half an hour and still felt groggy. I wished I could just lie down on the floor, but I somehow found the energy to get up and walk back to the apartment.

FRIDAY, DECEMBER 6

Friday evening, I walked into the apartment around six to the smell of hamburgers frying. I became ravenous in seconds and went directly to the kitchen. Robert was there with Charlie and Dave. "So you guys finding out where the pots and pans are?"

Dave came back with, "Not really. Aren't you going to cook for everyone when we move in?"

"I'll gladly cook one meal for you. Afterward, if you can get off the toilet, you won't want me to cook another," I replied as I opened the refrigerator.

We exchanged a few more good-natured insults as I fried my own burger while the frying pan was still hot. They were sitting at the table, just about finished eating.

"You going to the game?" Robert asked as I put a lid on the frying pan to keep the grease spattering to a minimum.

"Oh right!" I exclaimed, sounding marginally more excited than I felt. "Season opener at home and against the archrival, how could I forget?"

"We could risk our reputations and let you join us," Charlie said. He liked trading insults more than Robert, Dave, or I did.

"Good point," I said. "I'll eat and join you later. That way, the Tri Sig girls won't see me with you when you walk in, and they'll still lust after your bodies." The Tri Sigma sorority was mostly knockout girls who dated jocks and majored in art.

The three of them finished and were talking about schoolwork as I took the burger out of the frying pan. We were out of hamburger rolls, so I used four slices of bread, two for each side of the burger. I opened a beer and, rather than crowd in at the table, stood leaning back against the sink.

The three of them got up a minute later, made some comments to me, and walked out to go to the game. As I watched them leave, an odd sensation struck me. I felt separate and detached from them, as though they were characters in a movie I was watching. Then I wondered which of the four of us would be the first to die. It was a morbid thought, and I felt guilty for thinking it. Besides, I was the most likely to die first, and what of it?

I sat down at the table, turned on my radio, and picked up a copy of the student newspaper one of them had left behind. Natalie hadn't mentioned having a story, but I leafed through the paper to make sure. The lead story was about the resolution of support for worldwide student causes. The story included the full text of the resolution. It was short and innocuous: *The students of Middlesex College support the world's students in their struggle for equality, justice and peace.*

I couldn't see how anyone could object to such a vague statement, but the story quoted students who said the resolution condoned criminal behavior and anarchy. I didn't read the whole story.

There was a story on the sports page previewing the night's basketball game. "Roundball" was the biggest sport on campus, and Middlesex teams had made playoff tournaments for the past six years. The newspaper story predicted a close game and urged a big student turn out in support of the team.

Then a story on page 5 of the six-page paper caught my eye. The story was four inches long at the bottom right of the page. The headline read "Former Student Dies in Vietnam." I shouldn't have, but I read the story anyway.

The article said the guy's name was Thomas Redford. He had enlisted when he was a junior and had seven months left on a two-year hitch when he was wasted. I worked out the dates and figured he was a sophomore the year I was a freshman. After repeating the name to myself and thinking about it for a moment, I concluded I had not known him.

"This guy is unusual," I said to myself. He must have had school figured out if he had finished his junior year. It was unlikely he was drafted for poor grades like Pete and me, and the story specifically said he'd enlisted. What would motivate someone to jump school with one year left to enlist and get their shit blown away? The strongest possibility was that a girl had dumped him and he had done the old French Foreign Legion routine.

The story next said he was killed in Ta Nin, north of Saigon, of wounds suffered while in combat. The story didn't give his unit, but I guessed he was a grunt, but then he could have been an engineer. The story reminded me of the time my unit was mortared while we were eating breakfast. Would my obituary have said, "Died of wounds suffered while eating greasy eggs"?

Pushing the paper aside and finishing my beer, I wondered if the paper would have given this guy, Redford, a bigger story on the front page if he had been a graduate or in a fraternity.

It had been foolish of me even to read the story.

I stopped dillydallying around and left for the basketball game. From the number of students on the sidewalks, I judged that the field house was going to be crowded. There was a small crowd at the entrance, but it turned out not to be a ticket line. A group was parading around holding makeshift signs urging support for the resolution of student causes.

Inside the field house, the teams were finishing their warm-up drills. It was already stuffy in the gymnasium, which had the usual smell of locker room and hardwood floors. Members of the school band were also tuning up. I didn't see Robert and the others until Robert gave me a wave. I climbed up to them, the bleachers rattling at my every step.

Just before the game, an unusual parade came into the field house. The group of demonstrators that had been out front, about fifteen students, was escorted in by campus security and sat at the far end of one set of bleachers. Officer Cooper and one other campus cop sat below them.

The game began and went very well for Middlesex. The newspaper story about the game was wrong; it was going to be an easy win. My view of the cheerleaders wasn't good, but then the only good view was under their skirts.

During the first half, I spotted Natalie, Laura, and others in their circle of friends sitting across the floor from us. I hadn't seen Olivia, so I suspected she was on the same side as I was and hidden in the crowd. She wouldn't miss a popular event like this.

Just after the halftime horn blew and the crowd cheered the team into the locker room, the demonstrators got up and lined up at the edge of the court. The campus cop was stationed at the head of the line, and Officer Cooper was at the other end. The demonstrators began to chant "Support international students," "Support student power," "Support the resolution," "Support women's rights." They held up their signs, and the line began to move around the perimeter of the court. After an initial curious silence, the crowd began to give a mixed response, some cheers and a few laughs.

The marchers completed one lap of the court, but they didn't return to their seats. Instead, they started around again, and as they did, they switched signs. They had been holding two signs together, and now they swapped the one behind to the front. The new signs were mostly antiwar, with a few supporting women's liberation. They yelled chants to go with the new signs. "Stop the war!" "Make love not war!" "No nukes!" "Equal rights for women!" "End the draft!"

The odd spectacle turned semi-serious. There were immediate boos and yells from the section of the bleachers where the jock fraternities and ROTC guys sat. When the line of demonstrators passed in front of these guys, some popcorn and paper cups were thrown down on them. A marcher shouted back, "FTA, all the way," which was answered by "Commie punks" and a few bars of "God bless America." The security escorts immediately pushed the protesters along, and at the end of their second lap, they went directly out to the lobby.

A few minutes remained before the second half started, so I walked around to the other side to talk to Natalie and her friends. I sat down next to Laura. "Did you people know that was going to happen?" I asked. Natalie was on Laura's other side.

"Sure," Laura said. "They've been negotiating with the dean all week. It worked out great!" She sounded so satisfied she might have been a marcher herself.

"Who were they?"

Natalie leaned forward and answered across Laura. "They're what's left of the SDS."

"And I think they were terrific," Laura added. "There was no confrontation like on other campuses, and they worked within the rules."

"Well, I can't argue about that," I told her. "Considering how blasé this campus is, the popcorn throwing may be as violent as it gets."

Natalie leaned forward again. "Mike, would you help me out Monday at the student senate meeting? I want some pictures, but I'll be too busy taking notes."

She knew there was no way in hell I'd be at the meeting unless she asked me. But she was making an honest request, and I couldn't refuse.

"Sure," I responded. "I suppose it'll be a hectic meeting for you." My voice was flat but not negative, and I kept my facial expression neutral. I hoped.

"Great!" she said with a perky smile. "There is one thing. You'll have to use a camera with a flash, not the reflex."

"Okay. It'll be a good experience."

I went back around the court and rejoined Robert and the other guys for the second half of the game. Midway through the fourth quarter, Middlesex was so far ahead the second string was put in. The band played, and the cheerleaders clapped and jumped, and we won easily.

It was a relief to get back to the apartment that evening, kick off my shoes, and flop down on the couch. As Robert and the others bustled in the kitchen getting something to eat, I lay on the lumpy old couch and didn't even turn on a light or the TV. A lot had happened in one week. The demons were catching up, and there were fewer places to hide. I was running, but where to?

SATURDAY, DECEMBER 7

Saturday afternoon, I went downtown to buy a sweater. I didn't have a suit or sport coat, and I wanted to look at least somewhat dressed up for the concert. I went back to Stewart's of Middlesex and bought a maroon cardigan to go with a white shirt and black dress pants I already had. The sweater wasn't cheap, even on sale, but my VA check had come, and I had built up a little cushion, so I could afford it.

Holiday shoppers crowded the store, the same as the week before, and a long line of squirrelly kids and tired-looking adults snaked back from Santa Claus's throne up on the mezzanine.

After paying for the sweater, I continued walking around the store. This time, I was looking at things to buy other people. At least this year, I could do a little something for some people, regardless of how trivial. Most importantly, this year, I could kiss my mother and tell her "Merry Christmas."

Just as I had the week before, I walked past the perfume counter. The fragrance there was staggering, and I wondered how the salespeople could work there all day. I stopped and smelled the sample of Golden Autumn again. The store was busy, so no salesperson approached, and I put the bottle back down. There was a display of holiday corsages at the end of the perfume counter. The corsages were made of dried flowers, ribbon, and tiny Christmas ornaments. I bought one of them, and I hoped it would go with whatever Natalie was wearing that evening. The corsage temporarily appeased my conflict over a gift. I would reconsider the perfume again next week.

That evening, I was surprised by Natalie's reaction when I gave her the corsage. "Oh, it's lovely!" she burst out. "How sweet!" She held it up to her dress. "You're so thoughtful!" Then she gave me a quick peck on the cheek and went to a mirror. We were in the lounge of her dorm, so the other girls there came and complimented her.

I had expected her to be pleased with the corsage but not to make as big a fuss about it as she did, so I just watched from a distance as one of her friends helped her pin on the corsage. Natalie was wearing a knee-length dark blue satin dress with the zipper in the back. The sleeves were short, and the neckline was low but not daring. She appeared elegant though modest.

My interest in her clothes was purely analytical. I was calculating how to deal with the zipper and other obstacles. The situation could have been better, I thought, but I would be able to deal with what I saw.

She put on her coat, and we took the short walk to the fine arts building, where we found the town's genteel citizens crowding the lobby. Slow-moving bald-headed old men in black evening jackets escorted old matriarchs in fur coats. The younger professional couples mixed in and chatted respectfully with the old money. The college was an island of culture to the sophisticated townspeople.

The auditorium was nearly full, and since the seating wasn't reserved, we found seats near the back but in the middle. I noticed a few students in the crowd and eventually spotted Robert and Rose Marie, who had come earlier.

"I think this will be a pleasant evening," Natalie said after we had settled into our seats. "I'm going to escape into the music tonight. You won't mind if I seem far away will you?"

"No, not at all," I said. "Enjoy yourself."

"I need the time away," she said as she leaned slightly closer to me. "I'm not going to think about schoolwork, campus troubles, the war, famine—none of that. Just the music. My ears and mind belong to Handel for the next two hours."

To my relief, the two hours went faster than I had feared they would, and the music and voices engaged me more than I expected. Handel's inspiration was divine.

We met Robert and Rose Marie in the lobby during intermission. "Has he fallen asleep yet?" Robert asked Natalie.

"Nope!" she answered. "I think he's actually enjoying himself." She looked at me with raised eyebrows and a smile as she spoke.

"I'm fighting to remain conscious," I said. "Who knows how well I'll do in the second half?" I suppressed a smile.

The conductor had said at the beginning of the concert that the program would be shortened, and only selected movements from parts two and three were to be performed. That was lucky for me, since I did have to struggle to stay awake during the quieter parts after the intermission.

Timing was critical after the concert. Women's curfew was at normal time, midnight, which left us less than an hour and a half together. The same thought must have been on Robert's mind as he and I walked side by side as fast as Robert's handicap would permit. Natalie and Rose Marie walked behind us and talked about the performance. Only a few thin clouds blocked the stars that evening, and the moon was just a couple of nights past full. It was cold, well below freezing, and we all exhaled frosty plumes of air.

When we got back to the apartment, we were a pack of hungry wolves. Robert and I had done some grocery shopping that afternoon, however, so there were a couple of bags of potato chips, soda, and other snacks. We all piled into the kitchen and began to munch.

Dave and Ellen and Charlie and Fran were already in the living room when we arrived. They joined us in the kitchen with the snacks they had brought. My radio played the local rock station. The scene in the kitchen was enjoyable, but I had to approach Natalie as quickly as possible. When she left the kitchen for the bathroom, I came up with a scheme that was moderately subtle. I stood at the door of the kitchen, and when she came back down hall, I stopped her.

"Say, if I were a reporter on your paper and was writing a review of tonight's concert, I wouldn't be at all complimentary."

She feigned surprise. "I thought you enjoyed it!"

"No." I was trying to sound serious. "Not at all."

"Well . . . what can I do to make it up to you?"

"Okay. Well, uh, I don't like to collect my debts in public. Let's go down here and settle up."

I led her directly to my bedroom. The stigma of forbidden entrance had been broken by her previous visit. I didn't turn on a light. We stood in the dark behind the closed door and embraced. I moved my left arm around her and slid my hand up her back while my right hand settled on her left hip and our lips nervously explored each other's. She made a contented sigh, which encouraged me. I turned my hand slightly to the inside of her hip.

"Ah ha," she said, "what kind of shakedown is this?"

"A very pleasant one. Let me show you." We stepped to the bed and sat down. I kissed her again, and we lay back without resistance or hesitation. I rolled to the inside against the wall, and we faced each other lying on our sides. "Are you ticklish?" I asked her, hoping to disguise my true intent. Without waiting for an answer, I tickled her high on her ribs and under her arm.

She twisted and squirmed and hoarsely whispered, "Stop!"

I needed to set just the right tempo. If I went too fast, the entire effort would collapse in sudden indignation and insult. If I went too slowly, I would run out of time. My objective was to stimulate one of her three most sensitive spots.

Her neckline wasn't quite low enough, so I would need to get the zipper down about four or five inches to get a sleeve off her shoulder. I gave her a noisy kiss on the side of her neck that made her giggle while I sent my right hand around her back and flipped up the tiny tab of her zipper, unlocking it. The strain on the zipper from twisting and pulling on the dress might cause it to unzip by itself. At least I hoped so.

Such plans work well for a rational mind, but my power of reason was fading in the scent of her perfume, a lilac scent. We kissed, and I ran my fingers through her hair, pressing firmly and kneading, eliciting more contented tones from her. Her dress somehow came loose at the shoulder, and I was able to kiss her lower on her chest. "You're a mischievous boy," she said, and I assumed she knew her zipper was open.

"Just for you," I murmured, not slowing my pace. "Just for your enjoyment."

Working my hand into her bra from above would require a feat of contortion, since we were facing each other and on our sides. Rather than go to any exaggerated and likely alarming maneuvers, I simply curled my fingers in behind the bra and continued progressively downward stroking her with the backs of my fingers.

Her reaction was a low humming and the alternating squeezing and relaxing of her hand on my shoulder. Finally, my fingers touched her erect nipple. She drew a deep breath and twisted like she'd been shocked. I moved my hand away but then brought it back, eliciting another sigh of pleasure.

"Unbelievable," she said in a strained whisper. To my amazement, she pulled up her knee and swung it on top of my hip, laying her leg on top of mine. I hadn't intended to press beyond what I had already accomplished, but I could quickly change my plan. I knew where the apex of her sensitivity was and how to stimulate her to the point of losing herself. The question was, how willing was she?

Again, I dipped my hand inside her bra and, at the same time, gave her a deep kiss while, as subtly as possible, moving my leg further between hers. Each stroke of my hand and fingers encouraged her to move, and as we moved together, I raised my knee. She shivered and pulled away slightly when my knee made full contact with her, but she didn't pull her leg back. In a moment, I let my knee press against her again, and she answered with a thrust of her own.

I slid my hand down between us and over my knee. Then I raised the knuckle of my index finger. My next contact was precise, and Natalie drew a sharp deep breath. I applied gentle pressure with a fluttering movement from side to side.

Natalie's breathing quickened. Then she abruptly grabbed my shoulders and shoved me away, only to tumble backward off the bed herself.

I was stunned. Had the bed collapsed? I rolled to the edge and reached down. "Are you all right?"

"Yes, yes, I'm okay," she replied in the strained, breathless voice. I was confused.

The bed hadn't broken. Like a buffoon, I pressed for some explanation. "Are you feeling okay?"

"Yes, yes, I'm fine."

I didn't respond, and my ignorant silence prompted her to blurt out, "Look, I just didn't want to do that."

"Oh," I said. "Sorry. You fooled me."

She was standing up now and straightening her clothes. She managed to reach the zipper herself and pulled it up. "Let's get some air," she said. "And something to drink."

I turned on a light, which made us both squint, and before we left the room, Natalie checked her clothes. We didn't say anything to each other. No one was in the kitchen. Luckily, there was ice left, and I got us each a cold drink.

Natalie looked at her watch and said, "That's good. I thought it was later." It was eleven forty, and we would make her curfew with no trouble.

To make conversation and relieve the strain between us, I said, "Women's hours are ridiculous. No wonder students are rebellious." She made a curt but polite response. The conversation was artificial. Silently, we put on our jackets and walked out through the living room. No lights were on. Charlie and Dave and their dates had already left, and Robert and Rose Marie were wrapped up on the couch. We went directly out into the winter night.

We walked a quarter of the way to her dorm in silence before I thought of something to say. When I did speak, it sounded contrived. "Are you warm enough?"

"Yes. I'm fine. It's just a short walk, and there's no wind."

I considered talking about Christmas, but I didn't really have anything to say. It wouldn't be fair to talk about a happy time when neither of us was happy. The further we walked, the more frustrated I felt. Fortunately, my frustration didn't turn to anger. I fell into depression instead. Natalie said nothing.

As we approached her dorm, I wondered how the hell I was going to say good night. Shake hands? I made no effort to lead her off into the shadows but walked with her up the steps to the well-lit porch. She stepped to one side of the door, turned, and gave me a serious look like she knew exactly what she was going to say.

"Mike," she said. Then she paused and looked away. When she continued, she looked down, not at me. "Life has been extremely hectic this fall. I need time to think." She looked up at me now. "I hope you understand."

I didn't say anything but simply shrugged.

When she realized I wasn't going to speak, she tried to change the mood. She smiled broadly. "Thanks again for the corsage! It was very sweet and thoughtful of you."

She popped up to me and gave me a quick kiss on the cheek. I didn't lean down to accept the kiss. When she stepped back, I did too, putting even more distance between us. "Okay, well, good night," I said. Then I turned and started down the stone steps.

"Mike!" she called out. "Don't forget Monday night. If you can make it . . ." Her voice trailed off.

I turned. "Yeah, right. I'll be there," I said as I raised a hand in acknowledgment and went on down the steps.

So off into the dark I walked as always, wishing I had my weapon with me. Here I was, repeating a scene from two and a half years before. At least Olivia had given me signals for days, maybe weeks, before dumping me, signals I had refused to recognize. This time, Natalie was warm one moment and jumping out of bed the next. "Time to think." What the hell did she mean by that? And why did she still want me to help her Monday?

WEEK 12

DECEMBER 8, 1968–DECEMBER 14, 1968

MONDAY, DECEMBER 9

Monday started around 4:00 a.m. when, for no reason at all, I just woke up. There was no dream this time, I just woke up. After half an hour of lying in bed with my mind racing from thoughts of Pete, Natalie, school, the army, my parents, and back to Pete, I got up and boiled a pot of water for oatmeal. The kitchen was cold, so I lit the oven and then left the oven door open. I only had on a pair of camouflage green underwear and a pair of socks, so I went back to the bedroom and pulled a blanket off the bed and then sat at the kitchen table wrapped up like an Indian chief. I read my *Hornblower* book while I ate the oatmeal. When I'd finished, I considered going back to bed, but since the kitchen was warm now and my bed would be cold, I decided to stay in the kitchen. I folded my arms on the table and put my head down, hoping I'd fall asleep the way I had in the library. It was no use. My mind was still galloping.

Natalie hadn't flatly told me she didn't want to date me. That much, I thought, I understood. But I was confused because everything had seemed fine until she'd jumped off the bed. I concluded that it was my fault. I knew too much and had pushed her too far. I was a product of my experiences of war and debauchery.

But then, I thought, there was the possibility she had fallen for one of those rich, pompous big shots, like the one she had gone to homecoming with, and she was using my aggressive behavior as an excuse to end our relationship.

If my behavior was the cause, I told myself, I could apologize to her, change my behavior, and even take more interest in campus activities. If I decided Natalie was worth the risk, I could change. But I was shit out of luck if she had simply decided another guy had superior qualifications.

Finally, I just came to the conclusion that the mystery was beyond my power to solve. The best action I could take was to move on. There were girls taking the birth control pill who would jump in bed with me, not out of bed. I would be better off if women only meant sex to me.

Before the sun rose that morning, God took mercy on me and put me to sleep at the kitchen table.

A couple of hours later, my peaceful dreamless sleep was broken by Robert shouting into the kitchen, "Hey! Don't you have a nine-o-clock class?" He was standing in the kitchen door. "It's eight forty. I'm leaving."

Then he felt the heat and came into the kitchen. "What the hell are you trying to do?" he asked. "Bake yourself or burn the house down?" He slammed the oven door shut and turned off the gas. He didn't wait for the answer but bolted down the hall and out the door, his limp making the usual odd rhythm when he walked fast.

I spent the rest of the day running late. After one class, I slipped on wet grass as I was cutting between sidewalks, muddying my hands and soaking one leg of my pants. Recovering from that fall made me late for my next class.

Later, during lunch, I discovered that my watch had stopped, but luckily, I wasn't late for my one-o-clock geology lecture.

That evening at the apartment, I hurried through my dinner and left early for the student senate meeting. The campus clock tower chimes rang six fifteen as I walked into the student union. Although it was dark, it was a busy time on campus, with people walking to and from the dining halls. When I walked into the game room, I panicked for a moment, thinking the meeting had already begun. Nearly all the chairs that had been set out were occupied, even though the table, chairs, and lectern for the senate members were still being set up. With that large a crowd, I knew I was in for a tough night. I noticed a window that was open a crack and went over to it and opened it a bit more. Then I scanned the room for Natalie. After circling the floor and not seeing her, I waited near the entrance she was most likely to come through.

In a moment, a gaggle of student senators filed in. I realized they must have met in their office next to the newspaper office before coming to the meeting. I wondered if the senators carried knives and, if so, which of them was Brutus.

Natalie and other newspaper staff members came along after the senators. She stepped up to me and said, "I'm glad to see you! This will be a big help."

A range finder camera with a flash unit attached hung by its strap from her shoulder. She also carried a steno notepad and her purse. I held the notepad and camera as she dug flashbulbs out of her purse. "It's the newspaper's camera," she said, "and I could only find ten bulbs."

"Well, that should be enough," I replied. "I'll be able to get all the senators and a few of the crowd."

She gave me quick instructions on how to operate the camera and then said, "I'll be getting interviewers after the meeting, but you can give me the camera then. I have to lock it up in the office."

"Fine," I said. "We'll see how it goes."

"Okay, I'll see you after. I want to get whatever I can before the meeting starts." She went on into the meeting.

I walked around the room judging from what angles I could get the best pictures then took the last empty folding chair, folded it, and put it in a far corner where I could get it later if I wanted to stand on it for a better view. Soon, the room was clearly divided between the pro-resolution and anti-resolution students. The same fraternities that had booed the marchers at the ballgame sat together on one side of the central aisle. The scholarly fraternities and sororities and others favoring the resolution grouped together on the other side of the aisle. There were slightly more pro-resolution people, although it was hard to tell.

The student body president, a tall guy with wavy hair from one of the jock fraternities, called the meeting to order and explained that this wasn't a normal senate meeting. "This is a public hearing," he said, "an open forum for the senate to hear from the student body." His tone was serious. "We have set up a microphone at the back of the room." He pointed to it. "We will alternate speakers, a pro-resolution speaker followed by a speaker opposed. Two ushers will control the speaking sequence. Please be courteous to them and the other speakers." He paused a moment and continued. "Now this is important." He paused again. "So as many people as possible may speak, each speaker will be strictly limited to ninety seconds. Take a moment before you speak to make notes so you use your time wisely." He paused again. "Now I will read the resolution." When he finished, applause rippled through the audience, mainly from the pro-resolution side of the room.

I had taken a picture of the senators seated at their table and one of the president while he was speaking, and then I went back by the microphone. All the chairs were filled, and there were people standing in the back of the room. There were faculty members there too, my political science professor being one of them. People who wanted to speak began to shuffle into two lines as a guy and girl acting as ushers directed them into place.

The first speaker stood at the microphone. After the usual squeaks and whistles came out of the sound system, she addressed the assembly. "I represent many campus women tonight when I suggest the following modification to the resolution. We feel the resolution should read *struggle for equality for man and for woman*. Putting those words into the resolution would specifically note women's struggle for equality." She paused and shuffled her notes. "Now I wish to make a personal comment to all my fellow students. We are privileged to be students at this point in history—1968 has been the pivotal year. Students have asserted themselves. If we're old enough to be conscripted to die for our country, then we're old enough to participate in governing our country." Applause began, but she raised a hand and quickly continued. "Each of us has a personal decision to make. So make the decision you will be proud of in the future when you tell your children and others about 1968. Thank you." Strong applause from both sides of the room lasted until the president called order.

The room had become stuffy, prompting people to take off their coats and jackets and drape them over the backs of their chairs. I moved among the people in the back of the room, positioning myself so I could get a view down the length of the line of speakers. I took a couple of pictures.

The next speaker was a tall guy wearing his fraternity jacket. As soon as he reached the microphone, he received cheers from a cluster of his brothers. "I believe this resolution condones criminal behavior," he said in a firm voice as he read from an open the spiral notebook. "By simply saying we support the efforts of students without being specific about what efforts we do or don't support, we support criminal actions. We must not support actions like the French students rioting last spring that tore up their city. Those French students randomly destroyed millions of dollars of private property. I urge the senate to insert words to the effect that we support only lawful protests. The resolution must support law and order."

The speaker received cheers, shouts of approval, and applause from one side of the room. It occurred to me that an atmosphere of a sporting event had taken hold.

I recognized the third speaker. He was a senior named David Vaughan, a member of the campus intellectual brain trust. He had been in the demonstration at the basketball game, so I assumed he was a member of the SDS. I remembered him from my freshman year, when he was elected to represent the freshmen in the student senate. He had been an organizer from the start.

Vaughan began at a rapid pace in a calm voice. "I'm ashamed of my school. This resolution requires no debate. This is a simple, mild statement of support for students who have risked injury and imprisonment to oppose oppressive régimes. These Czech, French, Mexican, Spanish, and our fellow American students have given a noble character to this year. History will record their efforts for posterity." His voice was becoming shrill. "I predict that if the senate doesn't support this resolution, the students will. A petition will be circulated among the students, and more importantly, there will be public displays of support. These displays of support will make it dramatically clear that Middlesex students are not timid children to be manipulated by a fossilized administration."

With no hesitation, Vaughan suddenly changed the target of his attack. "The previous speaker is idealistic and naïve. It's impossible to change unjust laws while working within those laws." At this point, the student body president interrupted, saying the speaker was out of time, but his rant continued. "The wealthy ruling elite have constructed a network of unjust laws simply to maintain power. The distribution of wealth and power will never be changed by working within those laws."

The ushers came up and took the microphone away, but Vaughan stood his ground, still speaking. Applause and cheers came from the SDS contingent.

A muscular, crew-cut ROTC cadet officer came to the mike next. At least he wasn't in uniform. "My name is Lee Roberts," he said, "and I'm speaking for our campus ROTC." A loud cheer and encouraging grunts from his supporters drowned out his voice. After a moment, he continued. "This resolution sounds noble, but our enemies are not noble. They are patient and observant, and they're watching the antiwar movement. By passing this resolution, we will reinforce their conviction that the American people don't have the courage to stick it out. The enemy will fight harder and greatly increase our casualties. Simply put, this resolution endangers our troops. There are many former Middlesex students in Vietnam at this moment. These are people you have met, gone to class with, and watched play on our teams. I urge the senate and my fellow classmates not to support this resolution." Whistles and applause marked the end of his plea, but copying the SDS speaker's stunt, Roberts didn't give up the microphone. When the applause died down, he turned and told everyone what he thought of David Vaughan. Pointing at Vaughan, he shouted in a booming voice, "And I believe the anarchy the SDS supports makes them as great an enemy of our Middlesex alumni as they face on the battlefield. Our Middlesex soldiers would consider that individual as dangerous as a Viet Cong general."

Pandemonium broke out. Supporters of each antagonist jumped out of their seats and started shouting at each other. Vaughan confronted Roberts, face to face, reaching for the microphone and bellowing, "You're full of shit! You're just a play soldier. How do you know what the troops in Vietnam feel? You've never been there!"

Now Vaughan and Roberts both had their hands on the microphone, and their faces were just inches apart. I had moved in and taken two pictures, cursing the flashbulbs as I fumbled to pop in a new one. It wasn't as bad as reloading my rifle while under fire, but the time it took made me anxious.

Roberts yanked at the microphone and shouted back at Vaughan, "That's a laugh! You don't know anything about the military, let alone Vietnam."

I'd move moved behind Roberts by this time, facing Vaughan. I was ready to take a picture of Vaughan's response when he suddenly looked straight at me.

"Okay," he said, "let's ask someone who really knows about the war. Let's find out what a real veteran thinks." Vaughan moved past his adversary and stepped up to me. "You! You're a vet. I've seen you in your army jacket. Were you in Vietnam?"

I didn't answer but lowered the camera and backed away. My moving away from him seemed to encourage him. He stepped right up to me and demanded an answer. "Come on! Were you in Vietnam?"

The crowd behind me stopped me from moving back any further, and I had to stand in the circle of noise and look at Vaughan's angry face. "Yeah, I was there, but leave me out of this!"

"Leave you out? You're the warrior he wants to be." Vaughan pointed at Roberts. "Tell us what you think of this resolution."

Later, I remembered that it was hot in the room, and I felt like I was in one of my dreams, but I couldn't wake myself. I let go of the camera, and it hung from my shoulder by its strap, which left my hands free. "I'm not talking about any of this," I said as assertively as I could. "Get away from me!"

"What?" Vaughan shouted. "What about the killing you did? Aren't you proud of killing women and children? Tell us what you think of the resolution." He was right on top of me. He jabbed the microphone up into my face. He had gotten too close, and the mike hit me in the nose.

The hard metal object striking me blanked out my mind and ignited an eruption of energy. Both my arms shot out, and my open hands slapped him flat on his chest. My fingers curled, gathering wads of his jacket. I yanked him toward me with so much force that I saw his head snap backward in reaction. My arms pulled him in tight. Vaughan's face, shocked expression and all, was an inch from mine. Then my arms released their energy, and I flung him backward. His head fell forward, and the chain he had around his neck hit his mouth, and he went backward into the crowd. As he fell backward, he stumbled on someone's foot and fell on his ass.

Only then did I become aware of the shouting, squealing, and cursing going on around me. Luckily for me, we were among the ROTC group, and I also heard laughs and cheers.

Vaughan sat flat on the floor, looking up, his eyes wide and his mouth open. Then his mouth began to work even harder than before. "See? See? The military makes them crazy. We've got to do something!" He scrambled to his feet.

I stood there long enough to see him get up and to know he wasn't going to try to be a hero and come back at me. When Vaughan realized he was in the wrong crowd, he began shuffling backward toward his own people while still shouting. I let the crowd fill in around me and immediately left the area.

I knew there would be consequences, even though I hadn't seen Officer Cooper or any of his boys that evening. I wanted to leave immediately, except I had to return the camera to Natalie.

As the student senate president called for order and the buzz from the crowd started to quiet down, I circled to the front of the room. Natalie was standing near the senators' table. "Natalie!" I called to her. She turned to me, her mouth open, but I spoke again before she could say anything. "Would you take the camera now? I've used all the flashbulbs. I need to get out of this madhouse."

"What happened back there?" She took the camera.

"Just a little pushing, that's all." I began stepping away from her.

"Was it you he was taunting?"

"Yeah. But it was no big deal. Hey, I've got to go." I could see her silent, empty look as I left.

I forced myself to walk at a normal pace as I went back through the cafeteria and outside, finally free from the noise. The cold air enveloped me and gave me the same sensation I remembered from taking a swim in a chilly stream.

Now that Pete had gone, I had no place to go, except back to the apartment. As I walked along, my emotions alternated between satisfaction that I hadn't taken any crap and fearing I had become an uncontrollable street fighter. When I got back to the apartment, I was just disgusted with everything, both the jerks on campus and myself for getting involved with them and losing my cool.

The apartment was empty. Robert was probably at the physics lab, his second home. I turned on the TV and watched *Gomer Pyle* for no more than two seconds before clicking the knob on to the *Merv Griffin Show* which I watched for five seconds before turning the TV off.

An unusual urge came over me. I wanted to study. It was the best way to forget what had happened. So I spread books and papers out on the kitchen table and spent a good hour thinking about nothing but the work in front of me.

This interlude ended when I got hungry. For whatever reason, I decided to hard boil some eggs. While I was waiting for the water to boil, my mind wandered back to my problems. Since the dean of men had dragged me in because he suspected I had messed up Holden's car, he would certainly have me back on the carpet for this screw-up. Getting expelled might be a good thing. Who knew?

My mind continued to race in circles. If I left school, I still wouldn't follow Pete, but I wouldn't go back home either. Anyway, if I did ask my folks to come back home, they would threaten not to let me come back, though after a scolding, I would be welcome. If I did go back home, I might get some prestigious job, like pumping gas or being a janitor at my old high school. It wouldn't matter. Now that my perspective had changed, many things that had seemed immensely important didn't matter so much.

My self-absorbed thought was interrupted when I heard the front door bang and Robert came into the kitchen.

"Hey, is it true?" he said without even a greeting. "Did you get into a ruckus at the senate meeting?"

"My god!" I exclaimed. "Did the campus crier go around ringing a bell or something?" I turned back to the stove and picked up the pot and poured the water out and ran cold water over the eggs so I could begin peeling them.

"Well, something like that," Robert said as he opened the refrigerator. "Tommy Matson came into the lab and told us. He knew you were my roommate. What happened?"

"David Vaughan, the guy who's always been something in student government, well, now he's into the SDS, anyway, he and I got into a shoving match, and he ended up on his ass."

"What started it?" Robert asked as he slapped some bologna on bread.

"He was mouthing off about me being a killer." I concentrated on pealing my eggs.

"A killer?"

"In the army. I was a killer because I was in Vietnam. None of it matters. Let's just skip it." I had to change the subject. "What the hell do you and the others do over in that lab all these evenings? And don't tell me there are no women there."

"There aren't, except when they come over to get us out of the place."

We continued to make a mess of the kitchen as we talked. I steered the conversation away from anything school-related. There was a moon shot scheduled for the twenty-first of the month, just before Christmas, and I got Robert to explain why the mission wasn't going to land on the moon. Talking to Robert calmed me down as talking to him always did. Robert always showed up when I needed him the most.

Eventually, Robert went to bed, but I sat reading in the kitchen until I figured he was asleep, and then I went in the bedroom, took off my shoes, and lay down with my clothes on and wrapped the top blanket around myself. The next significant task of my day was trying to end it, trying to get to sleep.

It was difficult to be dishonest with myself in the dark. To leave school without finding what I was looking for would be a big disappointment. I was looking for a complete explanation of human behavior. I wasn't crazy. I felt I was actually making progress. Each class I took solved a separate and complete puzzle. The trick was seeing that each puzzle itself was a piece of the bigger human puzzle. The pieces all fit together, were related to one another. But this wasn't being taught. I had learned the relationships myself. I would be defeated and depressed if I had to leave school before finding the complete explanation.

I was still lying in the dark thinking these thoughts when I came to my senses. The reason I gave myself for wanting to stay in school sounded like a con from the school's admissions department. I was indeed crazy to think about human nature. I was giving myself a line of bullshit and, what's worse, believing it. It was human nature to try to blow someone's shit away before they blew you away. Human political nature created the conditions where thirteen- and fourteen-year-old girls lined the streets of Vietnam trying to sell themselves to GIs so they could get something to eat. And just as bad was the eighteen- and nineteen-year-old GIs spending their last dollar of military payment script to wear out those girls.

Human nature was a public that had grown oblivious to one hundred and more killed in action a week. It was the human traits of pride and arrogance that kept politicians from admitting a mistake and continuing to flush GIs down the toilet.

To hell with the Renaissance man. To hell with school.

TUESDAY, DECEMBER 10

As I crossed campus Tuesday morning, I watched well ahead on my route, since I expected Officer Cooper would be gunning for me. Cooper always wore a suit and a fedora hat, so he would be easy to spot in the stream of students. My luck held, though, and I made it to the classroom building without seeing him.

Natalie was standing beside the steps waiting for me. She had never done that before.

"How are you?" she asked. "Were you hurt? You should have told me what went on back there." She spoke rapidly, and I could hear the insistent tone to her voice.

"Nothing went on," I replied. "Just some pushing and shoving." If she wanted details for a newspaper story, she would have to get them from someone else.

She persisted. "The ROTC crowd said Vaughan hit you. Did he?"

We were pushing our way up the steps and into the building with what seemed like half the campus and everyone was in a rush. Instead of answering her questions, I asked one of my own. "Did campus security show up?"

"Yes," she said. "They asked questions and then stayed close to the microphone for the rest of the meeting." She paused. We were about to go in the classroom. "I'm worried you'll get into trouble because I asked you to help."

I didn't look at her. "You asked me to take pictures. The rest was my own doing."

We sat in our desks and joined the rest of the class in peeling our jackets off, opening notebooks, and squirming to get comfortable.

The class dragged. It seemed everyone was either asleep or almost asleep or high on caffeine and unable to sit still. As I sat there, I thought about how this was one of the classes I would miss if I were expelled. Literature was an escape, a time machine, a way of sharing experience I couldn't have myself. The next best thing to actually freezing your butt off in Alaska was to read Jack London.

After class, Natalie and I left the building together without speaking. She didn't say anything until we were out in the chill air and the crush of people around us had thinned. "The film should be developed by tomorrow. You'll have to come over to the office and see what you got. How did the camera work for you?"

Her mentioning the camera irritated me. The commotion of the meeting was the natural subject for us to talk about, but I was trying to forget the incident.

"I don't know," I said crisply. "Like you said, we haven't seen the pictures."

"I think they'll be okay."

We were at that point along the sidewalk where we would either go our own separate ways or go further together.

"Say," she said in a perkier tone, "how about coffee?" She had never been the one to suggest coffee before.

"No. I've got some studying to do. I'm way behind, and not studying last night didn't help."

What I said was true, of course, but it was some childish desire to be perverse that really motivated my response.

Anyway, she would only want to talk about the night before. She was on the newspaper staff. She wanted to gather material for a newspaper story.

"Oh okay." Her voice showed mild disappointment. "I've got work I should do too."

We said good-bye, and I crossed the street to the library. I was sure she was headed for the newspaper office.

Cooper had obviously looked up my class schedule. It could not have been a coincidence that he was standing in the lobby of the geology building when I walked in for my Tuesday afternoon lab. Fortunately, I saw him before he saw me, so I was able to look nonchalant when I walked up to him, stopped, and looked right at him.

"Yes, Mr. Collins," he said, "I do want to speak to you." I just nodded, and he went on. "Have you checked your campus mailbox?"

I was not in the mood for polite entry conversation. "So I suppose I'm off to the woodshed for another paddling by the dean?"

Cooper's face tightened, but he did not drop his congeniality act. "I'm going to talk to the dean later this afternoon," he said. "I'd like to hear what you have to say about last night."

People were pushing past us, rushing to lecture halls and labs, so we stepped out of the way, and I said my piece. "That loudmouth Vaughan got smart with me, and I pushed him off, and he fell on his butt."

"Specifics would help me," Cooper said with no expression to his face. "If you want help."

I took a deep breath and looked away. "Well, for one thing, he called me a baby killer, which I'm not. And he just kept coming at me, even when I backed off."

"Did he hit you?" Cooper was serious now.

"I was poked with something. Maybe it was as much an accident as anything else. It wasn't like a deliberate punch. But it set me off." I was keeping control over my voice.

"Did you antagonize Vaughan while he was down?"

"No!"

"Did you leave after he went down?"

"Yes. I just left. Well, I gave a camera back to the newspaper people, and then I left." I looked down the hall toward the labs. The lobby and hallway were empty now.

"Okay," Cooper said, walking away. "Just check your mailbox. You do have an invitation."

I turned quickly and hurried down the hall to my lab. After my lab, I went to my campus mailbox in the basement of the administration building. My appointment was for four o'clock that afternoon.

Even though I'd already told myself I was going to have another round with the dean, it was a shock to have it actually happen. The incident with Vaughan wasn't a big deal. There had been no blood, no injuries whatever. It must have been an injury to his ego though.

Even though it might be my last Tuesday on campus, I deliberately went on with a strictly normal Tuesday routine. I shot pool in the student union game room where I had created the commotion the night before. The pool tables and Ping-Pong tables were back in place. No one said anything to me about the senate meeting. Of course, the vets I played pool with didn't say much about anything.

I walked over to the administration building when my watch read three fifty-five. As I stepped around a corner in the lobby, Vaughan and one of his buddies walked past me from the hall leading to the dean of men's office. We passed each other so quickly, and they were so busy talking in agitated voices that they didn't recognize me. Maybe the dean had just chewed Vaughan out.

The dean's secretary, who still reminded me of an old schoolteacher, was sitting in the identical pose as the last time I was there. Her dress was the same dowdy style as before too. She invited me to take a seat in an old uncomfortable wood chair, and some minutes later, the dean opened his door, looked at me, and motioned for me to come in. He walked behind his desk and sat down, and I sat in another straight-back chair set to one side of his desk. It was hot in his office, and the dean was in shirtsleeves, with his tie slightly loosened.

He leaned back in his chair and gave me a discerning look. "Mr. Collins," he said, "I'm disappointed that you're back under these circumstances." I just sat there. He began to fidget, tapping a pen on what, again, must have been my personal files. "I hear there was trouble at the student senate meeting last night. What is your explanation of the incident?"

"One of the SDS demonstrators called me a baby killer and then stuck his hand in my face, so I pushed him off, and he fell on his . . . backside."

As he didn't prompt me for more details, I guessed he was satisfied with what Cooper had told him. After a short pause, he continued. "The incident that brought you here the first time involved similar behavior. Two incidents show a pattern." He leaned toward me and lowered his voice. "Mr. Collins, you're no longer in the army. The school cannot tolerate enlisted-man barracks behavior. I would have thought your military training would have made you more mature and disciplined." He inhaled deeply and then delivered another blast. "And more importantly, I absolutely will not let this campus deteriorate into chaos the way other campuses have."

I turned my head and looked out the window. Snow flurries were being tossed by erratic winds.

Since I didn't say anything, he started again. "Your friend, Mr. Henning, didn't try to rejoin the school community." Hearing Pete's name pulled my attention back, and I looked at him with a frown. The dean continued, saying, "I think Henning's leaving has removed a distraction for you. You were lucky not to have gotten more involved with him and his habits." I stared at him. He seemed pleased that he had irritated me. "Yes, we know what our students are up to."

"Even when they're adults?"

"He was a student at this institution. Remember what I said to you in October? Character is important to this school." He straightened in his chair. "Your first visit here was a warning. This time, I'm putting you on disciplinary probation."

He picked up a sheet of paper on his desk and read a few paragraphs listing the conditions of the probation. If I got in trouble again, I would be expelled. The probation would last through the spring semester. There would be another meeting with him in the fall when the probation might be lifted.

I signed the document, and he gave me a copy. "I'm sending your parents a copy of this letter," he said. "It would be wise to phone them before they get it."

"Yes. Certainly."

"You're not being singled out in this matter." He didn't seem to expect me to say anything. "Mr. Vaughan was also disciplined." He let a moment pass and then began his closing rhetoric. "Unlike Mr. Henning, your midterm grades and the comments from your professors show you're motivated and are participating in school activities. You can succeed if you bring your behavior in line with your fellow students and leave your past behind."

He looked at me again, and I nodded.

"Okay." He stood up. I stood up. "That's all I have to say."

He didn't offer a handshake this time, and I left without saying anything more. I walked across the street to the library and sat on the same bench near the front entrance where I had sat when I reviewed my political science test.

For a moment, I watched people walking in and out of the library, all loaded down with books, and wondered if they had problems too. So my character wasn't right. An enlisted ruffian man didn't fit the school's image. I took a deep breath and looked up at the overcast gray sky. Since that was the case, I decided I would rejoin my past rather than leave it behind. I would reenlist and go back to Vietnam.

A fog lifted in my mind. Now I could see all the events of the past months fitting together. Reenlisting would solve the problem of my dreams; they would come true or not. My social compatibility problems would also be solved. I would be with other worthless enlisted men concentrating on staying alive. I wouldn't have any women problems, since there wouldn't be any round-eyed women where I was going, and my relationships with other women would be devoid of affection.

The dean had sounded proud that he'd gotten rid of Pete. A true educator, that man was. He might make dean of the college someday.

It was easier for the school to spy on Pete and connive with the local cops than to help him. It wouldn't have been much trouble to have arranged a tutor or have meaningful discussions with Pete about his future. But that wouldn't have been good business. A business had to an image to protect.

I spent the evening lying on the couch at the apartment watching TV and eating popcorn. Red Skelton had Ozzie and Harriet Nelson on his show as guests. I wondered how the Nelson boys had avoided the draft. Later, out of desperation, I watched *The Doris Day Show*.

I thought about calling my parents but then decided not to. If there had only been the probation issue, I would have called my mother, but I wasn't ready to talk about reenlisting yet. It would be better to wait until my induction date was confirmed. Then I could tell my parents what was going to happen.

I repeatedly thought about Natalie and repeatedly drove the thought of her out of my mind. If she didn't care about me, then my leaving wouldn't matter. If she did care, I still had other problems to deal with. Life would be much simpler if a man had some definite way to tell how deeply a woman cared about him. I couldn't help but grin. If I could invent a love thermometer, I would be rich!

Having decided not to tell anyone of my plans, the only thing left was the question of when I would take the ridiculous plunge and see a recruiter. It was put-up-or-shut-up time. I decided to do it the next day. The longer I thought about it, the more likely I was to chicken out. There was a recruiter at the main post office downtown. I decided to pay him a visit after my geology class.

WEDNESDAY, DECEMBER 11

My alarm went off as normal Wednesday morning, and I followed my normal routine. But no matter how normal the routine, I still had the sensation of pending doom, the same nauseating sensation I'd had before I was inducted into the army two years before, the same nausea I'd felt at the end of every leave I had ever taken. This time, it was all of my own doing, but the feeling was the same.

Typically, Natalie and I didn't see each other on Wednesdays. Our schedules kept us on opposite sides of the campus. To be sure we didn't bump into each other this Wednesday, I went directly back to the apartment for lunch. I didn't even go near the student union. I didn't want to meet her and risk spilling my emotions on her.

My geology lecture was from one thirty to two thirty. As pointless as it might be, I went to the class. I enjoyed geology. I would never be a geologist, but it was interesting how geology shaped geography and how geography shaped history and politics.

The pivotal moment came after class. Either I walked downtown and saw the recruiter or I folded my cards in the face of my own bluff. A great urge came over me to run away and disappear. The trouble was I'd still be with myself. Pete had probably felt the same way, but then he had Patty.

I was the last person to leave the geology lecture hall. I was feeling mildly schizophrenic by that time, with the abnormal part of me convincing the more rational part of me that I would be just talking to the recruiter and there would be plenty of time to back out of the commitment.

The post office was a plain two-story red brick building on the street that ran beside the Chadicoin River, a short walk from the bridge where Main Street crossed the river. I read the date, 1934, cut into the building's cornerstone as I walked up the wide concrete stairs leading to the large double doors. The building had the usual flagpole in front and looked like a functional public works project.

Inside, there were only a few people waiting at the long wooden service counters in the lobby. I saw no offices in the lobby then noticed a large sign beside the stairs to the second floor that read *Armed Forces Recruiting Center*. There was a poster on the wall next to the stairs showing four men and a woman dressed in the uniforms of each of the services. The girl was a Navy WAVE. They all had huge smiles.

The second floor was a long hall lined with offices. Each branch of service had a separate office, and each office had an identical door with a frosted glass panel and the name of the department stenciled on it. The army recruiter was third. As I reached to open the door, I hoped it would be locked.

The door opened into a small office with one window, the recruiter's desk, some racks of promotional material against the one wall, and five chairs across the recruiter's desk. I thought the recruiter was optimistic to put out five chairs. The required pictures of Lyndon Johnson and Secretary of Defense Clark Clifford hung behind the recruiter's desk, along with the standard-issue motivational posters tracing a heritage of the U.S. Army. I recognized a poster depicting a Revolutionary War soldier from other army offices I'd been in.

The recruiter was on the phone, so I immediately sat down. The office was too small to for me to remain standing without being intrusive. When he finished what was obviously a personal call, he stood up and came around the desk to greet me. He was a tall thin staff sergeant dressed in his green dress uniform with the yellow-and-black patch of the First Air Cavalry on his right shoulder. I stood up, and we shook hands.

"I'm Staff Sergeant Hopper," he said. "Welcome to my shoebox office! How can I help you?"

"Mike Collins," I said.

"Mike, nice to meet you. What can I do for you?"

Anxiety made me nearly breathless, so I spit out the words without equivocation. "I want to reenlist"

"Great! Great! The best move you could make. Absolutely!" Then my words began to sink in. He looked puzzled. "Reenlist? Reenlist, you say?"

"Right. I've been out about six months. That's not too long, is it?"

"No. No, absolutely not, I can fix you right up."

The good fortune of having an easy mark drop into his lap had startled him, and his mind was just catching up. "Well, now let's get right to work."

He moved back behind his desk and sat down. "Pull your chair up close here," he stuttered, trying to remember my name. "Mike, yeah, pull your chair up, Mike, and we'll get going here."

The guy would be a used-car salesman if he ever got out of the army. He shuffled through the papers covering his desk and came up with a blank tablet and began to write. "Let's see, Mike, Michael, that is, and your last name again was?"

"Collins." I used a supportive tone to mask my disdain.

"Okay, Mike, what was your rank and military occupational specialty when you separated?"

"I was a Specialist Five and a combat engineer, 12B20."

"Combat engineer!" He finally looked straight at me. "That was hard, dangerous work. How long a hitch did you have? Enlisted or drafted?"

"Drafted. I was inducted in July 1966."

"Well, being an engineer, you probably did a tour in Vietnam."

I said I had, and we went on to exchange bullshit about the war. He had done two tours, one in early 1964 and 1965, the second in 1967. After getting the war out of the way, he asked me again about my military occupational specialty.

"So what MOS do you want to go for this time? You've got your choice now, soldier!"

"I'll go back to being an engineer, the same as before. But I want to be posted back to Vietnam."

He squinted at me. "You want to go back to Vietnam as a combat engineer?"

"Right." I squinted back at him. "Is there a problem with that?"

"No. No. Not at all." He tapped his pen for moment. "What is your idea here? You know you can't be guaranteed any specific unit over there." Then he got to the point. "There's no Vietnamese woman involved in this, is there?"

That was a connection I hadn't expected. "Oh god, no!" I said with a big grin. I leaned back in my chair. "No, I didn't get wrapped up or anything like that."

"Fine." He still looked skeptical. "Have you had any trouble with the law since you've been back?"

I wasn't amused any longer. "No, and the background check will confirm that. And my DD 201 file will show no disciplinary actions at all." Hopper was trying to find out if I was a pothead trying to get back to Vietnam for the easy grass.

"Okay," he said, "what have you been doing since you've been back? Working?"

"I've been going to school at the college. Look, if your quota's full, I'll go to a recruiter over in Athens or down in Cincinnati." It was strange talking to an E6 that way. But I was still a civilian.

Sergeant Hopper stiffened up. "I just need to know what's going on here. This is serious business. We only want quality people."

I nearly snickered at that remark, considering the quality of people caught by the draft dragnet. "Okay," I said after a minute. "I suppose my situation is unusual."

Hopper put his head down and started to write again. "Not really," he said, looking back up at me. "Lots of guys can't find work after being discharged. Or they come home to find their girls pregnant with Jody's kid." He looked down and began writing again. "I don't need to know what burr is up your ass."

His remark was what I expected from a staff sergeant. We went on to cover the details, but he kept writing on his tablet, not filling out forms. He also glanced at his watch a couple of times.

Fifteen minutes after I had walked in, Hopper was anxiously wrapping things up. "Well now," he said, his voice a bit too hearty, "I've got some typing to do. I'm afraid it's too late in the afternoon to finish. Can you come back tomorrow afternoon at, say, two o'clock to sign papers?"

"Sure," I said. During our discussion, Hopper had assured me he could get me an induction date in January. After four weeks of reorientation training, I would be back in Vietnam in the early spring. I left the post office carrying a folder of instruction sheets about my induction, a checklist of things to do to get ready, and some forms to fill out.

I wasn't in the mood for the Main Street holiday atmosphere, so I walked back to the apartment by side streets that were lined with the empty storefronts.

Back at the apartment, I found Robert, Charlie, and Dave in the kitchen making an early spaghetti dinner. I didn't feel sociable, so I just dumped my papers in the bedroom and made a quick pass through the kitchen to get a beer.

After casual greetings all around, Robert asked me about dinner. "You want some spaghetti? I can add more."

I didn't want the strain of conversation. "No, no, thanks," I said. "I'm heading back out. I just dropped off my books."

Dave tried to start an exchange of wisecracks, but I didn't respond. I took my beer out to the living room, turned on the TV, and clicked the dial around until I found *American Bandstand*. Then I flopped down on the couch.

As I had expected, Robert wouldn't let me sulk without trying to kick me out of it. After a few minutes, he came into the living room. "Are you sure about dinner? Another handful of spaghetti is no problem."

I put on a friendly demeanor and gave him a bright glance. "No, but thanks. Actually, I ought to be leaving. I appreciate the offer . . . really . . ." My voice trailed off.

He took a step forward. "Was there fallout from Monday night?" He was pressing for the real issue.

I looked up at him again and then gave him as much straight talk as I could. "Yeah. The dean of men reamed me out yesterday afternoon. I'm on probation again, disciplinary probation this time."

"Well, that's bullshit, and you know it. They're just trying to be hard-assed. It's nothing to worry about. Some jocks are on and off probation a couple of times before they graduate."

"It's no fun though."

Fortunately, I didn't have to say anything more because Dave called from the kitchen. "I'm straining the spaghetti! Come and get it."

Robert gave me another boost as he left the room. "Just keep at the books and this will all blow over."

I felt like a real scumbag for not telling him what I was up to. After he was back in the kitchen, I got up, put on my army field jacket, and left the apartment, leaving the TV on.

I went back to Mike and Sam's pizza joint. I'd felt comfortable there the night I'd shot pool with the other vets, so I figured I could kill the evening there and not have to talk to Robert, Natalie, or anyone else if I chose not to.

When I got to Mike and Sam's, *The Jonathan Winters Show* was on the TV behind the bar. It was a relief to just sit there, watching the show, eating pizza, and drinking beer. I watched *Green Acres* and *Beverly Hillbillies* too. I also talked football with Mike, who was tending bar. We were both pleased the Browns had won their division. Mike didn't care for all the new teams in football. He said it was because a lot of rich people wanted to get richer.

Some college students came in around ten and sat around a table and had a pizza. They looked like freshmen or sophomores, and I didn't know any of them. I hoped they didn't know Natalie. I stayed at Mike and Sam's till the evening news started at eleven.

When I walked up to the apartment, I could see the lights were out, which was a relief since I didn't want to talk to Robert. I went in and walked cautiously into the bedroom and picked up the folder of enlistment papers I had left on my dresser that afternoon. Robert was sound asleep. I took the papers to the kitchen so I could look them over, fill out what I could, and make a list of what I needed to get done.

But the minute I turned on the kitchen light, I saw a sheet of notebook paper laid prominently on the kitchen table and anchored by a saltshaker. It was in Robert's handwriting. *Mike, Natalie called, call her back. 7:10.* Further down was a second note. *8:40, Natalie called again. She said she is not on the story! Call her.*

"What the hell?" I muttered to myself. "Not on the story?" Natalie could only mean that she wasn't writing about the senate meeting ruckus. If she wasn't writing the story, then why was she's so anxious to talk to me?

It was very possible—almost certain—that she knew I'd been dragged in front of the dean. Vaughan had been chewed out before me and was running his mouth when I saw him leave the administration building. The news must have flashed around among the campus insiders and gotten back to the newspaper staff.

I felt a mixture of irritation and guilt. There was no reason for her to feel responsible for what happened at the meeting. I had told her that before class. Still, I felt guilty. She was a genuinely honest person. She was sincerely concerned about me.

But I was through taking risks with women. Besides, there was more involved here than just her. I would tell both her and Robert after I had finished what I had started.

I sat down at the table and spread out the enlistment papers. Some of the forms were the same ones I'd filled out at my first induction. I was tired, and when I began reading the Department of Defense forms, I quickly faded, so I staggered off to the bedroom and, for the second night in a row, went to bed with my clothes on.

THURSDAY, DECEMBER 12

A dream woke me about two thirty. It was about Vietnam again. It was all garbled, but I could tell it was another variation on my being the last GI in Vietnam. I got up and washed my face and took off my clothes. When I went back to bed, I fell right to sleep. I slept until Robert's loud voice yanked me out of my deep sleep.

"What *is* this shit?"

I rolled over and looked up to see him standing in the door waving a fistful of papers. It was eight thirty, and he was dressed for class.

"Are you trying to get back into the army?" He had found my enlistment papers on the kitchen table where I'd left them.

"Yeah, that's right."

"Oh, for god's sake. You're going off the deep end here." He sighed deeply and turned to leave then said over his shoulder, "Well, I haven't got time to discuss this silliness right now. You had better call Natalie. That's all I've got to say. You hear me?" When I didn't respond, he just said, "Jeez!" and picked up his books and left.

I rolled back over and stared at the ceiling. As bad as it seemed, this might have been the best way to tell Robert. I had no speech planned, no easy entry into the subject. This way, it was over. But I was a real shit.

There was no need to rush to get up. It was Thursday, and I had American lit with Natalie. I had already planned to cut the class and all my other classes for the day. But if I just lay in bed, I might fall asleep again, and I didn't want any more dreams. I got up.

Under different circumstances, I would have enjoyed a slow morning alone in the apartment. The only enjoyment I had was my shower. There was no one waiting to use the bathroom, no one to save hot water for, so I stood with my back to the showerhead and let the water pelt down on the back of my neck. The water was as hot as I could tolerate. I stood that way until the water began to cool. In a few months, I would be grateful to get a tepid shower standing in a plywood stall.

Around eleven fifteen, it occurred to me that Robert might come back to the apartment for lunch. I didn't want to talk to him, so I decided to go downtown, have lunch, and kill time before talking to the recruiter. The best place I could think of was the lunch counter at the Woolworth store. That way, I'd be off campus, and if I bought lunch and a few cups of coffee, I could kill two hours.

The temperature was in the mid-thirties, and it was cloudy when I left the apartment. I took a long route to get downtown, using side streets so I wouldn't go across campus. I had put the enlistment documents in a large mailing envelope to keep them dry if it rained while I was walking downtown.

I felt like a truant or an AWOL soldier as I walked along Main Street at noon. I couldn't remember being downtown at that time of day on a weekday.

Compared with Stewart's of Middlesex, the Woolworth store was unpretentious and nearly empty, which reminded me how five- and ten-cent stores were becoming dated. The lunch counter was about half full with businesspeople and workers from other stores having lunch. A waitress in a modest pink uniform took my order for a grilled cheese sandwich and french fries. I gathered up sections of newspaper left behind on the counter by other customers so I would have something to occupy myself.

After taking my time eating the grilled cheese sandwich, I had a piece of coconut cream pie and coffee. Then I read the local news sections of the paper, deliberately avoiding the national and international news in the first section, until it was time to leave.

The recruiter's door was locked when I tried it at one fifty-five. I saw an index card with *Be back in ten minutes* written on it stuck in the corner of the doors frosted glass window. Twenty minutes later, I was still pacing up and down the hall. I was getting irritated. I desperately wanted to get this business over with.

At two thirty, Sergeant Hopper and the navy recruiter came up the stairs laughing and talking loudly. Hopper greeted me with great enthusiasm. "Collins! Great to see you. Let's get in here and get this all taken care of. You have a great future ahead of you. This is the best decision you've ever done."

He was drunk. They had probably left for a liquid lunch at eleven. He fumbled with the key to the door and led me into his office, where he immediately opened the window, saying he was hot. Then he pulled his tie loose and flopped into his chair. "Well," he said, holding out his hand for the papers I was carrying, "what have you got for me?"

"I filled in what I could," I said as I gave him the papers.

He looked over the two forms I had completed. "Okay. This is a good start." He was shifting in his chair, trying to hold the papers steady. "I'm afraid I haven't been able to type up the papers for you to sign." He pulled out the tablet he had taken notes on the day before and a blank form of some kind. His head bobbed and swayed as he kept trying to look serious and businesslike.

"I really want to get this done today." I couldn't hide the disgust in my voice. "Can you type them up while I wait?" Looking at the guy, I knew it would be a big effort. It gave me a sadistic pleasure to put a staff sergeant on the spot. Plenty of them had given me loads of shit.

He stopped moving for a second and stared straight ahead with a blank look on his face. Then he snapped his head toward me and said with a grin, "How about this—you sign the form and I'll fill in the blanks later?"

"Sign a blank form?"

"Sure, sure. I have recruits do it all the time. It speeds things up." He gave me his sincerest used-car salesman smile.

"Well . . . what's on the form? What are you filling in?"

"Look," he said, the smile gone, "I got all the details from you yesterday." He slid the tablet around so I could see it. "And it matches right up with the damn form. Sign it and you won't have to come back here until I get your travel papers and an exact induction date." Now he was sounding more like a staff sergeant than a salesman for the army.

I leaned forward in my chair and read the form on his desk. It was all the standard name and address stuff, plus the terms of enlistment. The form had a second page, so I knew he could never do it in his condition.

"Okay," I said with a sigh as I looked around the desk for a pen. Hopper had gone stoned again. He was staring straight ahead. The movements of my hand movement picking up the pen snapped him out of it.

"Wonderful!" He watched me sign my name. "There! Now I don't need to keep you any longer. You're all set." He stood up and quickly steadied himself by putting his left hand on the desk as he offered me a handshake. I stood up and shook hands. His hand was cold and clammy, and his grip was what you would expect from a drunk. I couldn't make myself say, "Thank you," so instead, I asked how long it would be until he knew the induction date.

"Two weeks at the outside. Certainly before Christmas."

"All right. But I'll be calling to see if anything comes in early."

"Sure, sure," he said as he stepped around his desk and opened the door for me. I was getting a bum's rush.

Down in the lobby, I pushed open the large brass doors of the post office main entrance and stepped outside. The temperature had dropped dramatically and a light snow was falling. The flakes were dry and wispy, floating and whirling like they didn't want to touch the ground. I stood at the top of the steps for a moment and zipped up my jacket.

What a mess. Why was everything so difficult? I was just trying to unscrew my life, and instead, it was getting worse. That drunken recruiter was liable to enlist me in the WACs, a typical olive drab mess.

I still had some decisions to make and many other things to see to. I had to tell my parents sometime. That would be a delicate process. Then I thought of Natalie again. Did she care for me? It seemed I was suddenly caught in a vortex of worries. Moving like a robot, I went down the post office steps, turned left, and headed toward Main Street. I had only gone a few paces when I saw a girl coming toward me.

"Oh no!" I said out loud.

It was Natalie, and she was walking toward me with a quick and determined stride. I knew her being here was not coincidental. But before I could separate what was real from what I hoped I was imagining, Natalie was facing me.

"Robert told me you were here," she said. "And why? You haven't done it, have you?" Her voice was shrill and demanding.

Her tone offended me, and I became defensive. "Yes, I did," I said in what I hoped would be a strong voice. The words came out sounding squeaky.

She shifted her weight from foot to foot then pulled her hands out of her coat pockets, opened them to me in a pleading motion, and said, "Oh, come on. It's a joke! Tell me you're joking."

"It's no joke," I answered. A sick feeling was coming over me. The realization was creeping over me that I might have made an enormous irreversible mistake.

She looked at me a moment. "And you weren't going to say a word to me?"

"I didn't know what to say to you." I tried to back away, but she took a step forward. "But I was going to talk to you tonight."

"Oh sure, sure you were, after you did it! Great! Just great!"

She spun around and strode off with the same fast pace she'd used to approach me.

My feet felt planted to the sidewalk. With an effort, I broke them free and followed her. I could see her hair bouncing as she shook her head, and I suspected she was talking aloud to herself. She walked to the intersection at Main Street, where she would turn right to walk through town and back to campus. As she paused for the traffic light to change, she snapped a glance at me then turned and walked in the other direction on Main Street. She continued out on to the bridge over the Chadicoin River. I followed her as she walked out to the middle of the bridge, where she stopped. She gave me another look as she rested her arms on the high stone railing and looked down river.

I followed her out, stopped within speaking distance, and assumed the same pose as her, leaning on the railing.

"I don't understand. I just don't understand." She was staring straight down at the water.

"It's a lot of things," I said, also staring at the water. "A lot of things I don't understand either." I sighed. "Basically, I don't fit in here."

"And you think you'll *fit* back in the army? You hated the army! You know you did."

"It's more about getting back to Vietnam than being in the army. I'm going back to Vietnam."

She finally turned her head. "Vietnam! Oh, for god's sake. You sure will fit in just swell there."

"Well," I was still feeling defensive, "I sure don't fit in here."

"Why? Because you got in a scrape with a loudmouth know-it-all? Practically, the whole school cheered what you did."

"I'm on probation," I said as if confessing to a priest.

"So? Half of some fraternities are on probation for things like setting off firecrackers in the dorm. Big deal! You don't see them running off to the army." She hadn't looked at me again, but her voice was calmer now.

Cars hissed past on the wet pavement behind us. The wind was stronger out on the bridge, and it played with our clothes trying to seep through any opening to chill us. The snow created a white dotted curtain between us and the buildings of the town on our left. The scene looked like a black-and-white photograph.

"You don't know yourself," she said. She looked at me and blinked then continued before I could respond, which was good because I had no response. "You're not a warrior. You're a good photographer with a fine sense of composition." She was looking down at the water again. "You work well with light, and you can see different perspectives other people would miss."

"You lent me the camera," was all I could say.

"I've seen you," she continued. I've seen you in the bookstore looking through the big art books. I even know that you like Monet's water lilies the best. You spend more time on those pages." Her voice changed. She sounded like she was presenting evidence at a trial. "And I bet you didn't know that I saw you going into Dr. Herring's poetry reading and discussion group that evening in November."

I still didn't say anything. *Damn, she's good!* I thought.

Then she turned and faced me and asked me a direct question. "Tell me, Mike, why are you dating me?"

I looked at her, and our eyes met, and I answered without hesitation. "Because you are wonderfully unique. Because you have a beautiful and genuine personality. Because you're intelligent. And we like many of the same things." I paused, but our eyes held, and I said, "And you're very, very pretty."

She turned and looked down at the fast-moving water swirling around the piers of the bridge. Then she moved her hand and laid it halfway between us on the railing. "I don't know what will become of us, but I want to find out. Together."

I reached out and put my hand on hers and gave her a squeeze, and she turned her hand up and gave my hand a squeeze in return.

After a moment, I muttered, "There's still the army mess."

"Do you want to get out of it?"

"Now I do. I didn't want to get into that situation the first time, you know. I was drafted. I only went back to it out of desperation."

We had relaxed and moved closer to each other. Our shoulders were touching now. "Can anything be done?" she asked.

"Well, it will be like taking a bone from a mad dog, but I'm willing to try." I straightened up. "You can join me if you want to."

"Sure!"

We walked back off the bridge toward town. We walked side by side but didn't hold hands. At the intersection at the foot of the bridge, we turned right and walked the half block back to the post office. As we walked, I was thinking of explanations I could give for wanting my papers back. Nothing came to me, other than being damn insistent that I had changed my mind. Maybe I could claim to be a drug addict at my physical.

The lines of people in the post office lobby had gotten longer. Some people were holding packages wrapped in brown paper and tied with string. Others had large bundles of envelopes that I assumed were Christmas cards. We walked to the end of the lobby and up the stairs. "Would you mind waiting here?" I asked Natalie as we reached the hallway.

"Fine," she said with a smile. "Good luck!"

I went to the recruiter's door and found it slightly ajar. I couldn't hear any voices, so I pushed the door open and went in. Sergeant Hopper was slumped over his desk with his head cradled on his crossed arms, exhaling and inhaling with great sloppy gasps of breath. He had passed out.

God's grace was smiling down on me. All my papers were still right there. The problem was that some of the papers were under his arm. Without wasting any time, I picked out the blank form I had signed, gripping the exposed corner and steadily pulled it out from under him. Hopper's snoring continued as I slipped out the door, being certain not to pull it closed so as not to make any noise.

As I stepped into the hall, I held a finger to my lips, signaling Natalie not to speak. She gave me a puzzled look but didn't say anything. We walked to the stairs, and I folded the paper and stuffed it into my pocket.

"Are those the papers?" she asked.

"Yes," I said. "At least the only important one."

"So he was reasonable about it?"

"He was unconscious."

"What?"

We were down in the lobby now and could speak normally, but I didn't want to talk until we were out of the building, so I just gave her the hush signal again, and we left the post office. Outside, I told her, "He was drunk when I saw him to sign the papers after lunch—I mean, really drunk. He must have passed out right after I left."

"He was drinking during the day while on the job?" She sounded amazed.

"Well," I said, suppressing a chuckle, "it's not uncommon for military people to have a drinking problem." I hoped that life would leave Natalie naïve in certain respects.

Her voice became serious. "Won't he miss the papers after he wakes up? You could be in big trouble for taking government property."

We were passing a small park, and I looked through the bare trees out over the Chadicoin River and up at the bridge where we had stood a few minutes before. "If he calls, I'll tell him I never signed the papers. I'll tell him we argued about the papers, and as drunk as he was, he won't be sure what happened. Besides, you're not really in the army until you're inducted."

We were back at the intersection with Main Street where I turned left and walked out on the bridge again.

"Where are we going?" Natalie asked.

"I want to get rid of this form."

Back on the bridge, we stopped and looked down river. A flock of ducks rose, flapping and calling from the water near the far shore. The ducks flew toward us and then made a sudden sweeping turn and flew away, climbing into the darkening sky.

I took the enlistment form out of my pocket and tore it into tiny pieces. Then I reached out and dropped them. The small bits of white paper scattered with the snow and the wind and were quickly lost.

"That's the end of that," I said.

"Wonderful," Natalie said.

Suddenly normal feelings returned to me, particularly that I was hungry and cold. "Let's get a burger at the Hideout," I said, my voice more cheerful than it had been in days.

"Great idea! I'm starved."

Darkness fell as we walked back through town. The holiday lighting, hurrying shoppers, and falling snow added to our high spirits. We passed a jewelry store window full of sparkling diamond rings decorated with ribbons and bows. I didn't slow down and kept looking ahead. However, the perfume display in Stewart's of Middlesex's window did prompt me to speak. "I've got to get back downtown soon. I haven't done any Christmas shopping."

"That's terrible," she said. "Neither have I. Usually, I do all my shopping the Friday after Thanksgiving, but this year, I don't even have a list made out yet. If I shop here, I'll have to pack the gifts to get them home, or else wait and try to do everything the weekend before Christmas." She went on to speculate how much shopping she could do during the remaining days before Christmas. It was pleasant to hear her talking about happy times, and while she spoke, I was thinking how nice it was that now I would have a true Christmas.

We entered the campus through the main gate and walked up the wide sidewalk toward the old buildings. The smooth blanket of new snow had transformed the campus. Lights shone out of windows on the white snow. We stopped to enjoy the scene. "I should get up early and take pictures before the snow is trampled over," I said.

"That's a good idea," she said. "The paper always runs a few pictures of the campus in the snow."

I turned to her, put my hands on her hips, pulled her close, and said, "Thanks for coming down to the post office." As I spoke, a gust wind drove a few dried leaves across the snow beside us.

"So is that all the thanks I get?"

"No. I can do much better than that." I leaned down and gave her a long kiss, hugging her close. The wind came up again, and I turned her as we embraced so I would block the wind from her.

"It's warmer when we're together," she said as I kissed her cheek.

.